POWER

SISTERS OF WRATH

BOOK THREE

SIENNA SNOW

Cover Design: Steamy Designs

Editor: Jennifer Haymore/Silla Webb

www.siennasnow.com

ISBN - eBook – 979-8-88535-044-0

ISBN - Print – 979-8-88535-046-4

ISBN - Hardback – 979-8-88535-045-7

AI Disclosure

No generative artificial intelligence (AI) was used in the writing of this work. The author expressly prohibits any entity from using this publication for purposes of training AI technologies to generate text, including, without limitation, technologies that are capable of generating works in the same style or genre as this publication.

Tropes List

- Dark Mafia
- Antihero
- Arranged marriage
- Marriage of convenience
- Morally Gray
- Villain romance
- Forbidden love
- Possessive alpha hero
- Touch her and die
- Who hurt you
- Dark Beauty and the Beast Dynamic
- Damsel in Distress
- Virgin-like Awakening (heroine reclaiming her sexuality)
- Age Gap
- Obsessive love
- Healing Romance

- Only soft for her
- Dark protector hero
- Competence Kink
- Heroine in Danger
- Mutual Obsession
- Found Family
- Power Couple
- Dominant Hero/Submissive Heroine dynamic
- Dirty Talk
- Forced Trust

Author's Note
Content Warning

This book is a dark romance with subject matter that may trigger some readers.

- Graphic Violence
- Explicit Sexual Content
- Dominance themes
- Kidnapping
- Sexual Assault (SA) (off-page, backstory; heroine is a survivor)
- Morally Gray Characters
- Death & Loss
- Depictions of suicidal thoughts and depression
- Weapons & Violence
- Trauma & PTSD
- Death of a Parent
- Mention of Human Trafficking
- Revenge Killing

- Misogyny and Patriarchal Violence
- PTSD and Trauma Recovery
- Dubious Consent (Dub-con)
- Physical and Emotional Abuse
- Stalking and Harassment
- Panic Attacks/Anxiety
- Torture and Severe Physical Abuse
- Domestic and Emotional Abuse

ONE

C ALISTA

The bullet burst from the gun, producing a thunderous crack that echoed across the shooting range and sent a satisfying shiver down my spine.

The metal pressed hot against my palm, and each contour dug into my skin while the weight of the pistol felt significant and anchoring. I squinted, focusing my gaze on the paper target at the far end of the range, its surface crafted to replicate a human silhouette with clear lines defining the head and torso.

Spirals of smoke curled up from the barrel, tendrils weaving through the crisp morning air, brushing against my cheek like a playful whisper. The pungent, acrid scent stung my nostrils, potent enough to make me wrinkle my nose.

I had only been here a short while, yet already the target bore the marks of my precision. Tiny holes dotted the paper, the edges frayed and curling, each puncture a testament to my aim. Still, despite my steady hand, it wasn't quite as obliterated as I desired.

I steadied my breathing, drawing in a long, calming breath, and aimed with precision, squeezing the trigger once more.

The bullet zipped through the air with a piercing whistle, sending an exhilarating rush of energy coursing through my veins. It pulsed within me, an irresistible force awakening every nerve ending with a primal instinct. It was such an intense sensation that it seemed to seize my very essence, reminiscent of a siren's haunting melody drawing me toward the unknown. The world around me blurred as this rush consumed me, leaving only the rhythm of my heartbeat and the echoes of the shots in my ears.

That intoxicating feeling of control was nothing short of addictive.

"You might as well give in. You're never getting out of here…"

The persistent voices that had haunted my thoughts for nearly two years echoed with each deafening shot, a chaotic chorus accompanying the relentless slideshow of memories flashing through my mind—a testament to everything I had survived.

With each squeeze of the trigger, my hands bucked,

sending another bullet down the range and another nameless face flickering in my mind like a ghostly apparition. I had tried to banish those phantoms, those voices, and the horrific images that haunted my dreams, but they clung to me like shadows at dusk.

Every day, I visited the shooting range, allowing the smell of gunpowder and the crack of gunfire to become my soothing companions. Yet, despite my best efforts after each session, the memories persisted, stubborn and unyielding.

Frustration boiled within me as I tightened my grip and fired again. Another horror flashed before me, a vivid remembered pain stabbing at my consciousness.

The images flickered like a distorted, fuzzy, dark video with blurred, disjointed edges. Fear wrapped around me like a suffocating blanket, consuming me. The threats echoed, along with the brutal beatings etched into my memory. And the rest...the unbearable thoughts? No. I wouldn't let them win.

I released the trigger over and over, the recoil jolting through my arms a physical reminder of my defiance.

With each shot fired, every blast became a cathartic release, a desperate attempt to purge the past.

My fingers moved automatically as I loaded bullets into the chamber, expending nearly all the available ammunition in my relentless assault.

"Healing takes time, Calista..." My therapist's voice wove through my thoughts, blending with the taunts of my abductors.

It was a relentless loop that whirled in my head.

Time marched on, yet the trauma lingered, simmering like a pot left on the stove too long, refusing to evaporate, akin to an uninvited guest overstaying their welcome.

Standing in my booth, gun in hand, I transformed into a warrior, locked in combat not with a visible foe but with my past. An ugly past that loomed large, a shadow I desperately wished to escape. The fight wouldn't end until its grip on me loosened and it no longer dictated my life.

I longed for normalcy, a life unshackled by fear.

To return to the person I was before, when courage, boldness, and hope defined me.

When I was the old Calista Vitalis.

The Cali who was fucking joyful, before the darkness descended.

I couldn't recall the last time I felt a genuine burst of warmth or free, unburdened happiness. Every glimmer of trust I once had in people shattered into a thousand pieces when my sisters swept in and took me away from that nightmare.

It wasn't just a rescue. It marked the beginning of a painful transformation. I emerged from that ordeal forever altered, haunted by the realization that the person I once was had vanished, leaving me to wander down perilous, shadowed paths.

In those bleakest nights, with the silence of despair pressing in, I stared at the ceiling, grappling with the thought that ending it all might be the only escape from the relentless sorrow. But somehow, bruised and in despair, I fought with every ounce of strength to push away those taunts.

I refused to let them win.

I did it for my sisters, Laya and Avra, their faces a constant reminder of hope amidst despair, and for the family name that weighed on my soul like an unbreakable vow. And fueled by a burning desire for retribution, I fought to ensure that those monstrous kidnappers, the very architects of my suffering, would never claim another piece of me.

I wasn't the person I used to be. They had stolen so much—moments, memories, and parts of my spirit that could never be returned.

Yet, with each furious day spent training on the cold concrete of the shooting range, at the gym where sweat and determination molded my battered body into something formidable, and at dawn when I hauled myself out of bed, fighting against the weight of despair, I vowed with every heartbeat that they would never steal anything else from me.

The images still danced at the edge of my vision, and whispers of past horrors echoed in the silence. I clung to the hope that through grueling daily training and therapy, that paralyzing fear would one day dissolve into nothingness.

Still, my impatience prickled beneath my skin, driving me to the shooting range before sunrise and to the gym every day to perfect my fighting skills.

It may be obsessive, but I reminded myself that I was paving a way forward, each moment a step away from the darkness. In an unexpected twist that still left me in awe, I had secured a spot in Harvard's prestigious online MBA program, all because my sisters had dared me to take the plunge and apply.

Now, I was navigating my studies through the digital realm, staying with my sister Laya and brother-in-law Niko in the sun-drenched hills of Greece while focusing on my recovery.

As I took a moment to reload my gun, a familiar vibration buzzed in my pocket. The distinctive haptic pattern signaled that it was nearly time for my scheduled meeting with my sisters. Just one more round, I thought, and then I'd join them.

I shifted into a firing stance, feet planted firmly on the ground, and squeezed the trigger, watching as the ammo flew and the paper target in the distance burst apart.

A satisfied grin crept onto my face as I pressed the button beside me, bringing the shredded target closer. A small laugh escaped me when I saw the sheer destruction. The paper was riddled with holes, particularly in the areas of the head and groin.

I plucked the target from the clip, holding it up, and spun around to face my bodyguard. Sebastian, a towering figure with a steely gaze, was one of the Vitalis family's most trusted men, now tasked with shadowing my every move.

He was always there, never letting me out of his sight. Sometimes, it annoyed me, but I genuinely valued the security he and his team offered.

Being a Vitalis came with its own hazards, as my sisters and I bore the weight of a legacy riddled with enemies. The Vitalis name was both a blessing and a curse, a gilded cage with invisible bars.

From an early age, I understood the peril tied to my father's bloodline.

I was just a little girl when the truth of our vulnerability struck me like a lightning bolt. It was a dark night, one that reeked of blood and betrayal, and in an instant, I lost both my mother and father. In the aftermath, my only family consisted of my sisters and Vik, my father's second and most trusted advisor. They became my guardians and protectors.

They raised me to be strong, to fight, and to survive.

That strength bred a longing for independence, a desire to live like everyone else, to be carefree and unburdened by the name I bore. For a time, I had forgotten the ever-present danger of being a Vitalis.

Then we'd come back to Greece, the land of our ancestors, to reclaim all that was stolen from us and to stand tall in the face of those who sought to see us fall. I'd had only a vague notion of the sacrifices our ambitions demanded.

From the very beginning, I fought against the constant invasion of my space, determined to stand on my own. In the end, Vik had shaped me into a fighter whose accuracy exceeded even my sisters', regardless of how lethal their aim.

A chill crawled down my back, while an ember-like burn crept up the back of my throat. That day in the library had reshaped my reality. One moment, I was lost among time-worn art books, and the next, rough hands forced a bag over my head and dragged me away.

I had refused to let my security detail crowd me during class research, and the consequences had rained down.

Ozias Xenos, who was responsible for my parents'

murders and the reason my sisters and I fled to Prague, had orchestrated the kidnapping. I became a pawn in his quest for control and power and a tool for exacting revenge on his son, Elias, for betraying him and choosing Avra after their marriage.

Yet, I carried the burden for flouting well-established rules of safety in my world.

Sebastian's constant presence wrapped around me like an unseen shield.

Over time, our bond had evolved into an effortless friendship. I held the target aloft to display my shooting skill, and Sebastian's sly grin conveyed more than words.

"Aren't you supposed to aim for the head, Cali?"

I shrugged, a crooked grin pulling at my lips. "Some men need their balls shot off."

"I can't argue with that fact. But this?" He arched an eyebrow while tapping the target's crotch area. "You've obliterated this guy's entire pelvis."

"Yeah, well, he probably deserved it," I replied, passing him the handle of my pistol.

He arranged it neatly beside the other weapons I'd gathered that day.

"Ready for your meeting?" he asked, snapping the case shut.

I let out a tired sigh. "I suppose."

He arched an eyebrow. "That's hardly convincing."

I scrunched up my nose, muttering, "Let's get moving."

Minutes later, Sebastian guided us out of the parking lot, the car swallowing the road toward Avra's estate.

Today marked the turning point.

The day my sisters and I would confront the mighty "M" word.

Marriage.

Long ago, the three of us swore an oath to wed into influential circles and reclaim what was stolen after the coup against our father.

The traitors who betrayed Papa believed that, as daughters of Juno Vitalis, they could dismiss us.

We were no longer helpless children. We would claim what was rightfully ours.

The mafia patriarchs, shrouded in tradition and arrogance, never expected to be challenged by three determined women.

Initially, Avra had married Elias Xenos, followed by Laya, who wed Nikolas Galanis. With the first two moves made, it was now my turn. This plan for retribution had been set long before my abduction. I would not let my past alter our path. Even as my sisters offered me a way out of our marriage pact, I refused to step aside. I would not retreat. I wanted to choose my spouse on my terms.

I aimed to choose a process that resembled thoughtful dating rather than rushed decision-making. The man I selected would recognize my history, embrace the scars and burdens I bore, and see me as an equal shaped by challenges, not as a delicate ideal.

After a ninety-minute drive from Layla's giant estate in Nemea, the massive iron gates of Avra and Eli's estate loomed ahead. They swung open as Sebastian guided us to a grand mansion perched over the Aegean Sea.

The manor sat on the coast of Patras among vibrant gardens, a modest vineyard and dense woods looming on its sides with a sweeping ocean view as its backdrop.

Pulling into the driveway, I spotted Avra and Laya basking on a sunlit terrace overlooking the boat dock. I often teased Avra that if the role of Vitalis blood queen godmother ever grew tiresome, she could easily transform her home into a luxury retreat. The estate exuded an allure that promised to captivate the elite.

A sense of joy filled me at the sight of my eldest sister thriving in such beauty. I stepped from the car and absorbed every detail like a cherished painting. My feet carried me along the cool stone steps toward my sunlit sisters.

The morning light spilled across the entryway as I stepped inside and encountered a scene that eased the weight in my chest. My sisters' faces, graced with beauty that rivaled ancient goddesses, lit up when they saw me, just as I knew my own did at the sight of them.

In that moment, our bond felt etched into something unbreakable.

We had journeyed through hardship together: the loss of our parents, the forced exile to a strange land in our early years, and the burden of concealing our true selves for far too long. Each trial left us reaching for something solid, a taste of normalcy, a whisper of home. In foreign Prague, with secrets and dangers lurking, the three of us clung fiercely to one another.

I recalled countless moments when Avra and Laya had been my first call for comfort, and I knew that would never change. Yet now they had partners of their own. Avra and Laya had found love in Eli and Niko, drawing strength from their arms.

The thought of trusting a man myself seemed almost absurd.

How could I ever let someone guard my heart when betrayal had sculpted my doubts? Today, however, I stood on the threshold of confronting that very challenge. I exhaled and approached my sisters, pushing away the tightness in my stomach.

Laya was stretched out on a lounge chair, her legs bare in the bright sunshine. Her hand rested on the edge of the bassinet at her side, rocking her little boy who slept like a tiny angel nestled in a soft, white blanket.

"How's my favorite nephew?" I leaned down and kissed Laya's cheek, then looked at the serene face of the baby, Constantine Juno Galanis, named to honor our father and Niko's father.

"He's only pretending to sleep," Laya murmured, her voice low, her gaze fixed on the tiny face. "A single sound and he will scream at the top of his lungs."

I laughed, shaking my head. "He sure looks like he's asleep."

"Don't trust him." She sighed. "If I stop rocking, the spell breaks."

"I see." I turned to Avra, who was radiating a serene light. Expecting the imminent arrival of her child, she cracked a small smile as she caressed her rounded belly. As much as she complained about her growing size, the baby was all she could talk about most days. She was so excited to become a mother.

I knew Avra's and Laya's children would grow strong, cherished by love and shielded by our care.

Avra and Laya had sacrificed so much for our family. Their marriages had bolstered the Vitalis name, a choice made willingly to honor our ancestors.

Now, it was my turn to contribute in kind.

And yet, as they embraced partners, the idea of sharing such intimacy with a man filled me with disbelief.

Love, for someone like me, felt as unreachable as a fallen star, especially after the ghosts of abduction, rescue, and the shattering of my heart.

Avra stood up, her dark hair cascading over her slender shoulders.

"Hi, Cali," she said, pulling me into a warm embrace.

I responded, sitting next to her. "How's the baby bump coming along?"

Avra beamed as she stroked her belly. "Perfect."

"I can hardly believe you'll have a baby in just four months, and you don't even look pregnant."

"Laya says I will start expanding like a balloon any day now."

Laya raised an eyebrow. "That's true. You remember how I was."

"I'm prepared," Avra replied, lifting her shoulders.

"You say that now." Laya shook her head. "Wait until you're going to the bathroom every five minutes."

Avra promised, "It'll be worth it."

"Yeah, it is." Laya gazed lovingly at her son.

"Where have my warrior sisters gone? Now you both melt like soft butter." I sighed.

Avra's expression grew hard. "Hurt a single hair on our children's heads and our warrior spirit ignites."

I waved off the caution. "Calm down, there's no imminent threat."

"Then let us focus," Avra proposed, her voice shifting to business.

My heart sank at the reminder of the task ahead—a responsibility that was never easy to bear, yet one I could not shirk. "Fine, let me see them."

Avra retrieved a file folder from a satchel beside her and handed it to me. "Here are ten candidates. They are vetted. It'll be easier to choose once we narrow the pool down to two men."

"I insist on meeting them and deciding myself."

"Of course," Laya said. "If you choose none, we will continue our search."

Each candidate's photograph was paired with a background report. A few of them I vaguely recognized.

"I can cross out some already," I murmured, shaking my head and punctuating my words.

I separated three profiles based solely on appearance. It may seem shallow, but I wanted a husband I found attractive.

I needed a man who could reignite a spark in me, especially if I intended to take things at a measured pace.

"Appearance wasn't something I screened for," Avra informed me. "I thought I'd let you handle that. I'm not sure what your type is."

"I'm not sure either; however, I know these aren't it. They do nothing for me." I exhaled as if releasing an old disappointment. "Perhaps what once appealed to me no longer draws my interest."

"Trust your judgment when the moment arrives. There is no black or white." Laya's calm gaze urged me on.

I flipped through a few more pages, discarding more dossiers. "These seem too old. What would we ever have in common besides the lifestyle? Could we have a conversation about similar interests?"

Avra cocked her head. "Older men bring wisdom. Their experience holds a richness the young often lack."

I knew she was thinking of her and Eli. They had a ten-year age gap, and it worked, but then again, Avra was an old soul, and Eli wasn't as rigid as I expected of a man his age.

"Perhaps, but there's a chance they are more old-fashioned. I'm not sure I want to make that compromise," I said.

"The choice is always yours, Cali," Avra reminded me. "We are here to give you options, nothing more."

I focused on a photo of a brown-haired man with deep espresso-colored eyes. I discovered only openness and warmth as I examined his face for any signs of cruelty or harshness. His gaze was devoid of sharp edges and conveyed an inviting interest instead.

I flipped his page and read aloud, "Leon Boscos, twenty-eight. Three brothers, the youngest among them…"

"Oh, Leon! I think Leon is a great candidate, probably the best one of all, actually," Avra said. "He's handsome."

"Very handsome," Laya piped in. "And sexy."

"He does have a tragic history, although perhaps that will give him depth," I said, ignoring their superficial comments.

As I scanned further, the report revealed a grim story. He'd lost his family to a brutal attack.

We certainly shared some common ground there. His family estate was situated in Vouliagmeni, in the Attica region, on the southern outskirts of Athens, along the coast, which placed it fairly close to my sisters. More precisely, he lived just over an hour from Laya and under two and a half hours from Avra. f

"All right," I announced, taking his report from the pile and setting it aside with care. "He remains on the list."

I focused on the next profile, analyzing his serious expression. Though the angle might have revealed too much, his eyes conveyed a keen intensity.

"Dominic Lucianos, forty-one." I paused, considering. "A bit on the older side?"

Avra shrugged, her tone even. "Not really. He's one year younger than Elias."

I nodded. "And he is the youngest of his siblings."

"He attended school with Elias," Avra noted. "That connection brought him to our attention."

I inhaled deeply as the gravity of my decision pressed on me.

"He has sisters as well," I said with quiet resolve. "I will meet both Leon and Dominic, then judge for myself."

Sliding Dominic's paperwork alongside Leon's, I considered my possible choices. "Is this enough? Or should we look further?"

"Two provides a balanced start," Laya observed with a mischievous sparkle in her eye.

I snapped the file closed. "Great, then that's done."

Avra and Laya shook their heads with amused smirks.

"Such enthusiasm," Laya said. "It's almost overwhelming. I'm not sure how I can handle it."

"Hey, I'm trying," I replied, with a mock offended scowl. "I did have the option to run away and join the circus, but I decided to stay here."

"We appreciate you sacrificing traveling the world in a tent for us." Avra leaned back in her chair and rubbed her belly.

"I do what is best for the family," I cooed, and we all started giggling at the ridiculous turn in our conversation. "No, seriously, do you have any more information on Leon and Dominic? Have you met either of them?"

"I've only met Leon so far," Avra murmured. "Dominic remains a mystery to me."

"Likewise," Laya concurred.

Curious, I leaned in. "What did you observe about Leon?"

Avra's gaze flickered, hesitant. "He exudes a calm charm, but don't be fooled. In private, his nature shifts. He carries a history of unyielding ruthlessness."

"In our world, who isn't sharpened by violence?" I remarked, a wry twist in my tone. "I only hope he reserves that intensity for others, not me."

"Both men are good choices, but I think it's going to come down to how they make you feel when you are around them." Avra's penetrating gaze studied my face.

"Trust your instincts, Cali," Laya added. "The right choice will feel unmistakable."

"I have every intention of doing just that," I replied.

Both men exuded success and striking looks. Either could bolster our family name, or Avra wouldn't have included them at all.

I was set on meeting them both, giving each a fair shot, but Leon's image kept interrupting my thoughts, shadowed by Avra's caution about his reputation.

The thought of someone who wielded power with an iron grip captivated me. Such a man, exuding raw strength, was a magnet for my attention. It was as if he were born with these formidable traits.

In the looming presence of danger that accompanied me as a Vitalis, such a partner would serve as my stronghold.

After leaving Avra's house, my mind churned with thoughts of both men, yet Leon's face lingered, refusing to fade as I lay in bed that night.

The significance eluded me, yet it resonated deeply.

It felt like destiny, an unspoken connection, even though we had never crossed paths.

What did that mean? I wondered.

Two

L EON

I pulled the blue tie from around my neck and let it drop onto the bed, reaching instead for the sleek black silk one I had initially picked. The silk flowed effortlessly around my neck as I guided it beneath my collar, carefully crafting a flawless knot while observing my reflection in the mirror.

I needed to appear impeccably groomed and composed.

Today held significance, something I wanted everyone, particularly Calista Vitalis, to recognize.

The phone call informing me of her desire to meet and discuss a potential partnership had caught me off guard for a moment.

The concept of arranged marriages was a familiar one in

our circles, yet it was something I had never genuinely considered for myself. I had always imagined finding a woman more organically, with things naturally falling into place.

However, the idea of marrying a Vitalis sister was undeniably fascinating. Their family wielded considerable influence, and the recent return of the sisters, after years away, spoke volumes about their resilience and strength.

I had followed the stories of the territories they had reclaimed and the marriages of the other two sisters.

However, I hadn't realized Calista was contemplating marriage herself.

Given her past, it was unexpected. After enduring the horrific ordeals she had faced, I assumed she would prefer to remain single, allowing herself time to heal. But it seemed I had underestimated her readiness to move forward, to face the world anew.

Clearly, I was wrong.

I was genuinely flattered to be considered a candidate.

When Vik Remes, Calista's family representative and childhood guardian, invited me to join her for lunch in Glyfada, a charming coastal village just outside of Athens, I jumped at the chance. However, after a week of reflecting on the situation, my mind had become a jumbled mess of confusion.

Determined to prepare myself, I began exploring the extensive history of the Vitalis family, refreshing my memory of their legacy and influence.

The sisters appeared to have inherited not just their father's name but also his exceptional intelligence and sharp wit. I had met the other two sisters in passing before, and they stood out in my memory as articulate and confident individuals.

I expected meeting Calista would be similar. However, I couldn't help but wonder if her experiences made her unique.

Her abduction had ignited a storm of news across the syndicates, like a flash fire consuming everything in its path. When she was finally rescued, the whispers about her ordeal were so dark and grim that they lingered in my mind, casting a shadow over my thoughts.

The idea of any woman enduring a harrowing experience like the one Calista had faced ignited an intense fire. This seething fury seared through my veins like a relentless stream.

Yet, reflecting on her ordeal, I couldn't help but think that Calista might now have a profound depth to her character, a distinctiveness that her sisters might lack. All three sisters, alongside their devoted caretaker, Vik, had displayed remarkable strength and resilience. I admired their capacity to rise from the ashes and reclaim what was rightfully theirs with an impressive display of determination.

If anyone could understand the insatiable thirst for vengeance, it was undoubtedly me. I gazed into the mirror, and the reflection staring back was not my own but that of my father. With each passing year, my features seemed to mirror his more and more.

I wondered what he might have felt about this potential alliance, this intertwining of lives and destinies. Yet, I could never be certain whether he would have been in favor or against it.

He, along with the rest of my family, was brutally murdered, their lives extinguished in an act of unspeakable violence.

Everyone I cherished, my parents, my three brothers, their wives, and their innocent children, all ripped from this world in an instant.

The memory of that day hung over me like a dark, unyielding cloud.

The weight of survivor's guilt pressed down on my shoulders so heavily that at times it felt as though it might crush me entirely.

Before that tragic day, our lives revolved around joyful vacations filled with laughter and warmth. We spent carefree days on the sun-kissed beach, where the children built sandcastles, their giggles mixing with the sounds of the waves. Meanwhile, the adults savored wine, spirits lifted as they shared stories and games together late into the night after the kids had gone to sleep.

But everything changed in one afternoon.

I was supposed to join them for lunch that day, but an urgent meeting came up, one I couldn't ignore. It was a crucial deal I had spent months negotiating, and I'd finally reached the verge of sealing a contract that would expand our restaurants into a sprawling new mega-resort. Getting everything signed and sealed meant transforming our fortunes in a way we had never imagined.

The meeting concluded better than anticipated, with the developers inviting us into other ventures.

Eager to share the triumph, I hurried back to my family.

My heart raced with excitement, and I was ready to celebrate. However, when I arrived, everything I knew was destroyed. In my absence, a horrific attack had taken the lives of all of them. The news left me in shock and horror.

Afterward, regret consumed me, a persistent presence suggesting I should have been there.

Maybe I could have protected them. My being there might have changed things. This haunting sense of failure etched itself into my being, a weight I bore daily, as substantial as an iron cloak.

The day everyone I loved died, a piece of my soul withered with them.

Everything that followed felt irrevocably altered, as if the colors of my world had dimmed forever.

Investigations revealed a shocking betrayal. Distant family members, driven by greed, had orchestrated the violence, believing it would grant them control over the family business. They had not anticipated my survival, nor realized the depth of my father's foresight.

Julius Boscos, my father, was both wise and pragmatic. Recognizing life's unpredictability, he taught my brothers and me about business and the art of wielding power. His teachings became our armor, and even though he was no longer with us, his legacy continued to influence me as I navigated a syndicate world that had been forever altered.

After locating the individuals responsible and ensuring

they all faced a fate of immense suffering, I found myself shattered, coming to the painful realization that revenge did little to ease the constant guilt eating away at my soul.

Despite the emptiness left by revenge, I learned to coexist with that void, transforming my agony into a driving force to seize control of the company.

I was just twenty-one, and the world viewed me as too green, too untested.

They were right, in a way.

Yet, countless times, I had been the unseen observer during my father's tough business negotiations, absorbing more knowledge than most could imagine.

Initially, everyone underestimated me, and truth be told, there were moments when I doubted myself too.

Yet, there were moments when the depths of my ruthlessness caught me off guard. The pain that had once threatened to consume me became a wellspring of power, enabling me to tackle tough decisions with a steely resolve. Swift and unrelenting, I mastered the art of dealing with adversaries who dared to challenge me, wielding a blend of precision and keen insight.

I was far from the innocent figure they imagined. Suppressing my conscience during those initial, grueling years allowed me to act without a second thought, decisive and unyielding.

Over time, the legacy of my family not only stabilized but flourished.

Although my reputation suffered, I couldn't care less.

Being known as ruthless, cold, and unfeeling became an

asset. It instilled a sense of caution in others, making them think twice before daring to oppose me. My reputation and the fear it inspired effectively filtered out the weakest among my rivals.

All of this held true until today. The last thing I wanted was for Calista Vitalis to perceive me with fear.

As I stepped out into the crisp air and approached my waiting car, I thought about how to ease her worries over lunch.

While the idea of bringing her comfort filled me with determination, a deep anger churned in my heart for all she'd endured.

I thought of my nieces' bright, hopeful faces, now lost to time. If they had survived, they would be teetering on the edge of youth. The thought of them facing similar harsh challenges to Calista's sent a chill down my spine. No woman deserved to bear such cruel burdens.

As the busy streets of Thessaloniki unfolded before me, the cityscape gave way to a breathtaking vista.

The sparkling surface of the Thermaic Gulf unveiled itself, its clear turquoise expanse stretching toward the horizon on a day that promised brilliance.

I pushed aside the distressing images in my mind, resolute in viewing Calista Vitalis not merely as a victim of her history, but as the complete individual standing before me, unmarked by past wounds.

I made a quiet promise to myself to view her solely in the light she presented, rather than through the lens of shared losses and trauma.

I had no desire for her to see me as merely a man defined by sorrow.

Today, I aimed to treat her with nothing less than genuine respect and sincere courtesy.

A few moments later, I entered the grand lobby of the Electra Palace Hotel. I ascended toward the Orizontes Roof Garden, the rooftop restaurant where our meeting was set. Below, Aristotelous Square pulsed with life, while the expansive gulf unfurled like a boundless tapestry behind it.

Amid this splendor, my attention was irresistibly drawn to the imposing sight of armed, sturdy men encircling Calista. In one secluded section of the restaurant, deep maroon velvet ropes demarcated her space and that of her dedicated team.

I recalled from my research that Calista was rarely without a small security detail, yet the scale of protection now surpassed anything I had learned just weeks ago.

It was evident she guarded herself with a seriousness born of past betrayals or looming threats.

I couldn't help but wonder if this bolstered security was a reaction to a known danger or simply a reflection of her impassioned instinct for self-preservation.

Perhaps she suspected that my reputation alone might warrant caution even as I approached. After all, anyone stepping forward into an unknown meeting might feel compelled to ensure their safety.

In my case, I had arrived on my own, without an entourage.

It was evident that Calista posed no danger to me, and I

hoped that, in time, she would see that I was not a threat to her either.

My gaze swept over the crowd, navigating through the sea of broad shoulders and wide stances surrounding her.

When I saw her, I gasped, utterly astonished. Her beauty was not just striking. It was captivating and mesmerizing, compelling you to look away with effort.

The Vitalis sisters were renowned for their extraordinary allure, a part of the lore that enveloped their family.

The photographs I had seen had done her no justice.

She was turned away, granting me the opportunity to admire her without restraint. The sunlight poured over her delicate features, highlighting the ethereal quality of her presence.

She was petite, with a bird-like grace. Her full lips curled upward, a soft smile resting casually yet elegantly on her face. Her high cheekbones were accentuated by the gentle waves of her long blond hair, which cascaded over her small shoulders and glittered under the sun's bright rays.

At first glance, she appeared younger than twenty-two, a fact that had been my initial concern when I was asked to meet her. I was only six years her senior, but I knew those years were significant in shaping one's character and experience.

Then, as Calista turned her focus toward me, I experienced the powerful effect of her fiery green gaze as it locked onto mine with surprising intensity.

My breath caught in my chest as a surge of excitement raced down my spine.

The innocence I had expected was missing from her eyes.

Instead, I found a profound wisdom that spoke of experience and understanding beyond her years. Before me was a disciplined woman who had learned to measure her reactions, to keep her thoughts and intentions carefully guarded.

Her smile was polite, calm, reflecting the strength and confidence of a woman who knew her worth. I encountered not a single trace of nervousness. Her unparalleled beauty was overwhelming, leaving me breathless.

To my surprise, I felt a stirring in my pants, my cock twitching. I had never expected such a strong physical reaction at first glance.

I prided myself on being the calm, composed one, the person unshaken by social encounters.

Now, here I was, feeling like an awkward adolescent, my knees weak and movements clumsy, all because of a single, curious arch of her brow.

I advanced through the crowd of guards, their formation slowly creating a narrow passage just for me. At that moment, they looked less like soldiers and more like vigilant keepers of a rare treasure: the Vitalis sisters. They stood ready to protect with every fiber of their being.

My throat tightened as I neared her, and an enchanting perfume enveloped me, its rich scent imprinting itself on my mind. I could detect hints of lilac mingling with layers of gardenia and a subtle trace of jasmine.

She rose to greet me, and once again, I found myself captivated by her delicate features. Her movements were graceful and sure, an elegant invitation extended as she reached out her hand to shake mine.

"Hello, Leon." Her smile broadened, sending a surge of energy through me, as if her radiant face had the power to outshine the sun. "Thank you for agreeing to meet with me."

"The pleasure is all mine." I met her hand with mine, our clasp sealing the start of this encounter, and then gestured toward the chair opposite her.

Once she settled in, her chair tucked neatly underneath, I sat across the table. I observed her gaze fixate on me, her eyes bright and unwavering. Light surrounded her like water encircling a swan.

Her face radiated softness—full lips and lashes sweeping down—but each curve suggested a quiet determination. The contours of her shoulders revealed sculpted muscles straining against her blouse. A vein on her wrist arched like a taut string. This firmness betrayed years devoted to refining both body and mind.

Underneath her composed exterior, I sensed storms she refused to name.

Images flickered in my thoughts: the men who'd dared to harm her, their faces contorted in fear as she stood before them, calm as a judge handing down a verdict.

I imagined her palm sliding across a pounding chest, the quiet crack of bone under her command. My fists tightened beneath the table, each suppressed breath fueling a rogue ache for justice.

Alongside that cold fury, another ache rose, a longing to stand in her confidence, to earn a share of that unbreakable trust she bestowed on so few. My pulse hammered against my ribs, which were suddenly too tight.

Could someone forged in fire ever allow another soul to come near?

"Have you been to this hotel before?" Her voice settled me back into the moment.

I brushed my palm along the tabletop's carved floral pattern. "No. You?"

She tracked a seam in the wood. "First time. I've heard the cuisine here rivals the best in the city."

I offered a small smile. "Then I'm glad we chose it." The words tasted simple, but behind them lay everything I felt: admiration, protection, a desire to be the one she could finally trust.

She grinned once more, her expression radiant and inviting, and my heart skipped a beat. When the waiter approached our table, I almost sighed with relief, grateful for a distraction to latch onto.

If just the mere act of greeting her and basking in her presence had such an effect on me, how would I endure the next few hours without unraveling?

Once I ordered a bottle of wine, I shifted my focus back to her, quietly hoping my racing heart would calm. It was utterly captivating to see the sunlight flicker through her hair, creating a stunning glow.

At that moment, the breeze caught her silky strands, lifting them from her shoulders and revealing the smooth expanse of her long neck.

I swallowed hard, my breath momentarily caught at the

sight. It felt as if I was witnessing something forbidden, and a powerful urge to press my lips against her tender skin surged within me. I quickly averted my gaze, struggling to regain my composure.

"I assume you have a critical eye when it comes to restaurants," she remarked with a knowing smile.

"And why would you think that?" I inquired, meeting her gaze and maintaining an air of calm, despite the whirlwind of emotions her presence stirred within me.

She offered a casual shrug. "Because you're in the industry yourself."

"Ah, of course," I acknowledged. "I must confess, I do have high standards."

"When I picked this place, I considered that," she continued. "They've received excellent reviews, and I thought you'd appreciate something a bit more upscale."

"Well." I chuckled. "I hope you don't have the wrong impression, Calista. While I enjoy fine dining, I'm equally at home in more humble settings. One of my favorite places is a modest little café tucked away in Barcelona."

Her laughter rang out, a melodic sound that struck me as the most beautiful thing I had ever heard.

"Fair enough," she conceded with a nod. "And please, call me Cali."

"Cali..." I let her name linger on my lips, savoring each syllable's soft rise and fall. "What should we order from this luxurious establishment?"

Her fingers traced the edge of a leather-bound menu. She

tilted her head. "I was studying the offerings before you arrived. The lamb looks irresistible."

I flipped the menu open, scanned one page, then closed it with a decisive snap.

"I'll have that too." I offered a slow wink.

Her brows shot up. "You didn't even look at the menu, did you?"

"No," I admitted. As the sun slipped behind a cloud, the resulting shadow revealed her enchanting dark green eyes, now sparkling with tiny silver flecks. I could have gazed at them for hours.

"I trust you." I lifted one shoulder in a half-shrug.

She leaned forward, a teasing smile tugging at her lips, revealing a single dimple. "I have good taste."

"Which must be why you invited me tonight," I replied.

"One hopes," she shot back, raising her glass in a mock toast.

She swept her hair to one side, as the candlelight illuminated the graceful curve of her neck once more. A warmth unfurled inside me, making my cock grow harder with every second.

I blinked and raised the glass to my lips.

"So," I said, settling back in my seat, "I hear you're a formidable fighter, Calista...Cali."

"I work hard at it," she said, lifting her chin. "There's always room for improvement, though."

"Like perfecting a signature dish," I offered.

She folded her hands on the table, watching me. "I've heard you're a skilled chef."

"Sounds like we both did our research. My family business requires me to possess an elevated level of proficiency in the kitchen to succeed. My father made sure I knew everything there was to know."

She regarded me with careful silence.

"I make a mean lamb moussaka. It's my great-grandmother's recipe, inked in her own hand." I tapped an imaginary page on the table.

She traced a circle on the tablecloth with her fingertip. "You'll need to prove it."

"You want proof?" I asked, lifting a brow. "I believe I need to win this competition before I can prove that."

"It's hardly a competition," she remarked, shaking her head.

"Isn't it?" I countered in mock challenge.

"No, it isn't," she insisted. "I'm not exactly parading you around in swimsuits and giving out scores."

"Hmm," I mused, stroking my chin. "I think I'd have a decent chance at winning that too. Of course, it would depend on how many others I was up against."

She fell silent for a moment as she looked at me. Finally, she spoke again. "I'm only meeting with one other potential candidate."

The word "candidate" hung in the air between us, evoking images of a formal job interview. Perhaps that was what this was, in a way, on paper. However, sitting across from Cali, watching the sunlight dance through her wispy hair, felt far from any job I'd ever had.

"Just one other, huh?" I asked, feeling a surge of confidence. "That means my chances are pretty stellar. But you still don't get to taste my moussaka until you make your choice."

"So, you're not bothered that you're not my only option?" she inquired, arching a curious brow at me.

"Why would I be?" I replied with a casual shrug and a teasing wink. "I'm well aware that I'm a good catch."

"Oh,really?" she challenged, her tone playful yet inquisitive.

"Absolutely," I replied. "In all seriousness, I know my worth. But more importantly, Cali, I trust that you'll make the choice that's right for you, and that's what truly matters. Whomever you choose will undoubtedly be a fortunate man."

"And you're suggesting you're the right choice?" she queried.

"I'm not suggesting anything, Cali." I leaned in, meeting her gaze. "You said it, not me."

Her breath hitched, and she bit her bottom lip, her gaze never wavering from mine.

I sat back, nodding slowly as I savored the moment. Cali was breathtaking. She radiated strength.

Her intelligence was evident in every word she spoke. But it wasn't merely these qualities that drew me to her. It was the way she made me feel like a man in the truest, most primal sense.

She awakened something fierce and protective within me, a longing to both devour and shield her from the world.

And that was a feeling I hadn't experienced in what felt like an eternity.

THREE

CALISTA

The sea behind Avra and Eli's mini castle shimmered beneath the setting sun, each wave a stroke of gold and crimson crashing against the black rocks and sending salt spray into the air. In the distance, beyond the lighthouse, gulls called out.

On the ridge-high terrace, I pressed my palms against the cool stone bench with my legs folded beneath me.

I curled my fingers around a chilled glass of white wine, the condensation slick against my palm. My pulse hammered at the base of my throat every time a car door thudded in the driveway. Dominic Lucianos would arrive soon.

I forced myself to lift the glass, to trace the rim with my tongue, but the delicate essence of the earthy vintage left me unmoved. All my thoughts centered around Leon. His half smile, the confident tilt of his chin, and how his hand had brushed mine continued to set my mind aflame. Our meeting had exceeded every hope possible for an introduction.

A week had passed, and he remained front and center in my thoughts. It was ridiculous to react to anyone this way.

A hollow knot tightened in my chest at the thought of tonight's dinner with Dominic. I had given Eli my word I would come, yet forcing myself to think about anything except Leon was turning out to be damn near impossible.

Eli and Avra's villa crouched on a jagged promontory, stones rising from churning water. From the terrace, I felt the ocean's roar echo through my bones. Salt mist drifted upward, coating my skin, and a breeze snagged at the ends of my hair. Gulls cried overhead, their wings beating against the wind, but nothing in that wild landscape loosened the tension coiled beneath my ribs.

On paper, Dominic checked every box. He came from the powerful Lucianos syndicate family. He was well-known and highly respected in the banking world and one of the heirs to the Caldwell Banking Conglomerate. He already had an MBA, and Eli had pointed out that might be helpful and offer some common ground for us to talk about, since I was just about to begin pursuing a master's myself.

Despite all that, the fact remained that he was seventeen years older than I. I had no doubt he was much more experienced, in every sense of the word. That alone left me with a bit of unease. He was from an entirely different generation than me, for fuck's sake.

Outside of school, what would we even have to talk about?

Would he look down on me, I wondered? Would he think I was unsophisticated or naive? Would he be able to respect me as a woman? Would he respect my need for independence?

The last thing I would ever tolerate was someone talking down to me or disrespecting me. Would his age naturally create a skewed power dynamic between us? Would he dismiss me as green? Would he bristle at my stubborn streak?

I'd chosen him before doing the depth of research that I should have.

Late last night, curiosity dragged me back to the Caldwell website. Dominic's portrait crossed the homepage: broad smile, dark suit, hands folded in front of a boardroom window. Beneath it, boilerplate phrases on "Visionary Leadership" and "Commitment to Innovation."

But in a separate industry report, I found a footnote: Theo Caldwell, "the true architect of our growth," was credited with drafting every major deal and steering daily strategy. Dominic's name appeared again at the bottom as a signer of the gala invitations and the speech deliverer. A union built only on his profile felt hollow, more show than substance. His brother ran the daily operations of their empire. Dominic barely dabbled in banking himself. He wasn't running any part of the business.

All of this knowledge left me with the distinct impression that combining our families would not be much of a benefit to us, after all. In order to assist my family in any way, Dominic would still need to get his brother's approval first.

The idea of that was extremely unappealing.

I'd proposed canceling the meeting, but my sisters had insisted it was rude to do so to Eli's friend and that it was inappropriate not to meet with more than one possible candidate. Avra and Laya knew the meeting with Leon had gone exceptionally well. But they still thought I needed to weigh my options carefully, and they were right.

Maybe I was coming up with every excuse I could to delay this process.

Either way, the idea of meeting Dominic left me anxious and uneasy.

Now here I waited, ready for a refill of my wine with little hope of it dulling my senses to aid me in the patience I needed to plaster on my face for the evening.

He was seven minutes late, and with every passing second, I tightened my grip on the glass until the strain on my knuckles made them ache.

My thoughts wandered back to Leon. Outside of the fact that he was closer to my age, I felt calm around him almost immediately. The tension of that first conversation melted into easy banter within seconds, and his smile soothed some unexplainable ache in my chest.

He carried the air of danger most men in our world possessed, but this control around him made him seem more protective than menacing.

But what had unsettled me most was when he'd brushed a stray hair from his forehead and his eyes darkened for the briefest of seconds, my heart clenched, and warmth grew deep inside me.

To find an instant attraction with anyone, considering my past, was more than I had even dared to hope for.

Then, to add in the fluttering of butterflies in my stomach every time he flashed that dashing smile my way, it was as if I'd fallen down a rabbit hole.

Safety and comfort were something I truly never expected to feel from another man in my life, much less desire.

His presence didn't set off alarms. Instead, a calm hollowness closed over the space inside me I'd thought empty forever. I'd patched myself together one quiet night at a time.

Trauma had hammered nails through my trust, but Leon's proximity didn't pinch or prod. It simply rested, as if he'd found an unguarded door and sat on the threshold, waiting.

Later, I conducted in-depth research into Leon's background, searching through business journals and gossip about his dealings. They all said the same things: he was ruthless and single-minded. Articles praised his iron will and warned competitors to yield or disappear. But personal pages remained blank. No social media feeds or threaded rumors, only a man who walked alone and was fiercely loyal to a handful of companions.

He obviously kept a low profile and liked his privacy,

guarding it viciously. And I found myself respecting this stance.

"Cali?" Avra's voice slipped through the daydream, and I blinked at her pale face in the hallway light.

"Hey," I said, setting my wine down.

"Dominic's here." She gestured toward the open doors, where Dominic and Eli hovered in the foyer.

I straightened my shoulders. "Thanks, Avra. I'll come in to greet him."

She offered a slow grin. "Ready?"

I smoothed the front of my dress. "As ready as I'll ever be." My pulse fluttered against my ribs, reminding me I could choose where to place my trust.

Avra looped her arm through mine. "Enthusiasm everywhere."

I admitted with a shrug. "The lunch is on my mind nonstop."

"Maybe your heart's giving you a signal." Her lips quirked upward. "But hey, no pressure tonight. You step back whenever you want."

I drew in a breath, comfort blooming in her words. "You and Laya have been on my side since forever. I don't know what I'd do without you both."

She squeezed my arm. "Always."

We crossed the threshold into the foyer together, the muffled murmur of arrivals rising around us. I lifted my chin.

I had my own path to follow, even if it led straight back into Leon's orbit.

As we got closer, Eli and Dominic turned to look at us, and I observed Dominic while maintaining a polite smile.

He stood under the crystal chandelier, shoulders squared like carved marble pillars. His eyes gleamed bright blue against the shadow of the corridor, from a face beyond traditionally attractive, more on the side of overwhelming. When he smiled, his lips curled back in welcome, except the warmth that spread across his features never reached his gaze, as if the motion was more practiced and for appearances.

He had an impressive physique, with broad shoulders that conveyed strength. His large biceps suggested he regularly lifted weights. He sported a meticulously tailored bespoke suit crafted from the finest black silk.

His hair lay slicked back, each strand locked into place, giving him a shine that felt more varnish than style. Something about that look sent a prickle along my spine.

Before I could take a deep breath, he swept one hand around mine and pressed a kiss to the back of it.

Almost instantly, heat flushed over my skin, a tang of metal rose in the back of my throat, and it took all of my strength not to jerk my fingers free from his grip.

"Calista, it's an honor to meet you." His voice rolled out smooth and steady, the kind of voice that could hush a crowded room.

If his lips hadn't lingered on my fingers so long, I might have mistaken his charm for genuine interest.

But those eyes, cold as winter lakes, kept me from believing a single word spilling from his lips.

I withdrew my hand as calmly as possible, jaw tightening as my pulse drummed an erratic beat.

My head spun with questions, chief among them being how I would survive this meeting.

His gaze drifted down my body at a pace meant to trace every inch of me: the cut of my dress, the line of my hips, the curve of my waist. Each second stretched out until I felt exposed and uncomfortable under his scrutiny. Then he nodded once as though ticking a box on an inspection list, and a slow smile crept onto his lips.

The lascivious look on his face repulsed me to my bones.

I straightened my shoulders and raised my chin.

He must have read every rumor about me, my family's fall, the whispers of scandal, and yet he treated me like something to inspect in a cabinet of curiosities.

I shot a look at Avra. She dipped her head in perfect sympathy, her lips pressed tight, acknowledging our silence.

Relief warmed me in a pool at my feet. At least someone here understood.

Dominic folded his hands in front of him and took a step back.

"Nice to meet you, Dominic." I let formality rest in my voice like a shield.

Elias cleared his throat. "Avra and I have tickets to the symphony. We'll leave you to dinner. Our chef has prepared something special."

His smile offered escape. I'd known about the dinner before I arrived, but at that moment, every bite felt poisoned by embarrassment.

Avra brushed my arm. She stared at the parquet floor, as if willing the moment to pass faster. I glanced at the clock on the wall. It was too late to change our plans.

Elias lifted Avra's hand.

"It was good to see you, Eli," Dominic said, sliding one hand into his suit pocket. "Perhaps lunch next week?"

Eli offered a grin. "Absolutely."

Avra passed me a supportive glance. "Call me later."

"I will," I answered, forcing my mouth to curve into a smile.

They walked off together, their footsteps fading against the marble. A moment of quiet settled in their wake, and I turned back toward Dominic.

"The dining room is this way," I said, sweeping my arm toward the long corridor.

He stepped forward, hand hovering politely in midair. "After you."

I led the way down the hall, each footfall echoing through the gilded space. My throat tightened, but I willed myself forward. I'd invited him here. To turn cold now would be as discourteous as refusing the invitation in the first place.

Halfway to the dining room, I accepted a small truth: this dinner could go two ways. He might redeem himself, or we'd part with nothing more than a polite nod. Either outcome felt manageable.

As we neared the heavy oak doors, he paused beside one of the tall, gilt mirrors lining the walls. I halted behind him, watching as he adjusted his tie, straightening the knot, smoothing the silk. He tilted his head left, then right, examining every angle. A satisfied grin touched his lips, and he gave himself a single nod.

Then he met my gaze and froze, caught in the act.

I nearly snorted, but I pressed it down. I lifted my chin and offered the same polite smile I'd given him moments ago, waiting for him to turn and lead the way.

"I hope you're hungry. The staff left a feast for us." I pushed open the double doors and stepped into cool lamplight, my heels clicking on the marble floor.

He followed, lips parting into a whistle as his gaze swept over platters of glistening kofta, bowls of steaming rice, stacks of fresh pita, and dishes of hummus and baba ghanoush. "This looks amazing," he said. He drew nearer, sniffing the air. "Eli's chef is famous for his spetzofai."

I settled into a chair at the head of the table and motioned to a seat opposite. "Oh, yes. He outdid himself at our family dinner last week."

Beneath the chandeliers, steam rose in lazy spirals from every dish, carrying the warm, spiced aroma straight to my chest.

We sat. Silverware chimed against china. I stared at the food, wondering how long it would take him to stop small talk and strike a real topic. The question answered itself the moment I sank my fork into a kofta.

He cleared his throat. "So, you're looking for a husband, Calista?"

I lifted my gaze. "I'm weighing my options." I scooped hummus onto a piece of pita. "I hear you're in the marriage market too."

His shoulders lifted, one then the other. A grin tugged at his lips. "Sure. I don't need a wife, but do I want one?"

He held my stare as if I might supply the answer from across the table.

I watched a drop of olive oil catch the light on my plate.

"Look," he said, leaning back so the candlelight danced off the gel in his hair. "A wife would probably do me good. Pop out a few children, keep the family line strong."

I swallowed—a cool knot formed in my throat.

"I'm a busy guy," he admitted. "And in our world, men gain a certain sense of respect when they have a wife. So, having a wife would help my reputation and maybe boost my career a bit. I won't lie, having a wife around would make entertaining much easier."

"Why is that?" I asked, cocking my head to the side.

I had a feeling I knew what the answer was going to be, but I wanted to let him dig his grave even deeper.

"Well, because of all the shit involved," he said. I ignored his crude language and didn't blink an eye.

"Like what?"

"All that hostess stuff. Making sure everyone is comfortable and happy and has a drink in their hand."

"Couldn't your staff handle that? You're describing a waitress."

"It's not the same at all." He shook his head so emphatically that his hair broke free of the confines of the gel holding it down. "A wife can socialize, you know? Tinkling laughter? Flash a little cleavage? Flatter your boss in a corner, maybe let him slip a hand if he fancies himself bold?"

My fingers clenched the glass in my hand. I brought it to my lips, gulping until my lungs burned. What the fuck was wrong with him?

Bile rose in my throat, and I swallowed down every bit of water I could.

"God, sorry," he said, waving a dismissive hand. "That was inappropriate. You know. Considering."

Anger surged, fiery and ready to be unleashed. I leveled him with a look that dared him to repeat himself.

"Considering?" My heart hammered as a murderous haze clouded my eyesight.

My other hand drifted beneath the table, brushing leather against the dagger strapped to my thigh. One twist and his throat would part like silk. Blood would bloom across Elias's white marble.

He swallowed, a blush creeping into his cheeks. He looked sheepish, but not enough to stop himself from saying the asinine thing that was about to come out of his mouth.

"Considering what you went through. It's not exactly private—everyone's heard."

I let out a breath that felt too loud. My gaze narrowed, pressing him into silence.

He leaned forward, as if we were about to share a secret. "Tell me, Calista, since it's just the two of us. Were the rumors true? The ones about what they did to you? Because of the stories... God, they made it sound like you were torn apart."

I sat very still, the blade in shadow at my side.

My jaw slammed open, heat flushing my cheeks. How dare he? We'd only just met.

He lowered his voice to a conspiratorial murmur, as if that lessened the offensiveness of his words. "I don't mean to be insensitive, but you look really good."

He sank back in his chair, a thin sheen of sauce glinting at the corner of his mouth, and grinned like he'd just delivered a compliment.

"Seriously, you look great. You'd never know a thing by looking at you. That's why I asked if it was as bad as I heard."

His words fell between us like shards of broken glass. Beneath the table, my fingers tightened around the knife's handle.

I imagined the satisfying give of warm flesh and the metallic tang of blood scenting the air, then wrenched the thought away before it could escape.

"I'm not sure how to answer that, Dominic." I forced a brittle smile and met his gaze. "But let me assure you, the deepest scars are the ones you can't see."

He cocked his head. "Oh, you mean like..."

He scanned my body, tracing the line of my blouse, and I closed my legs, the table's edge cutting off his view.

"I mean psychological scars," I stated, my tone composed yet firm.

My palms itched to rise, to send every fork and wine glass crashing off the polished oak.

I was seething with anger now, and I wasn't doing much to hide it. How could he not notice? He seemed blissfully unaware of how he was affecting me.

He held up both hands, palms forward, flashing that smug smile. "I don't mean to offend. I was curious since we were talking about marriage. Sometimes those things break women. They don't always come back from it. Seriously, though, you look good. You don't seem broken at all."

A piece of lamb dangled from his fork as he watched me with the clinical detachment of a scientist observing a specimen. The chandeliers overhead rattled softly in the hush his words had carved out.

You don't seem broken at all.

The echo of his praise morphed into a blistering insult in my mind.

My pulse throbbed against my temples.

I pressed my lips into a thin line and leaned forward until the lace edge of my sleeve brushed the table.

"Don't worry about wedding bells, Dominic." I tilted my head, offering him a smile as brittle as cracked porcelain. "I have several suitors to consider. I'm nowhere near saying yes."

He shrugged, wiping sauce from his chin. "That's fine, but obviously I'm the best choice. You'll see."

I lifted my glass, rosé catching the candle's glow, and sipped cool wine before setting it down with perfect, unhurried poise.

"Will I?" I whispered, my smile unwavering.

Fuck this guy.

The low glow of the candlelight carved sharp angles across his face, and for a second, he looked nervous, a child caught with his hand in the cookie jar.

My sisters had taught me that true power thrums in silence. I let the room settle around us, the quiet pressing against him.

He swallowed, his confident smile flickering. He had no idea I'd already made the only decision that mattered. Not in a million years would I become Mrs. Lucianos. Not with a man who thought he could grade my life by the curve of my smile.

FOUR

L EON

Iason uncurled the blueprints across my cluttered desk, flattening the heavy rolls against scattered invoices, half-finished sketches, and last night's cold coffee swirls. A stained mug slid toward the edge.

I lunged, braced my palm against the desktop, and steered it back to safety. Dark liquid pooled in the saucer, droplets clinging to the rim.

"Leon, your office looks like a shipwreck," he said, tapping a stray takeout container off the corner. "How do you find anything in this chaos?"

I leaned back in my chair, feet propped on the leg of a drawing table. "Chaos breeds creativity," I shot back.

"Besides, you live in a penthouse that is larger than this entire floor, and it's crammed from floor to ceiling with items you won't part with."

He grinned, reaching for his reading glasses and perching them on the bridge of his nose. "We're both slackers, then. What we need is wives."

"No, that's what house cleaners are for," I corrected and tapped the blueprints with a pencil. "A wife is so much more complicated than that."

"I guess." He shrugged, shoulders lifting beneath his crisp shirt. "Maybe so. At this rate, I'll be forty and still flying solo. Perhaps a hybrid model—a spouse who also mops the floors?"

I set the pencil down and pushed the unruly stack of sketches aside. "That plan sounds outdated. You'd offend half of the world."

He jabbed a finger at me. "Says the guy waiting to be selected as a husband in an arranged marriage. You don't get more old-fashioned than that."

"Can we get back to these blueprints? I have to double-check every dimension before the permit office opens."

He lifted his glasses, slid them onto the bridge of his nose, and scanned the drawings. The fluorescent light above threw acute angles across the lines of the countertop, seating areas, and a raised stage for live acts.

Iason traced a corridor, paused, and tapped a beam's measurement. "These beams will need extra support if you plan to open that balcony."

I sank into the worn leather chair behind the desk.

Running my family's restaurant and entertainment venues felt like a storm I navigated daily. Iason had guided me through menu redesigns, seating layouts, and licensing battles —I couldn't imagine pulling it off alone. Even when he teased me about personal matters, he was my anchor.

While he studied the schematics, my mind drifted to Calista.

During lunch, a connection had sparked when I asked her about her studies. Her eyes brightened with enthusiasm, exuding a passion that energized the atmosphere.

In the days since, every image of her pulled taut like a bowstring, the tilt of her chin, the way light danced in her green eyes, the scent of her perfume.

I lifted a stray sticky note from the desk and twisted it between my thumb and forefinger. By the time I left the café, I'd called an organic grower north of town, secured six dozen white roses, and arranged their delivery to her sister Layana's estate. Layana's gates stood guarded by iron spikes and uniformed staff. Calista's address remained a secret. Tracing property records, cross-referencing social pages, and making discreet inquiries, each step confirmed that the Vitalis family took security seriously.

Iason peered over the plans. "If we reinforce that wall with steel columns, you'll keep the ceiling from sagging under all that equipment."

I pressed my fingertip to the blueprint's faded ink. "That'll work."

Then I looked away from the drawing frame to the cluttered office, at the peeling corners of posters from last season's acts, at the list of daily repairs scrawled on a scrap of paper.

"I need patience," I said, more to myself than to him.

"What was that?"

"Nothing." I cleared my throat. "Just considering next steps."

He tapped his pen on the desk. "Next steps for the project or next steps for you?"

I met his gaze. He already knew the answer.

A soft smile crept across my face. "Both, and right now, I'll start by waiting for permits, for the right moment to approach the Vitalis sisters, and for Calista to say yes."

"Leave the rest to me," he said. "I'll handle the permits. You handle romance."

I stood, set down my coffee, and felt something tighten and unfold in my chest. I would make good on those roses. I would earn a place in her family's trust. And I would wait, counting each day until I could call Calista my partner, in business and life.

"Well?" I leaned over the drafting table and traced the pencil marks on the blueprints.

Iason pushed back from his stool and folded his arms. His gaze dropped from the plans to me. "Leon, you ran these figures through every possible scenario before you handed them to me. We both know the numbers check out."

I tapped a finger against the edge of the table. "I like a fresh perspective."

He lifted one corner of the top sheet and let it snap back into place. The soft *thwack* echoed in the sunlit studio.

"Perfectionism suits you," he said. "No harm in that."

Satisfied, I picked up the rolled drawings and tied them with a leather strap.

"On to the next step," I said, sliding them under my arm.

My phone buzzed against my hip. I pulled it free, eyeing the caller ID. "Leon Boscos."

"Sir, it's Alex at Kanoula."

"Alex?" My chest tightened. He managed my estate with the precision of a surgeon. If he called me, something had gone wrong. "What's happened?"

"Can I get additional security onsite? Right away."

I exchanged a glance with Iason. His brow furrowed. "Tell me exactly what's going on."

I spent the next two minutes listening as Alex outlined a dispute at the restaurant—voices shouting, chairs scraping, the clink of glass.

When I tapped the screen to end the call, Iason was on his feet, coat already in hand. "I take it we need to move?"

He flicked off the light switch as we crossed the hallway.

"There's a brawl going on at Kanoula, if you can believe that."

"A brawl?" Iason asked. "What the hell?"

We reached my Aston Martin parked under the portico. I slid into the driver's seat, pressed the engine button, and the V12 rumbled to life. Iason buckled in beside me.

"You think this is about you?" he said.

"It wouldn't surprise me. Kanoula is a nice restaurant. Violence rarely breaks out in places like that. So, yeah, maybe it's about me."

"Why?" he asked. "You already eliminated the men who killed your family."

"That's true, but their names aren't forgotten. Rumors about my link to a Vitalis sister have already taken flight. Their enemies could be behind this."

He exhaled, fingers tapping the door panel. "They're not exactly predictable. There's no telling what those fuckers would do."

"Exactly," I said.

"Well, we can shut it down," he said. "Do you want me to call in reinforcements?"

I guided the Aston onto the driveway, then onto the main road. "Let's assess the situation before calling in reinforcements."

He remained silent for the remainder of the ride. Just a few minutes later, I arrived at the restaurant, where chaos overflowed onto the narrow sidewalk outside.

The restaurant was a cozy and intimate place, so the commotion spilling onto the street didn't surprise me.

As we hopped out of the car, I scanned the sea of people, trying to make sense of the situation. Through the windows of the restaurant, I homed in on the faces of two members of prominent syndicate families. Their presence only fueled my suspicion that this chaos might be centered around me.

"I see the eldest Polus and Manolis," Iason pointed out as we approached the crowd gathered outside to watch the chaos inside. "They've hated each other since they were kids."

"Yeah, they're going at it," I replied, just as the eldest Polus son swung his fist, connecting forcefully with the nose of my head chef, who happened to have gotten in the way as the fight moved in the direction of the kitchen.

Frustration boiled over, and I yelled, "Goddammit!" I pushed through the crowd and rushed into the restaurant.

Inside, pandemonium reigned.

Men were grappling with one another, while some customers and the staff huddled in the corner in fear.

My heart sank at seeing my beloved restaurant now a battlefield. Splintered chairs and shattered dishes were strewn across the floor, and all I could envision was the financial toll each broken piece represented.

Fury bubbled within me, and I needed to know who was behind this madness. I searched the room, finding Alex and the rest of the staff, who stood watching the chaos unfold. Relief washed over Alex's face when he spotted me and hurried over.

"Leon, should I call the cops? You told me to contact you first, and—"

"No," I interrupted. "Just guide the customers out through the back door and apologize. Tell them they can dine free for a year once we've sorted this mess out. I'll handle these assholes."

"I'll help," Iason chimed in, fists clenched at his sides, ready for action. "Who do I punch first?"

"Nobody," I replied. Determined to end the chaos, I grabbed an intact chair, climbed onto it, and took a deep breath. I shouted with all the authority I could muster, my voice cutting through the clamor. "Enough!"

To my surprise, it succeeded. Fists lost their force in the

air, chairs were returned to the floor instead of being smashed over heads, and all eyes shifted toward me.

I quickly evaluated the crowd, identifying nearly all as sons of the Polus and Manolis families. Since I regard the Manolises as my allies, I could only conclude that the oldest Polus had instigated this conflict.

"Who wants to explain why you're trashing my restaurant?" I yelled.

Nektarios Polus stepped up, dismissing my presence. He had been a scrawny kid years ago, but now he loomed over me like a giant. His shoulders were broad, and his biceps resembled melons. His face contorted into an ugly grimace as he glared at me. He'd taken quite a hit, and his left eye was rapidly swelling.

"This is all your fault!" He hurled the accusation at me.

I arched an eyebrow. "What have I done to warrant an assault on my staff and customers? Are you such a coward that you can't face me directly?"

I leaped off the chair, landing in front of him, staring him down.

"I'm here now, Polus," I stated.

Iason approached, planting his feet wide apart, fists clenched and coiled like springs ready to unleash a storm. Unaware of the chaos brewing, Polus continued to taunt, playing with fire as his words ignited tension. Iason, my business partner and steadfast protector, radiated a menacing energy, a clear warning that he could unleash fury if provoked.

But I could too.

"You've drawn your line in the sand, Boscos. Now you have to suffer the consequences."

"And what line is that?"

"Don't play innocent! Everyone knows what you're planning!"

"Outside of another restaurant, Polus? Please tell me what plans I've made that warrant you beating the shit out of each other in my restaurant."

"When you suggested marrying a Vitalis," he started, standing amidst the debris, perfectly upright in his charcoal suit as if he had orchestrated the entire scene, "you made it clear to everyone where your loyalty stands. You picked a side. Now, anyone who enters your restaurants is endorsing your decision, every choice you make."

I clenched my fists. "That's ridiculous. You know it."

"Are you saying it's not true?" Polus arched a brow. "You're not planning to marry Calista Vitalis?"

"I'm not saying anything of the sort. That's none of your business, Polus, and you know that."

I'd expected objections. My alliance with her would shift power across half the island, but I hadn't reckoned with Polus trashing my flagship location before I'd even had an answer. Did merely weighing her proposal justify this?

I swept a hand across my face, willing my fury back behind the dam of my teeth. My other hand hovered near the heavy brass kendo stick I kept behind the bar. Better to save that demonstration for when it mattered.

"It is our business," he insisted. "There are territories

involved. Business deals to consider. Certain consolidations can never occur if the Vitalis sisters are involved."

"I barely do any business with your family. If this is such an issue, then I can assure you I can eliminate any future dealings. Now, please get the fuck out of my restaurant and don't ever step foot near it again."

"You think you can tell us what to do? You think you can do whatever you want, without repercussions?"

I jerked my head toward the door and then toward the ruined decor, from the spray of wine on the walls to the splintered tables. "Did your Papa send you to do this, Nektarios? Is this a temper tantrum gone awry?"

Polus squared his shoulders. "I'm running the Polus syndicate now, and the Manolises need to understand the consequences of maintaining certain loyalties."

"I see." I stepped forward, bringing my face close to his and lowering my voice to a menacing growl. Anger and rage bubbled to the surface, threatening to break through my restraint. "Gather your boys and get them out before I jam your fucking head through the window. You don't want me to demonstrate what happens when you decide to fuck with me and mine. That includes my allies."

His face twisted. "Why put it all on the line, Leon? For a spent whore? Half this town got her in that kidnapping. Now you'll risk your name for a tainted cunt?"

I inhaled the bitter air, blood thrumming in my ears. Calista's name on Polus's lips was like poison. And I would see this through, no matter the cost.

My knuckles slammed into his cheek before caution had

a chance to speak. Bone crackled like breaking twigs, and bright red droplets arced through the air.

He stumbled backward, legs folding beneath him, and I was on top of him before he hit the floor. My weight pinned his chest to the scorched tile, and my fists moved in a brutal rhythm, each punch a hammer driving through flesh.

The world narrowed to the taste of blood on my tongue, the roar of my heartbeat in my ears, and the savage need to make him pay.

Around us, chairs clattered as Iason hurled himself into Polus's men. The crash of bottles and the thud of bodies hitting tables made the restaurant feel alive with violence, but every second I spent looking at Polus's face added fuel to the fire beneath my ribs.

He'd spat vile words about Calista, twisted her name until it sickened me. He deserved every wound I carved into his skin.

"Don't you ever speak of Calista that way again!" The words tore out of me.

Blood splattered across my forearms, dark and slippery, but I welcomed it.

I pummeled him, each fist smashing into his jaw, ready to drain the life out of him.

"I'll kill you!" I roared, my rage growing by the second.

He tried to gasp out a word. I crushed it.

"One more slip of your tongue about her, and I'll finish you right here."

My arms shook, veins thrumming, but I kept moving,

punch after punch, until his body slumped, heartbeats fading into silence under my weight.

Then I kept going.

A firm grip seized my shoulders and wrenched me back.

I staggered off him, chest heaving.

"Boss, it's over." Iason steered me backward, away from Polus's still form.

My gaze drifted over the ruined dining room, splintered chairs, shards of glass glittering in broken light, terrified staff pressed into a corner, faces pale as bone.

I took a step that felt like walking through mud. My shirt clung to me, soaked in blood that wasn't mine but felt intimate on my skin. I blinked, trying to clear the fog. Iason's hand stayed firm on my shoulder.

"Let's get some air," he said, voice even. "I'll bring our crew in to clean this mess."

I crouched beside Polus and nudged him with my shoe. His chest rose in a ragged breath.

Good.

He'd live to carry every broken promise back to the world that dared insult Calista. I stood, spine coiling with cold satisfaction, and turned to my staff.

"Alex, send everyone home. The restaurant is closed until further notice. All the staff will receive full pay, so tell them not to worry. I apologize that they had to witness this."

"Thank you, Mr. Boscos," Alex said.

He slipped out a side door with the others, footsteps echoing down the alley.

Iason and I walked outside, stepping over bodies strewn like discarded dolls. A small crowd had gathered under the flickering neon sign, but people scattered into the night at our approach.

"I'll wait here until our guys arrive." Iason took in my appearance, without doubt noting my soaked shirt and bruised knuckles. "Are you okay? You're covered in blood."

"None of this blood belongs to me," I replied, chest heaving. "He didn't land a single punch."

"I'm not surprised." He laughed.

"What about you?" I asked, pointing to his split lip.

"I'll manage. Are you okay to drive yourself home?"

"Yeah," I said. "Thanks."

A few seconds later, I climbed behind the wheel of my car. My knuckles throbbed with life. I turned the key, and the engine rumbled awake.

As I pulled onto the street, fury still hissed through my veins. Polus's insults had lit a fire I didn't even know I carried, and every mile fading behind me only fanned the flames.

A smile tugged at my lips as I thought of Calista.

How she was so important to me, someone not even my wife yet, and already worth any fight I had in me.

She still hadn't chosen, and I was already willing to protect her and defend her name.

I pressed my palm to the steering wheel, knuckles stiff, heart still thrumming with the taste of battle.

What would I do once we were married?

To what lengths would I go to keep her safe?

The answer settled behind my ribs like a promise: no boundary, no limit.

A weak man backed down.

My hands tightened on the wheel. I was far from weak.

Five

CALISTA

My heels clicked against the gleaming white marble as I wound through Laya and Niko's foyer.

Avra's baby nursery was coming together beautifully. I'd spent the morning browsing my phone for the perfect rug that would complement Avra's soothing colors and whimsical patterns. Each scroll revealed new options, and I envisioned how those textures and hues would enhance the cozy atmosphere we imagined for the little one's arrival.

My nose was still in my phone as I descended the stairs searching for Laya. We'd planned to go on another shopping expedition in the city, and it was time to leave.

I was so engrossed, I didn't notice the butler coming to me with his arms full of white roses in full bloom.

"Ms. Vitalis, these arrived for you," he announced, bowing his head.

He set the vase on a nearby console, and I looked up just in time to catch a single bloom drifting free. I cupped it in my hand, inhaling the way its scent slipped into my senses.

"Thank you," I said, lifting my gaze. "Who sent them?"

He touched a ribbon tied around the bouquet. "The card should say." He untied the silk loop and handed me a small envelope. "Shall I take these to your room?"

"Yes, please."

As he disappeared down the hall, I untied the ribbon, curiosity warming each finger, and slipped the card from its envelope.

The florist's name was printed on the corner, Petal & Stem.

This was the farm that had provided all of Laya's wedding flowers. They weren't cheap, and placing an order with them wasn't easy. I wasn't aware they created arrangements like these. From working at Laya's wedding, I assumed they only worked on large-scale events.

I eased the tiny card free and read:

Cali,

Our lunch together was the bright spot of my week. I can't stop thinking about you, and I hope I can see you again soon. Thanks for the sunshine. Call me anytime to chat, or...

Strogiká,
Leon

My heart skipped a beat, my pulse taking on a life of its own.

Strogiká—*fondly,* in Greek—curled at the end of his note like a secret revelation.

My fingertips brushed the handwriting, tracing each word as if it might vanish.

There, on the back, his phone number was inked, as if he had penned it with the same eager thrill I felt now.

I pressed the card between my fingers and imagined dialing, no pressure, just an invitation.

Leon's words hovered between us like soft music, nothing demanding or loud. He'd left the choice entirely to me. A gentle thrill spread through my veins.

I remembered Dominic's approach, overbearing tones and bristling insistence, and felt how differently Leon had reached out.

The contrast made me smile. I rose and tucked the card into my pocket for a moment when I could read it again.

Despite their similar reputations as ruthless and cunning, and sometimes violent, syndicate leaders, in person, the two of them were like night and day.

I was captivated by the contradiction between Leon's serene and patient presence and the intimidating reputation that followed him like a shadow. That intriguing space where light meets shadow in a person's life had always fascinated me.

To me, the painful traumas of life, while devastating, ultimately made one stronger and added layers of depth to a person's character and humanity that I believed were unattainable through any other means.

I'd come to understand this truth through my own painful experiences. But I saw this transformation in many others too.

My sisters and I endured the devastating loss of our parents and the shattering of the lives we once knew. Vik, who was very close to our father, took on the monumental responsibility of caring for three spirited girls in hiding while standing alone as a single man.

I observed it in countless others within the syndicates who had lost everything dear to them, their families torn away.

Something profound lingered after such loss, a deep and enduring change.

Most clearly, I recognized it in me after my rescue. I realized that the darkness would never completely vanish. It was now woven into the fabric of my being, altering me permanently, as much a part of me as my very skin.

Leon carried this darkness as well. He had suffered tremendous losses himself. His deep espresso eyes revealed the same sadness, shadows, and sorrow that I had come to know so well. If there was ever a man who could truly understand me and be attuned to my needs, it had to be someone like Leon.

An intense desire to be near him surged within me, almost overwhelming in its urgency. With a wide smile lighting up my face, I turned the card over again and dialed his cell number.

"Hello, Cali," he answered immediately, his voice warm and welcoming.

I furrowed my brow, perplexed. "What?" I said. "How did you know it was me?"

My private number was tightly secured, and I knew it wouldn't appear on his caller ID.

"I just had a feeling," he replied. In my mind, I could vividly picture him grinning and giving a casual shrug, and the image made my smile stretch wider. "Did you get the flowers?"

"I just did," I confessed, still a bit in awe. "They're magical."

"Fantastic!" he exclaimed with genuine enthusiasm.

"Thank you, Leon," I said, a wave of shyness washing over me. "That was very thoughtful of you. Your note was lovely too."

"I'm glad you like them," he said. "I wanted you to know that I was thinking about you."

My heart soared at his directness.

"You were on my mind too," I admitted, the truth spilling out.

Since our lunch, he had been a constant presence in my thoughts, which was quite remarkable and unexpected, given that I never imagined being genuinely interested in a man again.

Then, I asked, "You know what else I've thought about?"

"What?" he responded, eager to hear.

"That lamb moussaka you teased me with."

"Someday," he finally said, leaving the promise lingering in the air.

"Someday," I echoed, our voices mingling.

A gentle silence enveloped us, and I knew we were both wearing matching smiles. The sensation that filled the quiet was so delicate, so light and feathery, like a ray of sunshine dancing across my skin.

I think it may have been happiness. Pure, pristine happiness...

"Would you like to come over for dinner Saturday night?" I blurted out, the words tumbling from my lips before I could overthink them.

As soon as the words slipped from my mouth, I wished I could reel them back in.

My mind raced, questioning whether I should take the initiative and invite a man out. But then, I dismissed that notion with a roll of my eyes. That was such an outdated mindset.

After all, he was practically waiting for me to make the first move, even though we were still getting acquainted. Asking him over for dinner wasn't such a big deal.

"Are you asking me out on a date?"

"Yes."

"Where would you like to go?"

"I'm inviting you to my sister's estate. Laya and Niko have shown remarkable kindness and hospitality by allowing me to stay here," I explained.

"I've heard it's certainly big enough," Leon quipped.

"It certainly is. I have my own wing. It's quite impressive, and the vineyards are exceptional," I replied. "They're among the best in the region."

"I know well the remarkable empire Niko has created. It feels as though I'm being offered a glimpse into the vastness of my rival's operations. In comparison to what he oversees, my vineyard is relatively modest."

"Well, then, is he really your rival?" I questioned. "And besides, what's wrong with finding some inspiration to elevate your own work, Leon?"

He chuckled, a sound that made me feel light. I was relieved he found my comments entertaining. Many might have taken it as a jab at their pride. But Leon's self-assured nature allowed him to embrace the banter with ease.

"Fair point," he conceded. "It's a date!"

"Wonderful! How about you come over around seven?"

"I wouldn't miss it for the world," he replied with a warmth that sent a delightful blush to my cheeks.

As I hung up the phone, a sense of exhilaration washed over me. Leon was so at ease, so effortlessly engaging in conversation.

With my heart skipping in excitement, I moved forward, continuing my search for Laya. Each step was buoyed by the anticipation and thrill of what was coming.

"Hey!" Laya's voice shot through the quiet hallway.

I lifted my head, heart stuttering, to see her leaning over the banister at the top of the staircase. The late afternoon sun painted her hair in copper tones.

"Hey, there you are," I called. "I was just coming to find you."

I tucked a strand of hair behind my ear and let the warmth in my cheeks spill down my neck.

"Is that so?" she cooed, the amusement evident on her face. "Because it sounded like you were flirting with Leon Boscos on the telephone."

I pressed a hand to the receiver, my cheeks growing warm. "You heard all that?"

She dropped her shoulders. "I did indeed."

I rose from the carpeted landing and reached the bottom stair. "Is it okay if he comes over for dinner on Saturday?"

Laya's gaze swept the familiar walls, the framed sketches I'd made in college. "You live here, Cali. You can invite anyone over at any time." She descended the staircase step by step, each board creaking under her weight, until she stood before me. "So... Does this mean you've made your choice?"

I shook my head, running a fingertip along the polished banister. "I don't know. I've tried not thinking at all."

She cocked her head. "Are you sure? That conversation sounded friendly just now."

I let out a breath. "I like Leon a lot."

A gentle smile formed on her lips. "He seems like a good choice, for what it's worth."

"Thanks. It means a lot to hear you say that." My voice wavered. "I feel the same way. Obviously."

Laya folded her arms across her chest. "Then what's the problem, Cali? It seems simple."

A tight knot formed in my stomach. I twisted the sleeve

of my sweater. "But is it? I judged Dominic the moment I met him, based only on how he made me feel. Maybe I never gave him a proper chance."

She lifted a brow. "What's wrong with deciding by feeling?"

I turned toward the window and watched sunbeams drift across the floor. "That's not how you and Avra did it. You both chose for business reasons. Emotions didn't lead you. They were set aside."

Her lips curved, not mocking but gentle. "Is that really what you think?"

I met her gaze, most of my courage in my chest. "Well, yeah."

Laya shook her head, dark curls swinging. "I can't speak for Avra, but I knew I cared for Niko the moment he walked into that meeting. Those feelings only confirmed I'd made the right decision."

My shoulders eased their tension. I dropped my arms to my sides. "Okay."

She moved closer and rested her hand on my elbow, her skin warm against mine. "Cali, pay attention to your instincts. Observe how your body responds to others. It's a way to perceive things your mind may not comprehend. You can think until you're exhausted, but if something feels off, it is. I refer to it as our Vitalis superpower."

"Do you really believe that?" I asked.

She lifted her chin. "Mama talked about it when we were kids. She said never to doubt that instinct. I've never been wrong. You have it too—that's why you're torn. It doesn't have to be complicated. Meet Dominic again. You'll know if your heart flutters when you see him."

I smiled and closed the gap between us to hug her. She folded her arms around me and squeezed.

"What would I do without you, Laya?"

"Most likely die," she said.

I pulled back and hooked my arm through hers, leading her toward the front door. The air outside carried a promise of spring.

"You might be right," I replied. "Now, let's splurge on baby items. Do you think our little one will have that superpower?"

Laya's grin spread wide. "I certainly hope so!"

Six

L EON

Iron gates groaned open as I rolled my car forward, headlights catching their wrought-iron filigree. I guided the tires onto a ribbon of gravel and settled in.

The Galanis estate was massive.

Ahead, the manor rose like a fortress of sandstone, its turrets and arching windows dwarfing the hillside. My own vineyard, just a few tidy rows behind a low stucco wall, felt like a garden patch by comparison.

Beyond the house, vineyards tumbled over gentle slopes, each vine tied in neat lines that threaded through the grass. Clusters of grapes sat along them, ready to grow and ripen throughout the approaching Summer's sun.

To the right, olive groves spread into a soft green sea, trunks bent at odd angles under their silver leaves, promising hidden paths and cool shade.

I steered past a semicircle drive and cut around the far wing of the mansion. There, a low complex of buildings hugged the hillside. Cavern-wide doorways yielded glimpses of polished steel tanks, cylinders rising like sentinels, and gleaming pipes that snaked toward walls stacked high with centuries-old oak barrels. Their staves bulged with age, metal hoops mottled by time.

Workers moved in choreographed clusters: a man hefting nets into a press, another adjusting a hose, voices rising and falling against the clatter of footwear on stone and wood. Every corner of this place buzzed with purpose.

The operation proceeded smoothly and efficiently. Production schedules were posted on bulletin boards, fork-lifts maneuvered gracefully below the crate racks, and cellar doors opened at exact moments. I'd faced setups half this size and felt those familiar twinges of insecurity. Not today. I'd built niche experiences, boutique wineries, themed restaurants, and late-night lounges tailored to a select crowd.

My business thrived on intimacy. Galanis thrived on scale.

Still, scale didn't breed exclusivity. Plates in my restaurants could showcase his estate's single-vineyard reserve. His casks might rest beneath my bar's polished oak floors. I pictured summer tastings where my dim lanterns illuminated his wine's crimson depths.

There was ambition behind every thought. The Vitalis

family had stormed back into prominence: power brokers and social architects.

I wanted in on their momentum. And Calista Vitalis, soon to be my wife, sat at the center of that orbit. That fact pulsed beneath my skin more insistently than any spreadsheet or marketing forecast.

Her last call had sent warmth through my chest.

Colleagues had joked about the sudden lightness to my stride, but I knew it wasn't the market or a new contract.

It was her. My pulse skipped at the thought of her smile, the soft edge in her voice—anticipation, attraction, curiosity, each pulse a drumbeat of something uncharted.

I wasn't a soft or kind man, but something about Calista called to me.

I shut off the engine, and suddenly, the quiet felt electric. Gravel crunched under my shoes as I climbed the flagstone steps. Birdsong echoed from the olive grove, notes carried on a cool breeze.

At the top, the heavy oak door swung inward before I could lift my hand. A butler, tall, silver-haired, perfectly still, stood framed by the doorway, a silent welcome awaiting me.

"Welcome to the Galanis estate, Mr. Boscos," he announced, his voice resonating through the opulent entrance as he executed a formal bow. "Please, come in."

"Thank you." I stepped across the threshold and allowed myself to be enveloped by the opulence of the foyer.

The floors, a pristine expanse of white marble, gleamed under the light, while a grand staircase swept gracefully upward, an inviting path to the second floor. Nestled within the staircase's curve stood a statue of a nude woman, her form lending the space an air of serene elegance and timeless sophistication.

Across the room, a massive abstract painting burst forth with vivid gold, green, and white hues, infusing the area with a lively splash of color.

Just as I entered, a pack of four massive dogs bounded toward me, their exuberance palpable as they encircled my feet, tails wagging with uncontained joy.

"Oh, wow," I breathed, lowering myself to their level and extending my hands to pet them. They were shepherds, one with the distinct features of a Dutch breed, the others proudly representing Greek breeds. "Aren't you all beauties?"

I crouched farther, my hands roaming over their sleek coats as they vied for attention. Their friendliness was undeniable, their demeanor unbothered by the presence of a stranger.

Curious, I inspected the nametags dangling from their collars, chuckling when I discovered one of them bore the name Leontios.

It was the Greek word for fearless, a name I recognized instantly, for it was mine as well.

Rising to my feet, I noticed Calista entering the foyer, her presence commanding the room.

"Hello," she greeted me in a gentle voice. "I see you've made friends with the dogs already."

"I'm not sure I had a choice," I responded as I studied her.

Calista was a vision of beauty, her allure even more

striking than I remembered from our previous encounter. She wore a pair of crisp white slacks and a white silk blouse that opened tastefully at the neck.

My gaze traced the graceful line of her neck to the top of her chest, captivated by the gentle curve revealed there.

Her golden blond hair cascaded over her shoulders, framing her face with a natural elegance. As I absorbed the sight of her, the Dutch shepherd named Leontios trotted over to her side, standing with a protective air as she assessed me with a watchful gaze.

"Is that one yours?" I inquired, nodding toward the impressive dog standing loyally by her side.

"Yes, she is." Cali rested her hand firmly on the dog's broad back, as if to claim her as her own. I immediately knew a profound connection existed between Cali and this magnificent creature. "Her name is Leo."

"That's interesting because her name tag doesn't agree with you," I remarked, arching an eyebrow. The sight of her cheeks turning a delightful shade of pink was a small victory.

"I know, but I swear I didn't know you when I named her. Leontios is a girl's name, after all."

"I'm not sure about that," I said, feigning skepticism. "And if it's true, then my parents were tragically misinformed when they named me."

Her laughter was a melody that danced through the air, and when she shrugged, it was with such charm that I felt an overwhelming urge to hold her close and kiss her.

But I knew it was far too early for such an impulsive act. If I had any hope of getting closer to Cali, it would require a slow, measured approach. For now, I would have to suppress those impulses.

"Would you like to go out to the gardens? I'd love to show you around," Cali suggested with enthusiasm.

"That sounds wonderful," I replied, falling into step behind her.

We strolled through a lavish sunken living room, where a grand stone fireplace dominated one wall and expansive floor-to-ceiling windows offered a stunning view of the sprawling estate beyond.

Cali pushed open a pair of glass doors, and we stepped onto a terrace, the dogs trailing behind us, their paws pattering softly against the floor.

"Do you have any pets?" Cali asked, turning her head to catch my response.

"Yes, I have a shepherd of my own." I thought of my more-than-exuberant companion. "His name is Cosmo. You'll have to meet him sometime."

"I'd love to," she said, casting a warm smile over her shoulder. We paused near the stone railing, taking in the sight of the expansive rose garden below. "Maybe when you finally invite me over for that moussaka."

Her playful wink made my heart skip a beat.

"Absolutely," I agreed, struggling to maintain my composure in her captivating presence.

Sunlight spilled over her shoulders, each ray threading through her hair until it glowed like burnished gold. When she turned and smiled, her eyes curved into perfect crescents, and something in my chest clenched so tight I thought I'd stop breathing.

I pressed both hands flat against my thighs and drew in a measured breath. Let air fill my lungs. Released it without trembling. The confident businessman I'd rehearsed in my head dissolved when she caught my eye.

Instead, I felt like a schoolboy—knees weak, voice stuck behind a shuttered door. Even so, an odd calm settled beneath the chaos, a comfort I'd never known.

Cali led me down a sweep of stone steps, each slab worn smooth by untold footsteps. Vines marched off at the hilltop into the haze, with neat rows disappearing beneath distant pines.

A wrought-iron bistro table stood under a green umbrella, but Cali shrugged off her heels and sank onto the grass. She tucked her knees under her chin, and the two dogs flopped onto either side, noses nudging her hands.

"This is my favorite spot," she said, watching birds flicker between branches.

I eased down beside her, the grass cool against my suit trousers. A breeze carried a hint of jasmine from her perfume, the same scent from the last time we met, and I barely resisted the pull to lean in, to let that fragrance fill my senses.

"It's a beautiful view," I said, doing my damnedest to sound normal. "The vines look like ribbons laid out by careful hands, and those hills hold every story this land has ever told."

Cali tucked a loose strand of hair behind her ear. "Sometimes I spend hours observing the curve of each branch and listening to sparrows argue. My sisters tell me I'm wasting my time, that daydreaming leads to nowhere."

I remembered hiding in my grandfather's closet to escape chores, my eldest brother's exasperated sigh when I couldn't keep still. The ache of missing them tightened around my ribs.

"Isn't it every older sibling's duty to fuss over you?" I asked. "Mine drove me mad, but I'd give anything to have them back."

She turned toward me, expression open. "You miss them," she stated, not as a question but a fact.

Her honesty caught me off guard. Most people skirted around my family, as if speaking their names might break a fragile peace. I swallowed hard.

"I still reach for my phone to call my mother about the smallest thing, then remember she's gone."

Cali slid her hand over mine, palm warm against my knuckles. The grass whispered beneath us. "I understand," she said. "I miss my parents too."

A hush settled over us. She rested her fingertips against mine, and a warmth spread from the base of my palm to my collarbone. It felt like sinking into a familiar armchair after a long day, yet electricity raced beneath my skin.

Comfort pulled me inward as a thrill pushed me outward, two forces tangled until I could not tell one from the other. I pressed into the swirl of feeling, letting each pulse of wonder and surge of longing sweep through me.

I imagined every secret moment we might share in a sunlit kitchen, every quiet evening by a crackling fire.

If this marriage to Cali brought such wonder and peace, I would stand at the altar today. My chest ached with the closeness between us, raw and honest, grounding me in a truth I could not name but recognized without question.

I made a wish as her thumb traced my palm. When she was ready, I hoped she would choose me. Together, let us weave our lives into something enduring—a space filled with warmth and new memories created side by side.

I pictured her smile greeting me at dawn, familiar as sunrise, something I would crave each morning.

"I know you're thinking about it," she said, finally breaking the silence.

I cocked my head to the side. "What are you talking about?"

Her emerald gaze darkened. She pressed her lips together until they flattened. "My kidnapping. Everyone is curious. So go ahead and ask. It's fine."

My throat tightened. Words collected like stones in my chest before I found them.

"I've heard fragments of what you went through." I chose each word as if gathering pebbles in my hand. "But this"—I swept a thumb across her knuckles—"is your story. You share it only when you choose. I would never ask you to do anything that makes you uncomfortable."

Her entire demeanor radiated strength as she smiled at me.

I knew what she was feeling. I'd spent years after the deaths of my family members trudging uncomfortably through awkward conversations with well-meaning friends and colleagues.

There were times when I felt like I never wanted to discuss it again, but then that would feel wrong too. It was a delicate balance between needing to express your feelings and love for them and finding a way to move on once you'd been left behind.

To my surprise, Cali took the hand she'd laid on mine and turned it over, interlacing her fingers with mine before speaking.

"Thank you for being so kind. I know I don't have to talk about it. But...I don't know," she said, shaking her head slowly as she gazed out at the nature surrounding us. "Part of me wants you to know."

"I'm here to listen to anything you need to share. You're safe with me, Cali. Always."

Her shoulders dipped as if relief had slipped through her chest. A small tremor shook her lips into a half-smile. I closed my fingers around her hand, feeling the fine tremor of her bones and the fierce determination beneath.

She drew in a breath that rattled like loose stones.

"I was in the university library, in that glass-walled study just off the special research stacks. One other woman was at a long table carved from walnut, fixated on a blueprint. My security team stood beyond the glass panels. I told them to wait outside so I could think without them looming.

"I wandered toward a corner shelf and reached for a book on Gothic vaults when someone yanked me backward. I never saw it coming. A bag covered my face, and I felt a prick along my neck. My ears rang, and then the world went black."

I shook my head, a thread of rage beginning to surge through my body. A pounding in my head drummed a raging beat.

I stayed silent, giving her space to continue.

"When I woke, I was alone. Every wall pressed in, like stone had teeth. Darkness tasted of damp metal. My ribs ached from lying on the concrete slab. My breath came slow, every breath dragging cold through my lungs."

She paused as if to gather her thoughts. I let the quiet stretch until she spoke again.

"After hours that felt like years, footsteps echoed outside my cell. At first, they only watched. Faces pressed to the bars, silent eyes gleaming in the weak bulb overhead. I pounded on the door until my knuckles split and my voice shredded from my screams. Still, they said nothing. They only watched."

Her jaw clenched. "When they finally spoke, it was to shred my family's name. They accused my father of crimes he never committed. They threatened to hunt my sisters, to drag them in there and turn their bones to dust."

I swallowed, trying to keep from tightening my fingers around hers.

"I thought that was the worst. Then a second group appeared." She shivered hard, and I could see the vein on her neck pulsing rapidly. "They didn't stay outside the bars."

White-hot fury raced through my veins. In my mind, I was ripping the heads from these assholes' bodies.

"They beat me every day," she whispered, her voice cracking. "And they...they took turns—" Her voice dropped off.

This was excruciating.

"Cali," I whispered, squeezing her hand.

"It felt like it was never going to end..." She spoke so quietly I could barely hear her.

My heart broke for her. I wanted to pull her into my arms and hold her forever, but she was sitting rigid and still as if a strong wind might break her in two.

"Thank God for my sisters and Vik." She raised her head, tears on the tips of her lashes. "By the time they got to me, I was broken. I'd given up. I was frightened that I was going to die there."

"But you didn't."

"No." She sighed. "I didn't."

She faced me, and the intensity of her gaze made my heart clench. "But what they took from me, Leon, I can never get back."

"Calista, I am so sorry," I said, my gut twisting.

She waved her hand in the air, shaking her head.

"I'm not even talking about my innocence," she said, voice catching on the word, "though that vanished too. I mean my strength. Before...before it happened, I loved life like a free spirit. I fought for my freedom, marched into storms without hesitation. I found adventure everywhere I looked. Afterward, it was like someone yanked the wind from my lungs. I jumped at every rustle for months, convinced a threat lived in every shadow."

I leaned forward. "And now?"

She lifted her chin up, her jaw firm. "I'm gaining my strength. Not as quickly as I'd like, though. It leaves me feeling helpless, and that drives me crazy."

"I don't see you as weak," I said. "Calista, you're one of the strongest people I've ever met. I must admit, it's taking all my strength right now not to explode with rage after hearing your story. If it were up to me, I'd rip those responsible to shreds. But I recognize that you don't need anger from me right now. It's your story. Your anger. Your vengeance. But I can be here for you. I can be your friend. You can always talk to me about anything you want. But again, I never want you to feel the need to discuss anything that makes you uncomfortable."

I squeezed her hand again, hoping like hell that she could feel the depth of my sincerity.

"I would never be anything but gentle with you, Calista," I added, pressing my thumb against her knuckles.

She stared back at me thoughtfully before replying with a teasing smile. "You do realize everything you just said completely contradicts your reputation, right?"

I smirked. "Reputation's a tool. People see a wall of muscle and scars and think twice before crossing me."

She tipped her head. "Is that all it's for? My research has shown that you don't tend to have a lot of personal relationships."

I digested her words. "I will admit that I keep most people at a distance. But the right ones, the people who are supposed to be in my life, see past that tough-guy facade. They know the real me."

Her smile was as serene as an angel's, lighting up my heart.

"Am I one of those people?" she asked.

Her question was so simple, yet so complicated. How could I ever answer that?

"That's for you to decide. Can you look past what you've heard about me and discover who I really am?"

"I already am," she said.

I took a deep breath. Being physically close to her while having such an intimate conversation left my head spinning.

My pulse hammered as we sat side by side, the distance between us shrinking.

Her tone shifted, quiet and raw. "Leon...I think I could fall in love with you. And I'm not sure I want that."

I traced the outline of her hand with my thumb and smiled. If only she knew I was already there.

Seven

C ALISTA

Watching Laya cradle her son sometimes felt like watching the sunrise for the first time. Little Constantine's stubby fingers curled around hers, his tiny hiccup breaking the quiet. I'd expected him to light up our family, but the real marvel lay in Laya herself.

She had once navigated the world with a surgeon's precision, every emotion sealed away behind steel. Now, she slumped in the wooden chair, her face as soft as fresh dough, humming low as she rocked him.

When his eyelids fluttered shut, she pressed her lips to his forehead and whispered, "Sleep tight," as though the words could banish every fear he might ever meet.

I was beyond grateful I could watch her love bloom day after day.

"He actually slept through the night." Laya mopped milk from Constantine's chin with the edge of her napkin.

Avra leaned forward, one hand resting on the swell of her belly, the other curling around her latte mug. "That must feel like a victory," she said, her voice soft as sifting flour.

Sunlight poured through the café's front window, warming the checkered tablecloth and tinting every fork and knife gold. The scents of fresh basil and garlic curled around us.

I stared at Laya's contented grin and Avra's bright eyes. "I still can't believe you two are mothers." My thumb traced lazy patterns on the table's scarred wood. "It was just yesterday we were wandering cobblestones in Prague."

"Prague seems like another lifetime," Avra said, her smile wistful.

Laya tucked a loose strand of hair behind her ear and smiled down at Constantine. "And these changes—it all happened so fast. But look at this little guy."

"He's perfect," Avra breathed. Then she leaned in, watching me over the rim of her glass. "What about you, Cali? Have you settled on your own big decision yet?"

My chest tightened. I pressed my fingers to my temples. "Not yet," I said, letting my breath fall away. "I guess I'm still...undecided."

The lie landed on the table between us.

My knuckles tingled as if they wanted to tap out a confession. Something inside me, deep under ribs and bone, was screaming the opposite: that I already knew which door I had to open, even if every part of me trembled at the thought.

All I could think of was Leon.

Even my subconscious seemed to be working against me.

Last night, I had my first sexual dream in years.

Of course, Leon was front and center. His voice was low and gentle, his hands exploring every part of me I'd shut off for so long. In the dream, our bodies seamlessly aligned. A warmth surged through every nerve ending, creating a pleasurable ache in my chest.

I'd been blissfully slumbering throughout the night, kissing Leon, touching Leon...letting him touch me. We'd done everything, and he'd made me orgasm over and over.

When morning came, I woke to tangled sheets and a damp stain seeping through my pajamas. My skin felt hot, every nerve ending raw with yearning. I lay there, heart hammering, with frustration that what I'd held so vividly in sleep had slipped away at dawn. And in that moment, I knew I wasn't ready to hide from what my heart was demanding.

In Prague, my fascination with the opposite sex had soared to new heights. Under the guise of a new identity, I granted myself the liberty to delve into the vast landscape of sexual experiences, engaging with a variety of lovers. It was there that I came into my own, shedding layers of inhibition and shyness, embracing a newfound curiosity and desire. Each encounter felt like a revelation, a celebration of my sexual awakening.

Though my adventures might have seemed promiscuous, I approached each encounter with discernment, carefully selecting my partners and ensuring that I remained vigilant about safety, taking numerous precautions.

Most of these escapades were kept hidden from my sisters, aware that their perception of me as their timid little sister who required constant protection would clash with the reality of my newfound freedom. To them, I remained a fragile figure in need of safeguarding, but I saw myself as a vibrant woman at the pinnacle of her awakening sexuality.

However, the assault shattered that world completely. The sense of security I once felt, even within the confines of my own being, vanished, leaving me resigned to the belief that true safety in a man's embrace was an impossibility.

The mere thought of such intimacy turned my stomach, filling me with unease and discomfort...

Until Leon entered my life.

The dream I had about Leon stirred something within me. Maybe my earlier conviction that I would never again feel attraction was misplaced. All it took was the right person to enter my life.

The fact that thoughts of him occupied my mind even in sleep suggested a shift. Since waking from that dream, my thoughts had been a whirlwind of curiosity about what being with Leon might truly entail.

Would he be the type to linger in bed, savoring the exploration of each other's bodies with leisurely patience?

Or would he approach intimacy with a sense of urgency and efficiency?

Every fiber of my being hoped for the former. His

warmth and genuine nature hinted at someone who relished long, unhurried days entwined in the sheets.

The prospect was both exhilarating and soothing, offering a sense of comfort that I had long yearned for. The idea of resting in his arms, enveloped in the safety he seemed to exude, was deeply appealing, sparking a sense of longing and anticipation within me.

"I'm not rushing you, of course," she said, her voice calm. "But I saw how you reacted to Dominic when you first met."

My heart thudded. I pressed both hands to the edge of my chair to steady myself. "And?"

Her words pulled at the knot in my stomach. Dominic. I'd have to tell him soon that he was out of the running—an awkward conversation I couldn't stop dreading.

Avra folded her arms and leaned forward. "I did some more digging on my own."

"Did you?" My eyebrow shot up.

Laya closed her book and set it on the side table. "What did you find out?"

Avra exhaled, the sunlight catching in her dark hair. "I'll say it straight: I don't think Dominic is a good choice. He has a reputation for mistreating lovers—misogynistic remarks, power games. Nothing about him feels right for you, Cali."

Heat crept up my neck.

"I did some digging too." Laya came to stand beside Avra. "A few years ago, there was a rumor he was engaged. His fiancée vanished in the night. They say she ran off to escape him, then got quietly engaged to someone else so Dominic would give up the chase."

I pressed my palms together. "She must've been terrified."

Laya nodded. "Her family kept her whereabouts secret for months. She was very young. Their engagement never went public, so they hushed the whole thing."

I let out the breath I'd been holding. "That tracks with some of the things he said when we met."

"Like what?" Avra straightened.

I folded my hands in my lap and remembered our first conversation: the grand hall, pillars carved with dancing nymphs, chandeliers dripping with crystals. Dominic had smiled as if he owned everything in the room.

"He said he wanted a wife mainly to host his gatherings and to project an image—wife, child, perfect family tableau. He talked about us like we'd be props on his stage."

"That's fucked up." Avra's lips curved into a grim smile.

"I know," I agreed. "Then he started grilling me about the kidnapping. In a creepy way, to tell you the truth. I left feeling awful and dreading seeing him again."

Avra stood and shook her head. "Enough. Dominic Lucianos is off the list. You deserve someone who sees you as a person, not an accessory."

My chest loosened. I glanced at Laya, whose grin lit her face. "Really?"

"Absolutely." Laya held up both hands.

I sank back into the plush armchair, sunbeams pooling across my shoulders like liquid warmth, and for a moment, every tight coil of worry unwound. Relief spread through my chest until I could think of nothing else.

"That lifts a mountain from my shoulders," I said, letting the words tumble free. "With so few names left on that list, I felt I owed him at least one chance."

Avra leaned forward, elbows on the mahogany table, her gaze steady. "Remember, Cali, this choice belongs to you. Not to us, not to anyone else. You're choosing the person you'll spend your life beside. Choose with care."

I tucked a strand of hair behind my ear.

"I like Leon Boscos," I confessed, the corners of my mouth lifting despite my nerves. "He's on my mind from sunrise to sunset."

Laya's face brightened. "You're serious? That's fantastic!"

"I heard you laughing while you were on our phone call last night." Avra tapped a finger against her lips. "He had you spellbound."

I shrugged, heat creeping up my neck. "The old Cali wouldn't have felt guilty for skipping someone who didn't spark her interest. I don't know why I held on to that guilt now."

Laya slid her hand across the table and squeezed mine. "Maybe call on that old Cali when you need her. She knew how to guard her heart."

I drew in the scent of chardonnay from my glass. When I opened my eyes, the tension in my shoulders felt gone. "Thank you. I feel lighter already."

We burst into laughter, chasing the last threads of anxiety from the room.

"So then," Avra said, voice warm as candlelight, "it's Leon Boscos. You two will make a remarkable pair."

My pulse jumped. "I'll wait until after the charity gala to tell everyone."

In a few days, we'd host a children's benefit at the Greek National Opera located at Stavros Niarchos Foundation Cultural Center in Athens, our stage for unveiling the Vitalis sisters' return to power.

We selected this location due to its central position among many key regional players, making travel convenient. Moreover, its proximity to Patras reminded the syndicate families that I aimed to prevent any engagement rumors from overshadowing the fact that my sisters and I were among their equals at the table.

Avra hummed in approval. "Smart move. With two more families pledging fealty, half the territories answer to our banner."

"We've come so far in a turbulent but relatively short time." A joyful gleam lit Laya's eyes. "I'm proud of us."

"Mom and Dad would be proud too. We did it." I reached across the table and clasped their hands. "It feels odd how everything is falling into place."

Laya frowned. "Odd how?"

I rested my chin on folded hands. "What if this is an act? What if they're waiting to turn on us once we lower our guard?"

Avra closed her eyes for a moment. When she opened them, her calm felt like steel.

"You make a fair point. We should design a test to measure their loyalty. Until then, we watch every move."

"I'm with you," Laya said. "No one earns full trust until they prove themselves."

I drew my glass closer. "Thanks for not calling me paranoid. I used to hand out trust like candy. Not anymore."

Avra set her glass down and shook her head. "Trust is a badge you award only to those who earn it."

Laya raised her glass in a toast. "To the Vitalis sisters: sharp-minded and unbreakable."

Avra and I lifted our glasses against hers.

"Sharp-minded and unbreakable," we echoed, sealing our vow in clinking crystal.

Eight

L EON

Camera flashes stabbed through the evening haze as my driver guided the ebony sedan to a halt along the drive to the side of the Stavros Niarchos Foundation Cultural Center. A breeze scented with jasmine and limestone drifted around us, keeping the night from feeling too balmy and humid. Above us, the opera house's broad structure loomed large in the moonlit sky.

It had been designed to bring culture and history to the masses. On any other night, children ran carefree around the water features decorating the front exterior of the center, and the massive food court bustled with locals and tourists trying out various types of cuisines.

Tonight was different altogether. This was an invitation-only event with high security and guards at every point. There were no other events in the center but this one.

The gala, publicized as a fundraiser for children's education, felt less like charity and more like a contest of opulence. Crystal lighting glowed behind tall, sheer curtains billowing in front of windows, illuminating tables weighted with vintage champagne and tiers of silver candelabras. Guests poured through the entrance in waves: film stars draped in silken gowns, monarchs sporting jeweled orders across their chests, magnates whose names flickered across global headlines.

Inside, power and money coalesced in every gesture. Silk dresses caught the glow of crystal drops, and bespoke tuxedos fit shoulders like armor. Perfumes layered the air, amber, sandalwood, rare oriental blends, while voices traded gilded gossip in dozens of languages.

The crowd formed a living mosaic of influence, each face turned toward the next possibility: a handshake, an alliance, a rumor waiting to be wielded.

I slipped past a cluster of financiers arguing tax reform and made for the shadowy edge of the grand foyer, officially known as "the Book Castle."

I lingered by a tall, exposed metal and concrete column artistically designed for aesthetic beauty and structural necessity, fingers curled around a slender flute of champagne, scanning the room for Cali. During our last exchange, she told me she would arrive with her sisters and their husbands.

Our private phone conversations had grown into something I measured in hours, then minutes of anticipation. The texts were a mix of spirited debates on market volatility, heated discussions about geopolitical tensions, and everything in between. We had a spark I'd never felt among polished socialites or career politicians. Disagreement only deepened our respect for each other, every point countered with care, every concession weighed against principle.

However, none of the bonds we'd developed could spill over here. Every message we ever shared remained secured behind locked encryption. In our world, spies lurked everywhere, and nothing stayed secret without intent.

Knowing that only Cali and I shared the secret of our blossoming friendship filled me with a thrill of conspiratorial delight. It was a bond that felt intimate, as if we were both in on something special.

As I navigated through the sea of reporters and photographers gathered near the elevator banks, my gaze swept over each face, searching for those mesmerizing, jeweled eyes that had lingered in my thoughts since our first encounter.

Most likely, she was on the rooftop, called "the Lighthouse," of the building where the main event would take place. But once I reached the rooftop, a crowd of elegantly dressed guests continued to block my view.

Despite the challenge, I wove through the throng with determination, each step driven by my desire to find Cali.

The truth was, my primary reason for attending this event was to see her, though I intended to keep that to myself.

In one corner, I noticed Avra and Laya Vitalis,

surrounded by their husbands and a cadre of security person-
nel, engrossed in conversation with a group of equally
striking women. I scanned their gathering, but Cali was
nowhere in sight.

With a sigh, I paused and let the crowd flow around me.

I remembered Cali's words about her distaste for these
extravagant parties, with their superficial chatter and ostenta-
tious displays of wealth. She mentioned only attending
events like these because they were for a good cause and
brought in large amounts of money for charities.

More than likely, she found a nice hiding spot to avoid
the crowds. Looked as if I would have to find it.

A three-hundred-sixty-degree wrap-around open terrace
framed the main dining room. It gave breathtaking views of
the park surrounding the center and of Athens itself.

Somewhere out there seemed a likely place for Calista to
escape.

I made my way to the veranda and found the party had
overflowed into the open air, guests mingling with drinks in
hand while servers navigated through with trays of high-end
champagne.

I scanned the area, including every corner, and Calista
wasn't anywhere.

Maybe she was in the parks below. I frowned, knowing
I'd have to fight the crowds and elevators once again, but
made my way down.

Once I reached the main floor near the Book Castle, I
took a shortcut down a hallway with the closest opening into
the park. I descended a short set of stairs and walked around a

tall set of bushes. Just as I reached another grouping, a man's voice drifted from a gathering of tall trees, halting me in my tracks.

"Your family needs me," he declared. "You need to make your choice soon."

I paused, waiting to hear if there was someone who needed my help.

"Out of everyone, you and I both know I'm the best husband for you, Calista. Nobody else can provide what your family needs. We should announce our engagement tonight."

His words wrapped around me like a tightening noose, igniting a volcanic rage ready to explode.

Rumors had circulated that Dominic Lucianos might be the other suitor Cali was considering, but hearing it confirmed was another matter altogether.

And the way he spoke, dripping with entitlement and arrogance, made me nervous. Dominic was notorious for his overbearing nature, a man used to getting his way, particularly regarding women. Perhaps this was why the self-centered asshole remained single.

But there was no way in hell I would stand by and allow him to bully Calista like that.

I rushed in their direction just as Calista responded, "That's not going to happen, Dominic."

She faced him head-on, her posture a picture of defiance, her chin tilted upward with a mixture of irritation and strength.

In that moment, she looked more stunning than ever. Her blond hair was elegantly swept up with a few curls playfully caressing her cheeks, revealing her graceful neck and shoulders. Her strapless dress hugged her figure, accentuating her curves, and her cleavage seemed poised to spill over at any moment.

"Your attempts to corner and intimidate me are doing nothing to help your case."

My heart soared at her words, and I slowed my pace. She could take care of herself, and it might not be necessary for me to step in.

"I can tell you now that I won't be choosing you."

A grin tugged at my lips, satisfaction bubbling up at her rebuff.

But Dominic's reaction was far from pleased.

With a sudden, forceful grip, he seized her upper arm, yanking her closer, his face twisted in a sneer as he growled, "Not so fast, Calista."

I sprinted into action, closing the distance between us in just a few strides.

My shoulder crashed into Dominic's chest, and he staggered back.

I pivoted, guiding Calista behind me, my arm braced across her shoulders.

Dominic's hand remained locked on her arm, his fingers curling like iron bands.

Heat roared through my veins, each heartbeat hammering against my ribs. My fists balled at my sides, knuckles whitening, every vein in my neck throbbing. Blood pounded so loudly I could almost hear the echo on the paved path.

Calista's breath caught. "Leon!" she whispered, voice trembling through the tension crackling in the air.

Dominic sneered, mouth curling into a cruel smile. "What the fuck are you doing, Boscos?"

The world sharpened around us: Calista's pale cheek, the grit on Dominic's jaw, the distant hum of traffic. Every second stretched. I counted, torn between ripping him apart and waiting for her word.

A single fingertip pressed against my forearm—Calista's touch, light as a feather, firm enough to stop me in my tracks. I looked down, and her gaze met mine.

Her emerald eyes held something resolute, and even as her chest rose and fell, I knew.

"He's not worth it," she said, jaw set. "I've made my decision."

The certainty in her voice cut through the rage knotting my gut.

Dominic released Calista and waited as if she had chosen him.

Idiot.

I squared my shoulders and lifted my chin. "You heard her, Dominic. Now it's time you leave."

"Mind your own business, Boscos. This doesn't concern you." He jabbed a finger into my chest, causing me to stagger back a step.

It was clear he hadn't bothered to gather any information. If he had, he would have known I was in the running as well. Just as I was about to reveal this crucial detail, Calista's voice cut through the tension, leaving me momentarily speechless.

"It does. Leon is my fiancé."

My heart swelled with a mixture of disbelief and joy.

But I could dwell on her declaration later; right now, ensuring her safety was my top priority.

"You heard her." I raised my chin, challenging the jerk to go ahead and test me. "Leave now before I make you regret your very existence, Lucianos."

He let out a low, menacing growl, and his face twisted into a sneer directed at both of us before he turned and stormed off while muttering curses under his breath.

"You'll fucking regret this," he spat, his voice growing fainter with each step.

I stayed alert, making sure he didn't turn back, before shifting my focus to Cali, my heart pounding with concern.

"Cali, are you okay?" I scanned her from head to toe to ensure she was unharmed.

"I am now," she replied, her expression a mix of relief and exasperation. "Thank you for stepping in and getting rid of that asshole."

"Of course." A sense of relief washed over me. "I'm just glad I was here."

"Me too," she said with a smile, her fingers intertwining with mine.

If emotions could burst, my heart would have done so at that moment. I tucked a stray lock of hair behind her ear, looking down in wonder at the woman who would soon become my wife.

Could this be happening?

Was it possible that I was this fortunate?

I wasn't entirely sure if she had merely said those words to drive Lucianos away, but I couldn't deny how much I liked hearing them. The warmth of her hand in mine suggested that perhaps, just perhaps, she had truly chosen me.

NINE

C ALISTA

"We should sit in the park for a while." Leon tilted his head and gestured toward the moonlit path. His lips curved into a gentle smile.

"I'd love that." I allowed him to guide me to a nearby stone bench that looked over intricate patterns of trees and bushes laid out as far as the eye could see. The scent of the rich, green earth mixed with the salt of the sea filled the air.

We strolled to a bench and sat.

It happened so quickly that I hadn't had time to react. One minute, I'd been strolling around the grounds, eager to have a few moments to collect my thoughts, and the next, Dominic had cornered me behind a set of trees.

Before I could take a breath, he'd launched straight into a speech as though he'd stood on that spot every night rehearsing each line. He rattled off his accomplishments like they weren't the achievements of someone living in the shadow of his brother and family. He listed off his titles, his investments, and his political ties.

Then, he started in on my legacy, insisting there was no better choice for me, as if he were offering me a gift.

He passionately asserted that marrying him was the only way to secure the Vitalis reputation.

Every word felt like a weight pressing into my ribcage.

My pulse pounded, but I froze. Fingers trembling, I fished my phone from the pocket of my dress and slid my thumb across the record button.

I'd recorded most of Dominic's rant and was proud of myself for that.

But when he'd grabbed me so forcefully, my memory snapped open. All the trauma I'd gone through had come flooding back into the forefront of my mind, too many nights spent hiding, too many bruises I'd refused to name. Panic rose in my throat, bitter and familiar. My muscles coiled, ready to strike, but my voice went quiet.

If Leon hadn't walked up when he did, Dominic would have been on the ground holding his balls and wailing in pain.

Leon's arrival turned Dominic's fury toward someone bigger and broader. I heard the edge in the asshole's voice as he squared off against Leon, saw his shoulders inflate with wounded pride. He shouted over the scrape of their shoes on stone, a raw challenge corralling the darkness around us.

I started at the trees swaying in the night breeze.

"I was ready to put him in his place," I said, voice rough. "I shouldn't have hesitated."

Leon tipped his head toward me. "From what I heard, you'd already put him in his place."

I whispered, "As soon as he touched me, I should have fought. I spent months training for moments like that, and I let fear override every lesson."

I scanned the gravel at my feet, searching for the exact second I let my weakness overcome my extensive training.

"Hey, don't be so hard on yourself, Cali," Leon said. "You've gone through a lot. And most people wouldn't have been able even to utter the words you did. Dominic is an asshole, but he's intimidating, as well. From my perspective, you measured every risk, gathered proof, and stayed alive until help arrived. That took more strength than knocking him flat."

I met his warm gaze, discovered something steady within it, and felt the tension in my shoulders diminish.

"You are a nice guy, aren't you, Leon?"

He shrugged, shoulders rising in a reluctant arc. "I try. Some people disagree, but I'll always be good to you, Cali. I promise."

"Are you sure you want to marry someone as broken as me?" I whispered.

Leon leaned forward, elbows on his knees, his eyebrows

lifted in that look I knew so well. "Is that what you believe about yourself?"

His question settled over me like a silent weight. I stared at my hands, knuckles white against the fabric of my dress.

"Sometimes," I said.

He searched my eyes before speaking again. "I don't believe in perfection, Cali. I'm far from perfect myself. But the way I see it, you and I have endured a lot of similar traumas."

He lifted my hand, warmed it against his palm, then laced our fingers together.

My pulse throbbed. His hand felt solid and sure, a spark traveling through my veins.

His thumbs traced gentle paths across my knuckles. "If broken means we've felt life's hardest edges, so be it. Maybe our fractures match. Maybe we can help each other heal."

My heart swelled at his words.

Without hesitation, I cupped his face and pressed my lips against his, kissing him swiftly, confidently, and with intent.

He didn't hesitate, kissing me back. His lips were warm and soft against mine, and all the emotions I'd been trying to hold back rushed to the surface, overwhelming me and leaving my head spinning and my heart racing.

"Cali," he said. "You are the most beautiful woman I've ever encountered. You possess strength, intelligence, and kindness. To address your question, it would be the greatest honor of my life to become your husband. However, I want you to understand that I would never pressure you into anything you're unprepared for or don't wish to pursue.

Simply express your desires, and I will do everything within my power to make them a reality. Everything is under your control, and we will proceed at your speed."

My chest tightened at his words. When Leon spoke, my world contracted until only his voice was warm and steady, like an anchor in a storm. He was powerful and intelligent and sexy.

Most of all, he was kind. He had shown me nothing but complete respect. How could I not fall in love with a man like him?

His kindness cut through everything else. He treated me as though I mattered more than any mission, more than any title. In his presence, I felt less like a pawn on a chessboard and more like a woman worth every risk.

But terror knotted in my stomach. I wanted to plunge in headfirst, to let joy carry me away. Instead, my fingertips tingled, and my chest tightened, because I understood exactly why.

Fear.

The memory came unbidden: my mother's trembling hands as she read my father's letters during the siege, my father's fierce love having made them both targets. Our so-called allies had turned their loyalty into a weapon, gleeful to hold their devotion over them like a dagger to the throat. Love like that left you vulnerable in the worst way.

Pain.

It was such a mind-fuck. As much as I was afraid, I couldn't look at Leon without being excited at the same time.

The thought of moving through the world with him was thrilling.

The thought of marrying him...

Waking up in the same bed with him...

Going to bed together and all that entailed.

Suddenly, the dream I'd had about him the other night flashed in my head, and I felt the heat rise in my cheeks. Was it possible to feel shy and bold at the same time?

The urge to tell him what I was thinking overwhelmed me.

And yet, there he was, essentially telling me he was willing to be patient and let me set the pace of our relationship. Did he think I wanted to go slow? It would make sense that he would, given my background. After all, he was only being thoughtful.

But I couldn't help but wonder what he would think if he knew about my dream. What would he think if he knew I was considering sharing a hell of a lot more than a kiss with him?

I yearned to be alone with him.

To feel his lips on mine again. To feel his hands running over my bare skin, to feel safe enough to let go and lose myself in the desire I felt for him. After that dream, I'd felt like we'd already made love, and I'd been letting the images play in my head over and over, constantly aroused by the thought of it all.

That was what gave me the courage to kiss him like that.

The urge to confess, to spill all the images playing on

repeat in my mind, throbbed low and deep inside me. But he'd already told me I could set our pace. Gentle, patient, respectful. He didn't know I wanted more than a slow dance. I wanted to slide my fingers into his hair, to feel him shiver under my touch. I wanted to go back to his place as soon as possible. I knew he had two residences, the main one at his estate in Vouliagmeni and the other in Central Athens.

I drew a steadying breath, squared my shoulders, and met his gaze. "Is your house nearby?"

His pupils dilated, a slow smile curving his lips. "It's not too far from here."

"You said I could ask for anything." Relief and desire coiled together inside me.

His brow furrowed. "Always."

I leaned in. "Then I don't want to go slow. After the ball, will you take me there?"

For a moment, his expression stilled as if he'd been holding his breath. Then, pleasure spread across his face, and he stepped closer. His stubble grazed my cheek, warm and reassuring.

"Anything you want, always," he murmured, brushing his lips to mine in a soft, promising kiss, and then stood and pulled me up with him.

"Are you ready to join the others? I'm suddenly keenly interested in getting this over with as quickly as possible."

He winked, that mischievous glint in his gaze as he offered me his elbow.

I slipped my hand into his, smiling up at him. "More than ready."

Together, we walked up the staircase heading back into the ballroom in search of my family, my heart still pounding. But this time, excitement, not fear, led the way.

TEN

L EON

Cali shone above the crowd like the brightest star, every other guest dimming in comparison as she moved from one conversation to the next with effortless grace and charm. I watched her in silent awe, her every courtesy perfect, her every smile disarming.

As one of the favored Vitalis sisters, she drew attention wherever she went, and rightly so.

The Vitalis family's power surged through the syndicate ranks, their name once again commanding the respect of every other house. I took quiet satisfaction in how their security detail hovered, vigilant and unblinking.

Wherever Cali and her sisters ventured, their guards were

never out of sight. They had slipped up earlier, allowing Dominic to get dangerously close, but I knew better than to chalk it up to oversight. I suspected Cali had deliberately shaken them off.

The moment we stepped into view in the Book Castle, Calista's security detail converged on her, and she simply ignored their scolding stares and continued to the elevators and up to the Lighthouse.

I gazed upon my new fiancée with utter disbelief.

It had all happened so quickly.

Everything had moved so fast, and soon, after tonight, it would quicken even more.

The fact that she'd boldly asked me to take her back to my room was surprising. My first instinct had been to stop her, to urge her to take more time to think about it, and to slow down and get to know each other first.

But the gleam in her eyes warned me that such words would be disastrous.

It was clear to me that Cali was attempting to regain a sense of control in her life. She'd struggled with her actions in the incident with Dominic, as she'd explained. The fact that she wanted to claim her power wasn't something I was ever going to get in the way of.

If she needed me to help with that, I would never refuse. Even if it meant doing something I wasn't entirely convinced she was ready to do.

It wasn't up to me to decide that.

It was her decision.

Of course, I wanted to protect her—I always would—

but that didn't mean stripping her of agency. To do so would smother her, the opposite of what she needed. The path ahead would be narrow and delicate, but I would navigate it as best I could.

Calista was worth every careful step.

She was worth the whole wide world.

I chuckled to myself, watching her glide gracefully around the grand ballroom. Her smile was infectious, lighting up her face and those around her. Despite being a grown man, something about her transported me back to my teenage years, a thrilling feeling of sneaking around to do something forbidden.

Every so often, she glanced in my direction, a knowing spark flaring between us. It was as if we shared a secret language, silently planning our night together.

The sensation was a delightful rush, and I found it amusing how deeply it affected me.

"That's some smile on your face, brother," Iason commented, appearing beside me.

He had accompanied me to the event and had been waiting for me at our table when I returned with Calista.

"I'm sure it is," I replied, still grinning.

"Want to tell me what it's all about?" he asked, nodding toward the elegant blonde who had captivated my attention all evening. "I'm assuming it has something to do with that lovely lady you can't take your eyes off."

"She's my fiancée now," I revealed, feeling a surge of pride.

Surprise flashed across his features. "Excuse me?"

"It happened while I was outside," I explained the unexpected encounter in the park. "We're not telling anyone yet."

"That was fast." He clapped me on the back. "Congratulations are in order!"

He reached for a glass of champagne from the table, raising it in a cheerful toast.

"Thanks." I clinked glasses with him, the bubbly liquid fizzing.

"I gotta say, I'm surprised. And curious." Iason's brows furrowed.

"About what?" I asked, intrigued by his line of questioning.

"Is this just because you want a Vitalis princess included in your family line?"

I shrugged, a small smile playing on my lips. "That's not the only reason, Iason. But it's also not a hindrance, is it?"

"It could be," he mused, tilting his head as if weighing the possibilities. "Just be careful. Because now, your enemies have leverage against you."

"I'm well aware of that fact, and fully prepared to confront it as needed," I assured him, my voice steady and confident.

"Fair enough," Iason conceded, nodding. "I'm happy for you."

"Thank you, brother," I said, turning my focus back to Calista, who was socializing with friends. "I'm happy for myself, too. Calista Vitalis is an amazing woman, and I would be proud to stand by her side."

"Does this mean you're thinking of selling your house in

Central Athens? As a respectable man now, you could live on the estate full-time."

"Not a chance. Don't think I'm unaware of your plans. You can't have it. Calista and I will need it when we're in the city to avoid traffic."

"It's not like the estate is too far. It's about an hour with traffic, maybe two at most."

I shook my head. "That's not going to happen."

"It was worth asking." He smirked, raising his champagne glass with a grin.

I spent the rest of the evening with Iason, but my attention drifted away from the entertainment and the busy auction.

Instead, my gaze was captivated by Calista, who sat across the room, bathed in the soft light of the room.

Our brief kiss earlier had left a tantalizing imprint on my mind. I kept imagining the intoxicating taste of her lips, wondering how it would feel when my tongue explored the warm, inviting depths of her mouth.

The thought of her bare skin, smooth and soft, sliding against mine sent shivers down my spine.

I imagined the symphony of her moans, the sound echoing in my ears, as I envisioned her thighs pressing against the sides of my head while I indulged in her sweetness.

The mere thought of sinking deep inside her made my heart race and my palms sweat.

By the time the evening was over, I was a mess and feeling even more like a clumsy teenager while I attempted to hide my uncontrollable erection.

Just the thought of being with Calista made me crazy.

How would I survive the actual encounter without combusting from sheer anticipation?

As the crowd began to lessen, I exchanged goodbyes with Iason, lingering in the expansive Book Castle of the opera house with the remaining guests. The grand space was adorned with books of all types and photographs of artists, aspiring and well-known.

I made a note to bring Calista back here someday to see an opera, attend a community event, or maybe just try out the various vendors in the food court. It would be a good date night. It was exciting to think about all the things we would do together.

Yet the singular, throbbing thought of our plans for tonight occupied my mind. Upon hearing Cali behind me, I turned with a smile, excited for the evening to unfold.

She approached with her sisters, the crowd parting like a river as they strolled together, arm in arm.

"Have you chosen, Cali?" I heard Avra ask with a teasing lilt.

"Now that this event is over, I can tell you," Cali replied as she neared. "I have made a choice."

Laya clapped a hand over her mouth. "Oh my God! Tell us!"

Cali's happiness was infectious as she reached me, her fingers intertwining with mine, her touch reassuring and exhilarating.

With a beaming smile, she turned to her sisters and declared, "I've chosen Leon Boscos."

The confidence and certainty in her statement wrapped around my heart like a comforting embrace.

My face broke into a broad smile, joy radiating through my chest, warming me from the inside out.

"Yes!" Avra and Laya shouted in perfect harmony.

I turned to them, my expression solemn as I regarded them with deep sincerity.

"I'm honored Calista has chosen me," I declared, my voice steady. "I promise you both that I will treat her like the queen she is and protect her always."

"Welcome to the family, Leon," Avra said, her nod filled with approval. "Just make my little sister happy. That's all we ask."

"I will do my absolute best," I assured them.

"Shall we head out?" Calista inquired, smiling at me.

I nodded, unable to refuse her, yet aware of the curious glances her sisters cast our way.

"Where are you going?" Avra inquired, her eyes narrowing.

A rush of heat flooded my veins.

How could I possibly explain?

Your sister wants me to take her back to my house for a very intimate encounter.

Absolutely not.

Thankfully, Calista seemed to anticipate the need for a tactful response.

"We're going on a date. Unsupervised," she announced, cutting off any words I might have stumbled over.

"I see." Avra chuckled. "You're a grown woman, Calista. Enjoy yourself."

"I plan to," Calista replied, winking at her sisters.

I suppressed a groan before they walked away, leaving the two of us alone.

"Where's your car?" Calista's gaze locked onto mine with a confidence that reflected our earlier conversation. A thrill of excitement coursed through me, making my cock twitch in my pants.

"This way." I gestured, leading her outside.

Every step felt like a journey closer to a paradise I could only dream of. Inside, a storm of emotions raged as I grappled with my desires.

I longed to honor Calista with the utmost respect she deserved, but the way her thumb caressed the inside of my elbow was a whisper of intimacy that stole my breath away.

I yearned to strip away the barriers between us, to enjoy every moment of passion, but that desire conflicted with the gentlemanly restraint I wanted to maintain. In the back of the car, she sat close to me, so close that her fire-like heat radiated against my side, and her thighs pressed against mine, a silent promise. The air was thick with tension and by now my cock throbbed hot and hard with raw desire.

I breathed in her perfume, a sweet and musky scent that clung to the air, the same one she'd worn before. It was intoxicating, a fragrance that would forever be entwined with my memories of her and the desperate desire she stirred in me.

I reached for her hand, needing to be closer.

Her fingers were warm and soft, a stark contrast to the

hard, calloused skin of my own. The hunger and lust for her gnawed at me, a blaze that threatened to consume us both.

Yet, beneath the inferno was a cold pit of fear. I saw the echoes of old ghosts in her emerald irises, and the last thing I wanted was to be another one of them.

"Cali, is this really what you want, darling?" I asked as I turned to face her. "Are you certain? You can always reconsider. We could pause and grab a drink. There's a charming cocktail bar nearby. We could just enjoy a proper date. I promise I'm happy to wait."

She lifted her chin like a queen surveying her court, her lips curving into that confident half-smile.

The streetlight gilded her cheekbones. Her eyes, dark as obsidian, losing the green hue, shone with intention.

"I don't want a bar," she said, voice steady as silk. "I want you, Leon."

Her words stole the breath from my lungs.

She was so fucking beautiful. So stunning, I couldn't think when I was around her. And still she drew me, like a beacon of light in the darkness. It held a sensual promise, and a direct and unwavering pulse of desire and need shot through me.

"Rest assured, Leon, this choice is entirely mine. Clearly, you're not forcing me in any manner. Do you want me as much as I want you?"

The question hung between us, soft and impossible to deny.

I closed the space and brushed my lips lightly over hers,

tasting the sweetness of her breath. I held back the flood of desire that threatened to pull me under.

"There is nothing in the world I'd rather do than make love to you, Calista."

She kissed me in return, her urgency reflecting my own. When she released me, her dilated pupils betrayed her desire, glowing like embers poised to spark. The car glided to a stop in the driveway of my Athens house.

We rushed from the car and into the house without uttering a word. The moment the lock clicked, shutting off the rest of the world, an untamed energy surrounded us. It was a tense, living, breathing thing. She positioned herself on the living room threshold and stared at me. Her face was flushed, and her eyes full of undisguised desire that matched the storm thundering through my brain.

Her silk dress clung to curves I was aching to discover with slow precision.

"Undress me," she commanded, and I stepped closer, the final step toward the precipice of our future together.

Eleven

C ALISTA

The surge of brazenness that coursed through my veins as soon as I heard the door lock was electrifying, as shocking as an unexpected thunderclap that left me breathless and disoriented.

The Cali who had always second-guessed herself, always hesitated, seemed to have vanished into thin air. The woman who had grown restrained and shut off from the world was eerily silent.

The layers of armor I had built around myself, the icy facade I presented to the world, the mask that whispered for me to shrink into the shadows—all seemed to dissolve in that instant.

The attack had reduced me to a mere shadow of my former self, so much so that most days, I stared at my reflection in the mirror and struggled to recognize the woman looking back at me.

The memory of the Cali I once was faded more with each passing day. That Cali, who had brimmed with confidence and self-assuredness, who knew exactly what she wanted both in life and in her intimate moments, felt like a distant ghost from a dream long forgotten.

She was bold, fearless, and embraced her sexuality with open arms and unabashed audacity.

I longed for her return.

I missed her presence.

Yet, despite the daring flicker of boldness I had shown tonight, I remained uncertain if that version of Cali was still alive within me.

I desperately hoped that she was merely buried beneath layers of fear and caution, waiting to be coaxed back to life so she could embrace herself again in all her radiant glory.

Was I deluding myself?

As I stood there, my heart pounding, daring Leon to undress me with a silent challenge, was I truly ready for her to roar back to life?

I was pleading for the spark within me to ignite into a blazing fire, but was I prepared for the intensity of the flames that would follow?

There was only one way to find out, and I found myself standing on the precipice of that very opportunity, hoping fervently that Leon wouldn't falter.

By the way he fixed his gaze on me, like a wild animal contemplating the release of a caged beast, he seemed to be weighing the situation with careful consideration.

"Calista, darling," he said in a low rumble, "let's pause, just briefly, and talk."

I took a deep breath, determination coursing through me.

"First of all, is this a test?"

His question caught me off guard, sending a ripple of surprise through me.

"Yes," I replied quickly. "But not for you."

He cocked one brow, the corner of his mouth quirking up.

"Fair enough." He stepped back, hands tucked into his pockets. "May I make a proposal before we go any further?"

I crossed my arms, taking a step backward, further into the room, and then shifting my weight from one foot to the other. My pulse thrummed in my ears.

"Sure," I muttered, brushing a stray curl behind my ear.

The knot of impatience in my chest tightened even as his steady calm washed over me. It was a strange comfort I hadn't realized I needed.

He lifted his gaze, slow and unwavering. "I want us both to vow honesty. Honesty in everything, but especially about how we feel."

I waved a hand. "Of course."

My heart pounded against my ribs.

He shook his head, exhaling a quiet sigh. "No. I mean, really honest."

"Oh." The single syllable caught in my throat.

Heat bubbled up my neck. Talking about feelings was like standing naked in a windstorm.

I swallowed and forced a smile. "Okay, you go first."

He retreated a few paces so there was ten feet of empty air between us.

My stomach clenched, and every instinct told me to close the gap.

"My worry," he began, "is that you're moving too fast. Are you using this—us—to exorcise old demons, Calista?"

My fingers fluttered at my sides.

"God, no," I blurted, shaking my head, and then said with a hitch in my voice, "I promise that's not why. I feel... safe with you, Leon. I haven't been with anyone since..."

My throat tightened, and everything else I wanted to say dissolved in the wake of memories.

I inhaled, pushing through, and continued. "I used to feel fierce. Like my body was mine, like I was a goddess. I want that back. I want to feel pleasure like it's mine to claim."

He moved in my direction, closing the majority of the distance, and reached out, his thumb brushing my jaw.

"You are safe with me. Claim it all."

Warmth bloomed in my belly. A slow grin spread across my face. I lifted my chin, pursing my lips as if in a challenge.

My fingers found the tiny latch of my gold hoop earrings. I set them on the wooden side table nearest to me. The soft *clink* echoed as they hit the polished surface.

I leaned in, the air between us crackling.

Then I slid a hand behind my head, releasing the pin that held my curls aloft. A cascade of dark blond ringlets tumbled over my shoulders, brushing my collarbone. I tilted my head, feeling each lock fall like warm silk.

My heel tapped the floor as I took another deliberate step forward. His breath hitched, and his pupils swelled. I let a teasing smile curve my lips.

"I want to claim you, Leon."

Lightly, I slipped the slender chain of my bracelet past my wrist, watching it fall onto the table with a soft thud.

He froze as if the air had turned molten. He was rooted in place until I took one more step.

His foot scraped across the polished wooden floor, the sound a faint whisper in the charged air.

I reached back, my fingers finding the zipper nestled at the small of my back, and I tugged it downward, the cool metal gliding over my skin. Inch by inch, the dress surrendered to gravity, sliding over my curves and revealing skin that tingled with anticipation.

His breaths grew ragged, every inhale and exhale unsteady.

I stood there in nothing but my bra, panties, and stockings, the intimate apparel clinging to me like a second skin.

I advanced, leaving behind the discarded fabric, and approached him with purposeful intent, each step a wordless statement.

He backed away, shaking his head. "Cali."

My name came out rough and full of desire, making goosebumps pebble my skin.

"Are you afraid of me?" I questioned him, unable to hide my amusement.

It was almost laughable, the idea of this man, a reputedly fearless and unshakable being, intimidated by me.

"No," he asserted, firm yet tinged with something unspoken.

My smile widened, satisfaction curling at the edges of my lips as his answer emboldened me further. "Good."

The intensity of his gaze swept over me, a palpable heat that seemed to sear my skin with its fervor.

"Please be careful. I'm so afraid you're moving too quickly," he cautioned.

But he was only spurring me on, igniting a defiant fire within me as I closed the distance between us, driving him backward until he was trapped against a large armchair in the corner.

"Do I look like I'm afraid?" I placed a firm hand on his chest.

I pushed, sending him tumbling back into the chair, exactly where I wanted him to be.

He watched me, his gaze wide with a mixture of surprise and something deeper, as I allowed my gaze to drift downward.

My breath hitched at the sight of his erection, straining against the confines of his slacks, the fabric outlining it with tantalizing clarity and offering a delicious preview of what lay ahead.

Fueled by the audacious courage that proximity to him inspired, I dared to take the game further.

I climbed onto the chair and straddled his lap, allowing my hair to cascade around his face like a curtain.

I brought my mouth a hairsbreadth from his, brushing lightly against it, teasing, as my tongue flicked out briefly to taste the warmth of his lips.

He gasped, a ragged inhale rasping between his parted lips, yet his broad hands stayed firmly anchored to the leather armrests, knuckles whitening against the smooth surface, a restraint that was both maddening and electrifying.

I craved the brush of his fingertips against my skin, firm and demanding. I longed for his mouth on mine, a devouring claim to every inch of me.

His momentary hesitation was excruciating. I knew he treaded softly, careful not to overwhelm me, that he wanted to be gentle, but I wanted more than his caution...

God, I needed so much more.

It was one thing to be kind, but it was another thing to try to keep fear at bay when it didn't exist in the first place.

I bent toward him, pressing my breasts against his chest and kissing him with firm intent.

This time, I slipped my tongue between his velvet lips, seeking his taste, his heat. He met my advance, his tongue tangling with mine in a fevered dance as I moaned low against him.

His hand rose to my hip, the broad warmth of his palm scorching and sending a jolt of electricity rippling through my veins.

"Yes," I breathed, leaning into his touch. I murmured in his ear, "Leon, I'm fine. I promise I won't break."

He withdrew and stared at me as if he were searching for some hidden truth, shining like a star within them.

"I never want to remind you of any pain you endured," he whispered with unexpected emotion.

"Oh, Leon," I said, shaking my head.

I desperately needed him to realize that I envisioned no pain now.

Not that kind of pain, at least.

With him, there would be no true suffering. With him, even with the kind of pain that might take place, I'd experience only pleasure.

I dipped forward again, capturing his lower lip between my teeth and nibbling. "When offered willingly, pain can be much different than what you're thinking of, darling."

His eyelashes fluttered in slow beats, then the shadows of desire that lurked inside him flared into brilliant flames, sparkling with a delicious tension of light and dark that made me shudder with raw craving.

His hand slid up to the nape of my neck, fingers tangling in my hair.

"Fuck, Calista, you're killing me," he growled, crushing his lips to mine with urgent, hungry force.

I moaned as he collapsed into desire, exhilarated that his protective shell had shattered.

I yearned to see the man I sensed just beneath Leon's composed, careful exterior.

I didn't want his fury, only the fierce passion simmering below the calm surface. I longed to feel that unbridled intensity.

I broke the kiss and gazed into his piercing, dark eyes.

I craved to see the savage hunger of desire blazing there because of me.

Old Calista, new Calista...whoever I became, I needed to know he wanted me, wholly and completely.

And the burning lust in his gaze told me I was exactly where I needed to be.

I leaned forward, trapping his lower lip between my teeth once more, savoring the low, intoxicating rumble from his throat.

"Cali," he whispered, pulling away.

With a firm grip, he grabbed my hand and guided it to rest between his thighs, pressing my palm against the unmistakable hardness there.

It pulsed beneath my touch, so thick and long. Arousal flooded my core.

"This is what you do to me. I've never wanted anything more in my life than to lay you on my bed and slam my cock into you over and over, as hard as I can. And God, baby, trust me, we will get to that. But this time? This first time?"

He shook his head, his arms stretching out beside him as though surrendering to an invisible force, and drew in a deep, steadying breath.

A slow, sexy smile spread across his mouth, lighting up his gorgeous face.

"I'm all yours. Ready. Willing. Definitely able. But this time, it's all you. You can take your time, go fast, or do whatever your heart desires. You're in control tonight."

His words sent a shiver down my spine, a delicious

tremble that seemed to start from the core of my being and ripple outward.

His complete openness to me freed my soul as if he had reached into the depths of my spirit and untangled the chains binding me.

I wasn't broken.

I wasn't weak.

I was human... And nobody could take that away from me.

Without hesitation, I kissed him, deeply, passionately, pouring every ounce of sweet ecstasy his words had ignited within me into that kiss. It was as though he had found the key to unlock the cage I had been trapped in, even after my rescue.

Though I had been free for a long time, I had remained imprisoned in my mind, in my body. Leon's acceptance was the missing piece I had been waiting for. He was the one I'd always needed.

He wrapped his arms around me, matching the energy of my kiss with perfect harmony, his tongue dancing with mine, his hands running over my body as if he were trying to memorize every curve and contour.

I pushed against his clothes, a sense of urgency driving me to feel the warmth of his skin against mine. He leaned forward, allowing me to slide his jacket off, our lips never parting, my hips instinctively moving against his. The need to feel every inch of him became overwhelming, an insistent demand that couldn't be ignored.

"Please get up," I urged, jumping off him and peeling his shirt from his shoulders.

My fingers fumbled with the front of his slacks, clumsy with desire and nerves.

For a fleeting moment, the confidence I had felt began to waver, a tendril of fear threatening to surface, and I sighed a shaky exhale.

Sensing my hesitation, Leon gently clasped my hands, bringing one to his lips. He kissed my fingers tenderly, his eyes locking with mine. The reassurance I saw there meant more than I could ever express.

"Breathe, baby," he murmured. "We have all night. There's no rush."

I followed his instructions, feeling the warmth of his lips brushing against my hand, which brought a sense of calm over me.

With his free hand, he unzipped his pants, the metallic sound slicing through the quiet room, and allowed them to slide down to his ankles. He stepped back, carefully lifting each foot to free himself from the fabric, now standing in front of me clad only in his boxers. The boxers were a deep, inky black that molded perfectly to his muscular form.

My heart raced as I caught sight of his cock pressed thick and long under the fabric, throbbing with desire.

For me.

He reached for the waistband, fingers poised to pull them down, but I stopped him with a gentle shake of my head.

"No," I said. "Let me."

"My pleasure."

His lips curled into a crooked smile, a mischievous glint in his eyes. The sight sent a thrilling jolt of electricity coursing through me, igniting a spark that settled right on my clit.

As slowly as I could, I slid a fingertip under the waistband of his shorts, feeling the cool elastic material give way to the warmth of his skin.

He drew in a deep breath, the sound echoing in the quiet room.

With a teasing smile, I traced the edge, feeling the heat radiating from his bare abdomen. His muscles rippled beneath my touch, each spasm a testament to the tension building between us, and I delighted in the way they contracted under my fingers.

"This is a delicious torture," he moaned, and a shiver slid down my spine.

I pulled my other hand from his hold.

I let it wander down to his hip, slipping under the shorts with deliberate slowness.

As I pushed the fabric downward, his breath hitched and caught in his throat when the elastic band snagged momentarily over his cock.

I paused for a heartbeat, our eyes locking, before tugging the shorts farther down, freeing him as they fell to the floor.

This time, it was my turn to gasp.

His cock was beautiful.

The skin was smooth and taut, the throbbing shaft standing proud, its impressive thickness and length causing my eyes to widen in awe.

I swallowed hard, my nipples hardening with anticipation and a shiver running through me at the thought of him filling my pussy.

I reached up to his shoulders, once more pushing him back into the chair.

Leon sat bare and motionless, his gaze locked onto me like a predator homing in on its prey. His eyes were obsidian, pupils dilated, and the hunger in them sent an electric shiver cascading down my spine. Between his legs, his cock stood erect, a demanding exclamation point on his desire. The room was thick with anticipation, the air heavy with our mutual need.

I reached in front of my chest, releasing my strapless black lace bra. The fabric loosened, and my breasts spilled out, the bra falling to the floor in a whisper of lace.

Leon's lips parted as he drew in a deep breath. His gaze was a physical touch, a hot trail searing my skin as it moved over my body.

I hooked my thumbs into the waistband of my silk panties and eased them down my hips.

They pooled at my ankles, and I stepped free of them, the click of my stilettos echoing on the floor.

"Holy fuck," Leon breathed, shaking his head as his gaze roamed over me. Goosebumps prickled my nipples while a flush crept up my neck. "I've never seen... You're...you're a fucking masterpiece."

A smile tugged at the corners of my mouth, warmth spreading through me at his words.

I wanted to feel beautiful, to feel sexy, to know that he

saw me as I wanted to be seen. The lust in his eyes left me trembling, a hunger gnawing at my core, a restless impatience coursing through my veins.

I straddled him again, this time our bare flesh meeting, sliding together like silk on silk.

His cock nudged against my vulva, and I gasped at the sensation, a jolt of electricity sparking through me. I was already so wet, his shaft sliding against me, a delicious friction that left me shuddering.

He stared up at me, his face a tapestry of awe, love, and lust, all woven together in an expression so beautiful it made my heart ache.

I lifted my hips and reached down to wrap my hand around his cock. He was smooth, hot, and hard in my grasp. I squeezed, feeling his pulse throb against my palm as I guided him to my entrance.

His eyes widened, his mouth fell open, and he groaned as I began to slip him inside me.

I shifted my hips and leaned down to kiss him deeply as I pressed down, my pussy sliding down over his shaft as slowly as I could force myself to go. It was excruciating. I couldn't wait to feel him buried as deep as possible.

But I knew in the back of my mind that I would remember this moment forever. I wanted it to last. I tried to remember the way every single inch of him was introduced to my body.

Our tongues tangled together, our moans engulfed by each other's mouths, as his throbbing hardness filled me up inch by delicious inch. I spasmed around him, my pussy soaking him now, my juices dripping over his shaft. When he was finally buried to the hilt, he groaned loudly into my mouth, his cock twitching and pulsing.

"Leon, my God," I cried, tearing my mouth from his, a ragged gasp. I searched his eyes, seeing my own disbelief reflected back at me.

"God," he growled, his body trembling beneath me. "You feel...fucking amazing."

I pressed my thighs together, then arched my back and slid off him only to impale myself again on his rigid length. Each time he twitched inside me, a pulse of heat radiated up my spine. My pussy squeezed around him, slick and welcoming, craving the hollow fullness of his cock.

I bore down onto him, hips slamming, skin slapping skin. His pelvis lifted to meet every frantic plunge, muscles rippling beneath his tanned flesh—the room filled with the wet slap of our bodies and the frantic chorus of our moans.

Bending forward, I captured his mouth in a hungry kiss, tasting the salt on his lips as I fucked him, my hips rolling and bucking as delicious waves of lust washed over me. He grabbed a fistful of my hair, kissing me hard as he fucked into me.

Electric sparks danced through me every time our bodies met, a current of lust that crackled along our skin. Our naked flesh rubbed together, my breasts against the hard muscles of his chest.

His hands roamed my curves, thumbs carving circles over my hips, then sliding down to squeeze my buttocks as he thrust his hot, hard cock up into my pussy, over and over. I arched over him, surrendering to the delicious friction.

He curled his fingers around my hip bones, then pressed his thumb flat against my swollen clit, causing my brain to explode with pleasure, my body crashing over the edge, my pussy spasming. My muscles trembled and clamped down on him as my orgasm ripped through me in fierce, shuddering waves.

I cried out, my voice raw with release.

Hot waves of pleasure rolled over me, rendering me weak and limp against his body.

His thumb stilled against my clit.

He held it there, drawing out the aftershocks until I could breathe again.

"That's it, baby," he whispered. His pelvis ground into mine, cock still throbbing in my soaked, contracting pussy. "I love feeling you come on me. It's a fucking fantasy come to life."

He began circling my clit again, slower this time, teasing me toward that explosive brink.

His lips brushed my ear before his teeth closed over my earlobe.

"Come for me again," he commanded, low and rumbling.

Without waiting, he thrust his hips upward. I was rooted to the spot, every nerve ending ablaze as his cock plunged all the way in, then retreated and slammed back.

One strong hand gripped my side, fingers digging into the tender curve of my hip, anchoring me to his relentless rhythm. His thumb kept spinning on my clit in tight, maddening circles.

"God, Leon!" I gasped, nails digging into his broad shoulders.

"Do you like that?" he growled. "Are you going to come for me again?"

His voice, deep and urgent, sent shivers skittering down my spine. He was the most magnetic man I'd ever known, and his demand ignited a fresh hunger inside me.

"Answer me," he urged, thumb stroking faster now, pulling me toward the edge.

I could feel the tension coil in my core, ready to snap. Every inch of me burned with need as I tossed my head back and surrendered to the delicious storm he created.

"Yes, I fucking love it! Please don't stop, Leon. Make me come again," I begged, raw with unending need.

My strength returned, just a little, and I opened my thighs wider, feeling the slick heat as my pussy slid farther down his shaft.

I rode him, rising and falling with more intensity, meeting his powerful thrusts with my rising momentum. The sound of skin slapping against skin filled the room, echoing the fervor of our movements.

Overwhelmed by the flood of sensations, my pussy clenched and released in rhythmic spasms at the feel of him hitting the deepest parts of my body, the way he stretched me open so fully, the way his cock fucked into me so delicious, so raw.

"Oh God, I'm coming. Don't stop," I cried out, waves of

pleasure rolling over me, pulling me into a state of hypnotic, lustful bliss.

My body quivered, caught in the throes of ecstasy.

"That's it, baby, that's it," he growled.

His cock swelled inside me even bigger, and he moaned a low, primal, savage growl that rocked through my body.

"Cali! Cali! Fuck!" he shouted. His cock pulsed and exploded deep in my pussy, his white-hot seed searing my wet, spasming walls.

His body trembled against mine, both of us caught in a shared, feverish release.

We clung to each other, our arms wrapping tightly around one another, his cock still buried deep inside me. We gasped for breath, our bodies slick with sweat and satisfaction.

After a moment, Leon slid his hands beneath me and lifted me, carrying me up a set of stairs, down a hallway, and into a large, spacious room. In the center was a giant bed covered in a dark gray duvet. He moved to it, laying me down and settling in beside me.

On instinct, I turned towards him, and he pulled me into his arms. My head settled on his chest, the constant thump of his heart a soothing sound to my ear. He gently kissed my forehead as we were surrounded by a peaceful silence filled with unspoken understanding.

I longed to express everything flooding my heart—to tell him how safe and liberated I felt in his arms, how he had become my sanctuary. But words seemed unnecessary, as if he already sensed every emotion swirling within me.

"Leon, I have never felt more alive in my life," I said, knowing I spoke the truth.

He tightened his grip around me, nodding. "I feel the same, Cali. I really do," he replied, his words a soft affirmation.

As sleep began to steal over us, wrapped in each other's warmth, I knew with certainty that choosing Leon Boscos as my husband was the best decision I'd ever made.

TWELVE

L EON

TWO WEEKS LATER

My fiancée's lust was insatiable, and as the past two weeks proved, so was mine.

Every morning, light found us tangled in sheets, skin slick with sweat and the musky tang of desire.

I could still taste her on my lips from dawn's first kiss, feel the hot clamp of her thighs around my shaft. Four times before breakfast, we'd lost ourselves, and yet tonight, as I steered my Aston Martin down the winding drive to Laya and Nikolas's estate, my cock tightened in my trousers, aching for another taste of her.

The polished leather of the steering wheel pressed into my palms while the engine hummed low and hungry, mirroring the roar in my chest.

I replayed the memory of her breathy moan when my hand drifted along the curve of her waist, or the shiver that quivered through her when I brushed a fingertip under her jaw.

She'd whimpered once, tiny and urgent, when my fingertips brushed the hollow of her throat, so raw, so unguarded.

But I'd stopped, pulling back before the spark in her eyes could ignite my savage need.

Every fiber of me wanted to arch her back against the mattress, drive into her until her nails scored my shoulders and her moans carved my name into the air. I longed to claim every inch of her, to wrap my fingers around that soft column of her neck...gently, of course, and still firm, until the friction set her pulse racing.

But with each passing sunset, I forced myself to wait, letting her lead the rhythm of our bodies until she'd woven trust into the marrow of her bones.

Calista was worth any struggle of restraint.

Her skin glowed like warm honey in candlelight, and her laughter tinkled like wind chimes in spring. Even her quiet moments, hair splayed across her pillow, eyelashes faint shadows on her cheek, made my blood throb.

Thinking she would soon be my wife felt like winning a jackpot I never dared play.

Tonight, we'd join her family for dinner and linger under the same roof, becoming more than fiancée and groom—becoming one household.

I parked beneath a row of ancient oaks, their branches draping the cobblestones in dappled shadows. I stepped out, chest tight with eagerness, and smoothed the crease in my shirt, though my mind was still tangled in memories of her hip against mine.

It had been hours since I'd last seen her. I wondered if she'd slip her fingers into mine and remind me of what waited behind closed doors in the quiet between family greetings and warm embraces.

Would she catch the restless beat of my pulse when I brushed past her at the buffet table? Could she sense the low growl of hunger I kept caged, waiting for the moment her walls came down?

My greatest fear wasn't that I'd never taste her again. It was that I'd overwhelm her before she felt truly safe.

So I watered my lust in tiny sips, a lingering kiss at the nape of her neck, a slow stroke along her spine, always backing off before she trembled too hard.

In those stolen fragments, she'd matched my heat, arching into my touch, her breath quickening when my fingers tickled the curve of her hip bone. But each time I halted, knowing she'd someday beckon me to see the full force of that beast within.

I'd be the calm in her storm, the steady hand that guided her from hesitation into trust.

Everything else—my raging desire, my need to devour her —could wait until the moment she whispered, "I'm ready."

And then...then I would show her just how endlessly insatiable love could be.

She'd rushed out of my house in Central Athens to meet her sisters for lunch, her hair tousled, her dress wrinkled from where it had lain in a rumpled heap on the floor all night long.

We'd been distracted, exploring the pleasures of our bodies until the early hours of the morning, falling asleep in each other's arms when she'd meant to return home the night before.

When she'd woken up, slightly dazed and hungover from the bottle of wine we'd finished off the night before, my heart had melted at the sight of her sleepy expression. I kissed her forehead, felt the flutter of her pulse beneath my lips, and seconds later we were back at it again, skin on skin and undisguised need.

My phone had buzzed all morning with her teasing messages:

"Stop thinking about me," followed by a lipstick-kiss emoji, and later, "You're impossible," with a camera-snapping icon.

Each ping sent a jolt through my chest, igniting a coil of hunger in my gut. I sat through meetings with my mind hazy, tasting the echo of her perfume on my collar, imagining her low, throaty moans in my ear.

The tension between us was sensual and sexual and tantalizing beyond belief.

It was like every word we spoke to each other was laced with a lustful undertone, which left me in a state of heightened desire every waking moment. How the fuck I was going to make it through this dinner with her family with her being close enough that I could smell her perfume, I had no idea.

It would take every ounce of strength I had.

She was testing me at every turn, unknowingly.

Eventually, after we had moved past these challenges and were comfortably living together, I realized I would share all my struggles with her, and we would find humor in them.

The thought of building a life with Cali was exhilarating to me.

Developing a deep, intimate knowledge of each other, sharing private jokes, maybe creating a family with each other —I was looking forward to all of it.

As I parked the car and slid from behind the wheel, my heart raced with anticipation. I climbed the steps, and the door flew open before I could knock, my beautiful fiancée's beaming face greeting me.

Her face softened when she saw the wrapped baby gift in my hand.

"You're so kind," she remarked, accepting the gift from my hands and setting it down on the floor. Instantly, she embraced me before I had a chance to greet her, and I couldn't help but wrap my arms around her.

"I missed you!" she murmured in my ear, pulling me inside and closing the door. We stood alone in the formidable foyer, and I bent my head, brushing a kiss across her lips.

"I missed you too, even though it's only been hours." I

inhaled the fragrance of her lilac perfume, delighting in the pleasure coursing through my veins because I was close to her again.

It was impossible to keep my hands to myself, so I took this stolen moment alone to let them fall down to her hips, running across the curve of her ass as I kissed her again.

Her body leaned into me sensually as she moaned into my mouth. I grabbed a handful of her hair, letting my tongue delve into her mouth.

The sound of footsteps approaching made us jump apart like a gun had gone off.

She furrowed her brow and squinted, shaking her head as she muttered, "Fucking cock-blocking pains in my ass!"

I chuckled, glad to hear I wasn't the only one suffering.

Laya and Nikolas came out to greet me, and I picked up the gift and handed it to them.

"How thoughtful of you, Leon." Laya flashed me an approving smile.

"I appreciate the invitation," I said.

"Do you have a bag? I can have one of the staff bring it to your room," Nikolas said. "We've prepared the guest wing on the south side of the house for you."

"Thank you," I said. "My bag is in the back of my car."

"Say no more. I'll take care of it," he replied.

"Dinner is ready, if you're hungry." Cali smiled up at me. Her lips were still wet from our kisses, and the urge to lick her bottom lip overwhelmed me. I was certainly hungry, but I was hungry for Cali.

For now, though, food would have to do.

A few moments later, we were gathered around the dining table together, digging into a traditional Mediterranean feast of lamb and rice and everything that went with it.

"You still haven't made moussaka for me," Cali reminded me.

"I know," I said. "I will, someday, don't worry."

What I neglected to mention was that it took effort to make, and whenever Cali came over, we spent all our time in bed. I hardly had the opportunity to drink water or wine, much less to prepare a full meal for her.

She winked at me, and I knew she was thinking the same thoughts.

As she sat beside me, her thigh pressed warmly against mine beneath the table, a subtle yet electric connection sent my mind wandering to places it shouldn't go, not at this moment anyway.

The room buzzed with the gentle coos and babble of the baby nestled next to Laya, who juggled doting on him and nibbling at her meal.

Watching Laya and Nikolas interact with their child stirred memories of my own chaotic yet cherished family dinners. The way they seamlessly blended affection and responsibility resonated deeply with me, and it stirred a hopeful vision of the future I yearned to create with Calista.

Ever the devoted family man, Nikolas moved with an understated yet constant vigilance, his attention focused between Laya and Constantine, ensuring their well-being. His love for them was palpable, a quiet intensity wrapped around him like a heavy coat, signifying the weight of his dedication. It was the kind of love that spoke volumes without uttering a word. I felt a similar gravity when Cali was near, a protective instinct that settled into my bones.

The thought of how this feeling might intensify if we had a child together sent a ripple of unease through me. The instinctual drive to protect Cali was already a powerful force within me, and the idea of adding a child—our child—could push me into an obsessive spiral.

"So, Leon, I'm curious where your family stands these days," Nikolas inquired, his tone steady but probing.

"My family is just me," I responded, my voice tinged with the familiar ache of loss that struck my heart like a piercing needle.

"Of course, I understand." Nikolas nodded. "I didn't mean to imply otherwise. I was referring to the Boscos syndicate as your family."

"I've managed to uphold the power my family wielded before they were cruelly taken from me," I said, my words edged with determination.

"Are the Kotas and Gekas families still loyal to the Boscos name?" Nikolas continued, his gaze steady and unyielding.

I wasn't surprised by his focus on those particular families. The Kotas and Gekas were woven into the fabric of the Boscos lineage through my mother's side. My uncle, my mother's eldest brother, sat at the helm of the Kotas family, a patriarch with a commanding presence. My great-uncle Nimo had once led the Gekas family before his marriage. His wisdom and influence were legendary.

In our world, familial connections forged by marriage or birth held an inviolable sanctity. The Boscos family was renowned for upholding these bonds with unwavering loyalty. Uncle Nimo, in particular, had been a vital pillar during my rise to power. As one of the biggest investors in the Boscos empire under my leadership, he had guided me with a steady hand, filling the gaps in my knowledge that my father, taken too soon, hadn't been able to impart.

"Yes, they're my extended family, after all," I answered. "And, with my impending marriage to Cali, those two syndicates and territories that they rule will now be loyal to the Vitalis family, as well."

"I'm glad we can depend on their partnerships," Laya remarked. "This only adds to the strength of the power we're creating."

Cali flicked a lock of her hair over her shoulder and shrugged, her pendant swinging against the silk of her dress.

"That's good," she murmured, voice hushed. "Nothing in our world is certain. The more people we have behind us, the better."

I studied her, wondering what she meant.

Instead of prying, I tucked the question away for later.

I sensed she was referring to the protection of having multiple allies standing behind you. The world we lived in was violent and dangerous, spilling blood to sate their hunger for power. Trust lived on a knife's edge here, and reputation turned on a whisper.

Even murder.

We were all well aware of that fact. Each of us sitting at that table had experienced a great loss, except for Constantine. I studied his tiny body, in awe that he had no idea what kind of life he'd been born into. As the son of a Vitalis sister, he was a tiny human in great danger and would grow to be a man with great power.

Either way, seeing how his parents adored him, I knew he would grow up knowing he was loved. My parents had instilled that same sense of adoration in me, and not a day went by that I didn't miss them tremendously. Constantine would no doubt love his parents as vehemently as I had loved mine.

I was certain they would safeguard one another against any violent plots our enemies might be planning.

I looked over at Cali, my heart skipping a beat at the sight of her. I planned to protect her just as fiercely. Nobody would ever get near enough to her, or our future children, to harm a hair on their heads.

"We're looking forward to you joining our family, Leon." Laya smiled over at me before glancing at her sister.

They beamed at each other, seeming to engage in a silent conversation with just their eyes. I loved the closeness they shared. It told me that Cali was capable of understanding the importance of family. It showed me that she would take the responsibility of being a wife and mother as seriously as it warranted.

"Calista chose well."

"Thank you, Laya," I said. "I'm honored to become a member of the Vitalis family, and I vow to you that I'll take excellent care of your sister."

"I have no doubt," Laya replied. "Even though she'd argue she can take care of herself."

"I would agree wholeheartedly," I said, quickly glancing at Cali. She was clearly enjoying the conversation, smiling mischievously to herself. "But I'm available should she require assistance at any time."

"You really are the perfect choice if you understand that," Laya observed.

Under the table, Cali grabbed my hand and squeezed, the feel of her bare skin against mine sending my cock twitching and throbbing all over again.

I couldn't wait to get her alone.

But hours later, after everyone had gone to bed and the house had fallen dark and quiet, the disappointment I felt that I hadn't been able to do that without being completely obvious was hanging over me.

Lying in the dark guest bedroom, I longed to feel her against me again. Her beauty was unsurpassed, her sensuality unmatched by any previous lover. She left me beyond satisfied and in a state of constant hunger, the contradiction of the state of my body keeping me unsettled.

Soon, she'd be in my bed every single day.

I wondered if the intensity of my passion for her would wane after she was readily available to me. I suspected with a delicious dread that it would only further fuel my desire.

My hunger for Calista was going to kill me.

But oh, what a way to go. I chuckled to myself as I heard a knocking sound coming from the wall behind the fireplace in the corner.

Quickly, I grabbed my gun, alarm rushing through my veins in an instant. As the head of a syndicate, I was always on the verge of awareness, and this was why. My enemies could strike without any notice at all, at my most vulnerable moment.

That was why vulnerability wasn't an option for me. Ever.

When the panel beside the fireplace creaked as it swung inward, my finger snapped onto the trigger on instinct.

My breath caught in my throat. A pale rush of hair brushed into view, and my heart slammed against my ribs.

When Calista's face appeared through the narrow opening, my jaw dropped.

"Cali!" I cried.

She lifted her hands as if in surrender before dropping them with a smirk. "Easy there, Rambo. It's only me."

My pulse throbbed in my temples as I eased off the trigger, engaging the safety with a soft click, then laid the gun on the nightstand.

Flames flickered across her skin as I turned back to her, still unsettled with shock.

"Relax," she said, fully entering the room.

The faint sound of her bare feet touching the rug heightened my senses.

"Obviously, I'm not a threat."

"It'll take a minute for my heart to stop racing," I admitted, running a hand through my hair.

Her chin lifted, defiant and sly.

"Let's get it going faster," she said. "Undress me."

Her demand made my cock spring to attention.

I wanted—needed—to taste her again, to chase her curves with my hands. But after a few weeks of letting her lead, the urge to take control flared. I closed the distance.

She stared up at me, her deliciously puffy lips enticing me. The room was dimly lit, the glow from a single candle casting flickering shadows against the walls and bathing her beautiful skin in an eerie glow.

"Undress me first," I demanded.

"My pleasure," she whispered, lifting the hem of my T-shirt and pulling it over my head.

She let it drop and ran her hands over my bare chest, sliding up to my shoulders and down my arms. A shiver ran up my spine at the velvety touch of her fingers on my skin, the smoldering desire in her irises leaving me breathless.

"I didn't think we'd get any time alone together," I admitted.

She brought her lips close to mine, the words falling from her mouth with a smile.

"Did you think I could resist coming to visit you, knowing you're only a few rooms away?"

"We should be quiet," I said.

"I'm not sure that's possible," she replied as her lips brushed against mine and she pressed her body against me.

"Let's see." I grabbed two handfuls of her sweet ass,

lifting her and carrying her to the bed. I dropped her on it, delighting in the gasp that escaped from her lips. Her hair fell around her beautiful face, leaving her looking like an angel lying before me.

Cali lay back against the cool sheets, my body humming with anticipation as I trailed my fingers along the inside of her thigh, my touch featherlight. The air between us was thick, charged with an unspoken promise, and when she looked up at me, the hunger in her gaze sent a shiver down my spine.

She was wearing nothing but a short, loose black dress, the skirt riding up over her hips and revealing her bare pussy to me.

"You little vixen, you don't have any panties on," I said, drinking in the delicious sight of her.

I loved watching her like this—lips parted, chest rising and falling with shallow breaths, her skin flushed with heat. She was stunning, spread out before me, waiting, wanting. Her scent was intoxicating, warm, and inviting, and I reveled in how her muscles tensed as I traced slow circles along the sensitive skin of her hip.

"Why bother?"

Her smile was sexy and playful. Seeing her lying on the bed, so wantonly open, her sex on full display for my gaze only, left me trembling with desire for her.

I sank to my knees between her thighs, unable to wait another second to taste her. I kissed the inside of her knee, then lower, dragging my lips along her thigh in a path that made her tremble. I was in no hurry, savoring the slow descent, teasing her with my deliberate pace. My hands slid up, strong and sure, pressing against her thighs to hold her steady. Cali let out a sigh, her thighs quivering, her fingers threading into my hair as she arched toward me, silently pleading.

My mouth landed on her mound, my lips lightly engulfing her vulva before I pulled back, teasing her.

"Leon!" she exclaimed.

"Patience," I whispered against her skin.

Cali let out a breathless sigh, but it turned into a gasp as I nipped at the sensitive flesh of her inner thigh. I could hear her breath catching, her moans warm and teasing, sending sparks of anticipation racing through me. I was close to her pussy—so close—but still taking my time, reveling in the power I had over her body.

When my mouth finally met her mound, a cry escaped her lips. I groaned in response, the sound vibrating against her clit as I tasted her, slow and purposeful. My tongue moved with practiced ease, finding the rhythms that made her hips shake, that made her fingers tighten in my hair. I was relentless, my hands holding her firmly as I worked her clit with unyielding precision.

I could feel the way she responded to my mouth, how her body arched and trembled, how she tried to pull me closer even as the pleasure threatened to consume her.

"Leon, God, God..."

My name fell from her lips, breathless, desperate. I took it as encouragement, and my movements became more insistent and focused. Her thighs trembled against my palms, her breath coming in uneven gasps. I could feel her hovering on the edge, her body tight with tension, every muscle coiled in anticipation of release.

"Let go," I whispered against her skin.

Her body arched, her head falling back against the pillows as she growled and moaned. I didn't stop. I increased my speed, drawing every quiver from her beautiful center until she was left gasping and weak beneath me.

And then I started all over again.

My tongue darted forward, sliding against her clit. I let it slide down farther along her slit, dipping into her folds and slipping deep into her sex. I found her entrance soaked now, the taste of her nectar making me feel like I'd found the greatest treasure of humankind.

She tasted sweet and subtle, the excitement of her arousal seeping out of her generously. I lapped up every single drop with pure enthusiasm, my hunger for her rushing violently through me.

I licked and nibbled at her pussy until her thighs began shaking again, and then I sucked even harder, capturing her clit between my lips. Her hands pushed at my head, her fingers tangling in my hair.

"Leon! Don't stop, babe! Oh my God, yesssssss! I'm going to come again! Don't you dare fucking stop!" She hissed, wrapping her thighs tightly around my head and grinding her wet pussy against my mouth.

I slipped a finger inside her pussy, sucking hard on her clit at the same time. She shuddered and quivered. The sight of her, her head thrown back, her back arched, her gorgeous breasts on full display, was a fantasy come to life. She cried out as I bit down, slipping another finger, and then another, into her warm wetness.

She lifted her hips as I fucked into her harder and harder, my mouth still firmly attached to her rapidly swelling clit.

"Leon! I'm coming!" she cried, her moans ribboning through the air like the sweetest music. Her pussy spasmed around my fingers, and I kept fucking her hard through her orgasm, never letting up the pace until she reached down and grabbed my hand, holding it still inside her pussy while her orgasm subsided.

Her face was bright red with a slight sheen of sweat glistening on her forehead. As her eyes fluttered open, she gazed at me with pure joy.

Cali laughed, still catching her breath, as she gazed down at me with the most endearing smile.

"Come here," she demanded.

I had a thought that I'd never had someone tell me what to do as much as Cali did, but I was entirely happy with it. I would have never let anyone else talk to me that way, but if we were naked and happy, I didn't give a fuck at all.

I did just as she commanded, willing and eager to give her all she desired.

I slid my body up hers, the soft feel of her naked flesh against mine sending ripples of pleasure along my skin. Kissing her deeply, I pressed my cock into her center, hard and throbbing with raw desire.

To my surprise, she used my legs as leverage and quickly flipped me over onto my back before straddling me.

"Your training is excellent." Her long blond locks hung around her face as she brought her lips to mine again, creating a curtain of intimacy between us.

"I know," she said. "I've been practicing that move for a while."

"Now what?" I quipped.

The light I had come to love so much sparkled in her eyes once more. It was a playful mischief that made me feel weak. Whenever it shone, I could tell she was at ease, comfortable, and felt secure enough to reveal that facet of herself to me. It moved me profoundly. One day, I planned to share that with her.

But now was not the time.

"Now this," she replied, sliding her body down mine until she was kneeling between my thighs.

Immediately, she took my shaft between her lips, the quickness of it practically sending me through the ceiling.

"Fuck! Cali!" I groaned, my hands sinking into her hair.

She bobbed up and down my cock, sucking as her tongue twirled around the head. I watched her every move, in awe of the feelings she drew out of my body.

Slowly, the tension built inside me as she slid her lips up and down my shaft, her rhythm increasing until my hips were rising and falling in sync with her movements.

If she didn't stop soon, I was going to come in her mouth. I felt the pressure building—a hot drumroll in my veins—and I knew she sensed it too because her pace only quickened. Wet warmth slid around my length, and every thrust of her lips sent tiny lightning bolts of pleasure shooting through my lower belly.

"Cali, stop," I hissed.

She gave me a playful glance, picking up the pace and sending shocks of electric pleasure ricocheting through my entire body.

I'd been dreaming about sinking into her sweet cunt for hours. I wasn't about to waste my chance to do that by coming in her mouth. With a deep breath, I reached deep into my soul for the last ounce of control that I possessed.

"Cali, come here," I demanded, the need for control overwhelming me.

She looked up at me, whimpering in surprise as she pulled my cock from her mouth. I reached down, grabbed her under her shoulders, and lifted her up and over my body.

When she settled astride my hips, I grabbed the base of my shaft and positioned it at her entrance.

Her pupils dilated, lashes grazing her cheekbones like dark feathers. She swallowed hard.

I whispered, "I need you, Cali. Your cunt. Now."

I thrust up into her, the warmth of her body providing everything I would ever need in my entire life. Her slick entrance wrapped around my cock, inch by delicious inch, until I was buried deep inside her.

My heart hammered against my ribs. I paused, savoring the way her pussy walls fluttered and clenched me in a tender welcome.

She shifted, sliding back until the head of my cock peeked free, then arched forward. I caught her hips and drove up, thrusting until every inch of me was buried in her warmth. Wetness pooled between us, and I tasted salt and sweetness as our bodies ground together.

Cali went limp against me, her cheek pressed to my shoulder, letting me guide her hips up and down, my cock swelling inside her as she let me have control. Her moans brushed against my ear, the long locks of her hair falling over my face.

"God, you feel so good," she murmured, moaning my name.

I inhaled the sweet scent of her perfume, the smell of her, the feel of her, the sounds coming from her mouth, all intoxicating me and sending me into a blissful trance of sensuality.

My fingers gripped the tender flesh on the sides of her hips, slamming her up and down my raging cock.

The chemistry flowing between us was electric. Sizzling and sparkling, my body buzzed with excitement. I shoved myself even farther into her, desperate to get as deep as possible.

"I'm going to come again, Leon," she announced, sending shocks of pleasure straight to my brain.

"Do it. Come on my cock, Cali. Come for me, baby. I love it so much," I said, pulling her back so I could capture her mouth with mine. Her lips parted, allowing my tongue to delve deep inside, tangling with her own. She moaned into me, her hips grinding delightfully against my cock.

She rose and fell, searching for release, her head falling back, her lips falling open. I watched with savage hunger as a pink blush rose on her cheeks, and when her cunt tightened around me, I had to take a deep breath to keep the control I'd so desperately been trying to hold onto.

She spasmed around my shaft, warm, wet, quivering.

A surge of power hit me hard. Something about Cali, about being deep inside her, of having her beautiful pussy exploding around me, left me feeling like I was standing on top of the world, as if I were invincible.

I knew at that moment that as long as I had Cali to sink into at the end of every day, I would have the strength of a million men.

With the pleasure and feeling of power she gave me, I could have conquered a hundred empires, laid a thousand men out with the strength of my fists alone.

She made me strong...

She made me into the man I'd always dreamed I could become.

As I exploded deep inside her, the last remnants of control milked out of me, and waves of deep pleasure rolled through me, stealing my breath and strength in one fell swoop.

Amusement bubbled up inside me until I was chuckling.

Cali pulled her head off my shoulder and blinked at me, amusement dancing in her eyes. "What is so funny?"

"I was thinking about how powerful and amazing it made me feel to be inside you. Until I came, and then I was left weak as a puppy."

"Well, let's hope our enemies never break in right after we're finished making love."

I pulled her close, needing her next to me. "I'd never let anyone hurt you," I whispered in her hair.

"And I would never let anyone hurt you either. Especially in your weakened puppy state."

"My enemies would love to use this against me," I said, shaking my head.

"Don't worry, darling." She kissed my lips lightly. "Your secret is safe with me."

THIRTEEN

CALISTA

Leon always minimized his estate, calling it modest and highlighting the grandness of Nikolas's and Eli's homes. However, upon arriving at his Vouliagmeni residence for the first time today, I saw how much he had undervalued his property. Having spent time in his beautiful house in Central Athens, I should have expected something truly remarkable.

My driver navigated the winding driveway at a leisurely pace, allowing me to absorb the sight that unfolded before me. Situated just east of central Athens, Leon's estate was nestled on a cliff in the affluent suburb, where opulent estates dotted the rugged landscape.

The exterior showcased a stunning example of contemporary architecture, featuring a smooth, white stucco facade that appeared to harmoniously merge with the landscape. It overlooked the vast expanse of the Saronic Gulf, where the turquoise waters shimmered under the sun. The rhythmic crash of waves reverberated through the air, mingling with the briny scent of the sea and the gentle caress of the breeze.

The property was enveloped by lush, mature landscaping, creating an unexpected forest-like atmosphere despite its coastal location. Towering cypress trees swayed gracefully in the wind, their rustling leaves harmonizing with the ocean's symphony.

Leon's house was undeniably impressive, a testament to his wealth that he seemed to downplay with his modest demeanor. His natural humility made the opulence of his surroundings even more striking. I felt a sense of awe as I stepped out of the car, realizing that this would be my home one day too.

I felt a rush of excitement as I took in the angled lines of the house, the avant-garde sculptures placed strategically throughout the garden, and the short staircase leading to the entrance. Large pots brimming with vivid pink bougainvillea adorned the landing, their vibrant blooms climbing the house's facade.

The scene was breathtaking, and I couldn't help but feel a flutter of nerves mixed with anticipation.

Sunlight filtered through the magnolia trees as I crouched beside Leo, my loyal Greek shepherd. Her tail swept the grass in broad, happy strokes while she sniffed the air, nostrils flaring as she drank in every new scent.

I slid my fingers through the soft waves of her curls, feeling the warmth radiate through her coat into my palm, steady and comforting. Each delicate pant against my hand reminded me that I wouldn't face this next chapter alone.

Leaning back, I grinned down at her. "You know what, Leo? We're going to live here soon."

She tilted her head, one ear flipping forward, then let out a high-pitched whine.

"Don't worry," I said, brushing her ears. "You're coming too, my love." Her tail resumed its frantic wag as we looked up at the house ahead.

It was strange to think I'd be moving into a home this grand, especially without my sisters. They'd always been nearby. Vik too. It was going to take some getting used to, for sure.

I stood at the edge of Leon's sprawling estate, tracing the elegant lines of his mansion, a postcard-perfect vision nestled among manicured gardens. The grandeur of the place seemed almost ethereal, a world away from anything I had known.

Papa had been wealthy, but his riches paled in comparison to the opulence before me. Marble columns, intricate ironwork, and sprawling lawns evoked a sense of timeless luxury beyond my wildest imaginings.

The sheer scale of the life Leon maintained seemed incomprehensible. He had inherited the mantle of his family's business, a weighty responsibility for someone so young. I couldn't imagine the immense effort and countless hard choices he'd made to keep his family's empire together.

No wonder he'd garnered the formidable reputation

surrounding him. As the head of a syndicate with such influence and power, it was inevitable.

Papa had once presided over a vast and critical region, a position that ultimately claimed his life. Ruthless adversaries had gone to great lengths to annihilate him, leaving his loved ones vulnerable and destitute. In this world, survival demanded a merciless nature. You had to be unyielding, impenetrable, and perpetually vigilant. Otherwise, you'd be crushed. The system operated with ruthless efficiency.

Avra had told Laya and me about our mother's experiences. Mama often felt trapped, surrounded by an impenetrable wall of security, simply because she was married to the head of the Vitalis syndicate.

Papa was well aware that his enemies would seize any opportunity to reach him through her. Despite feeling like a prisoner, she accepted her lack of privacy out of love for him.

After our parents' deaths, when we fled to Prague, I too began to feel the restrictions as I grew up. Initially, I was too young, a mere child needing security and safety. However, once I entered adolescence, I craved freedom and the need to spread my wings and not always be under Vik's vigilant gaze.

Was I about to exchange one gilded cage for another?

A knot tightened in my stomach at the notion. Doubt crept in, whispering that perhaps this decision had been a mistake.

Just as uncertainty threatened to consume me, a blur of black fur catapulted toward us.

Leo tensed, ears pinned back in alarm, but soon relaxed,

her tail wagging in delight as the fluffiest dog I'd ever seen pranced around us.

The dog's glossy black coat was speckled with tiny white patches, a joyful distraction from my tumultuous thoughts.

"I see you've met Cosmo," Leon called out.

There he stood, leaning casually against an arched doorway that led to the back of the house, his posture relaxed yet exuding a quiet confidence. The sunlight streamed down, casting a golden glow over him, and the vibrant pink blooms surrounding him seemed to amplify his striking presence.

"I think Cosmo met us?" I glanced down at the energetic ball of fur still circling our feet.

Leon's gaze locked onto mine, his expression intense and smoldering, a contrast to the bright day that enveloped him.

My heart skipped a beat, and all the doubts that had been lingering in my mind began to dissolve like mist under the morning sun.

He dressed in casual jeans that hugged his frame just right, and a black button-down shirt with the sleeves rolled up to reveal the defined muscles of his forearms. The gentle breeze tousled his dark hair, a stray lock dancing over his forehead, accentuating the strong lines of his chiseled jawline.

A storm of emotions swirled in his deep brown eyes, mirroring the electric tension that seemed to vibrate in the air between us, leaving me a tad breathless.

The idea of being trapped in this moment with Leon, as if frozen in a secret moment of our own, suddenly thrilled me.

"Cosmo, come!" Leon commanded, his voice firm yet affectionate.

With a joyful bark, Cosmo bounded toward Leon, and Leo, who had been my shadow just moments before, eagerly followed, completely captivated by Cosmo's antics.

Leo, it seemed, would fit right in here.

Leon secured the gate behind him, then sauntered over to me with a smile that made my heart flutter.

I tilted my face up to him, my skin already tingling with the anticipation of his touch, the sweetness of his impending kiss.

"Cali, I need to ask you a serious question," he said, shifting the lighthearted mood instantly.

I blinked at Leon's face just inches from mine. I swallowed, and my mind clouded with confusion and curiosity. His gaze drilled into me, silent yet insistent.

He didn't wait.

"Tell me the truth," he said, voice low and urgent. "If you had the choice, would you rather plunge the blade yourself into the chest of the man who orchestrated your pain, or would you prefer to have someone else do it—wrap his still-beating heart in cloth and deliver it to you as a gift?"

My jaw went slack. A gust of ocean breeze tugged at my hair, and my heart thundered in my ears.

I no longer felt bile rise at the thought of him. Instead, I envisioned revenge and breaking him, just as he had attempted to do to me.

His role as Elias's father held no significance. Elias now

viewed him solely as his genetic donor. He'd help me gut him if given the chance.

"Leon..." I managed to say, utterly unprepared for the question.

He straightened, dark curls brushing his temples. "Ozias Xenos doesn't deserve another breath. I just need to know if it'll be your hand or someone else's."

"Leon—" I shook my head. "I'm flattered, I am. But honestly, I just don't know if revenge will change anything. I've spent so much time trying to move on with my life. Do you think it will make things easier?"

"I don't know. Perhaps it will change nothing for you. But my question still stands, because again, that monster doesn't deserve to draw another breath after what he did to you."

I turned away to watch the ripples drifting toward the wooden dock. The water gleamed like molten silver, and my chest tightened as I wrestled with his words. My sisters and Vik had offered me the same choice: say the word, and Xenos would be dealt with.

I'd insisted I wanted to do it myself, *when I am ready.*

Had I ever been honest?

Dark imaginings flickered through my mind: dragging him into a cold cellar, twisting a knife between his ribs, listening to his screams like steel on stone...or watching the life fade from his eyes as I toyed with him.

Each fantasy once blazed inside me. Lately, those visions felt like cold ashes, hollow and meaningless. Instead, I'd been painting my daydreams with brighter colors: cozy dinners by a fire with Leon, laughter spilling through sunlit rooms.

I craved a new chapter, a future untainted by blood. Could that future begin with my hands stained?

Well, there was only one way to know.

I drew in a slow, steady breath, tasting the crisp air.

Then I turned back to Leon, meeting his expectant gaze. A steely calm settled in my bones.

"Bring me his heart," I whispered.

Leon's grin was feral, his nod decisive. "Consider it done."

Every beat of my heart thundered in my chest when he spoke.

Warmth radiated from my core. This was exactly the kind of marriage I craved: strong arms that guarded without smothering, thoughtfulness that slipped in like a gentle breeze, respect that never rang false.

Leon slid his hands around my waist, pulling me so close I could press my cheek against the firm line of his shoulder. His cologne—earthy sandalwood with a hint of spiced amber—drifted into my senses, and I savored the taut strength of his embrace.

"It's so good to see you," I murmured into the cotton of his crisp white shirt, my breath catching on each syllable.

He let out a low chuckle. "I'm not sure I can let you go now that you're here."

"Then don't," I whispered back, tilting my chin to meet his gaze.

He gave me that slow, tender smile he reserved just for

me, the kind that made hope flood through every cell. "Come with me, please."

He wove my fingers through his and led me past the iron gate where the dogs had scampered off—ears flopping, paws pounding the flagstone path.

Beyond the gate, the house revealed its secret face. The terrace dropped away into a vast panorama of cliff and sky, anchored by an infinity pool whose water merged with the ocean's silken horizon.

Along the pool's edge, terracotta pots overflowed with magenta bougainvillea and scarlet geraniums, their blossoms nodding in the sea breeze.

I paused, palm pressed against the smooth stone balustrade. "Leon, it's breathtaking. Your description at lunch couldn't begin to capture this."

"I'm glad you think so," he said. "I find great peace here. When I'm stressed out from work, I sit here in the garden by the pool and stare out at the sea. It's so huge, it reminds me that whatever I'm dealing with is surely not as important as I'm making it out to be."

He guided me toward a white gazebo tucked into the corner of the terrace. Three marble steps led up to its shaded platform, where sunlight filtered through intricately carved arches, painting lacework patterns on the flagstones.

In the center, a round table draped in moss-green linen held a banquet: a basket of freshly baked brioche, a silver ice bucket cradling chilled champagne, plates of ruby-red straw-berries and slices of tropical mango, and at its heart a tall glass vase bursting with white lilies whose petals caught stray sunbeams.

My breath hitched. I spun in a slow circle, the hem of my dress swirling.

"This is pure magic," I exclaimed. "I feel like I've stepped into a fairy tale."

"Well, that's convenient." He sank to one knee so softly I barely heard the stone meet his tailored trousers. My spinning came to an abrupt halt.

A gasp escaped me when he opened a small black velvet box. Inside sat the most beautiful gold ring, adorned with an array of sparkling sapphires, rubies, and diamonds.

My heart skipped a beat, and I could barely breathe at the sight of it.

"Calista Vitalis," he said, voice trembling with devotion, "would you do me the honor of becoming my wife?"

Tears blurred my vision as emotion pooled in my throat. "Oh, Leon..." I covered his hand with my own, feeling the warmth of his skin beneath my palm.

"I know you picked me first, Cali, but I would have chosen you over any other woman in the universe. I want you to know that."

"Yes, of course! Yes!" I cried with joy.

He rose, the ring glinting between us, and slid it onto my finger.

I held my hand out, marveling at its weight and how the gems caught the light. "It's perfect—just like you."

Leon enveloped me in his embrace, and we shared a slow kiss, as the world faded away to the gentle connection of his lips on mine. When he eventually pulled away, I wiped the tears from my cheeks and kissed him again, resting my face against his chest.

"I hope you like it," he whispered, his breath warm against my hair.

I said, my tears warm and bright, "I adore it."

He pressed a tender kiss to my forehead. "I'm sorry it took me so long. I had it custom made—you deserve something as unique as you are."

"Thank you." I kissed him and then wrapped my arms around him. "You really aren't evil incarnate after all. You're more like a tender teddy bear."

"Don't say that around anyone else, please." He brushed a kiss across my lips. "I'm only like this with you, my darling."

"Lucky me," I said as he kissed me again, his arms wrapped tightly around me, his ring wound firmly around my finger.

FOURTEEN

L EON

Iason perched on the edge of the worn leather couch in my office, his shoulders tense, jaw tight, and fingers tapping a quick beat against the armrest. The afternoon sun filtered through the blinds, casting stark stripes of light over his angry face. Outside, fluffy white clouds drifted across a steel-blue sky, completely oblivious to the turmoil brewing within these walls.

"We can't let this go on," he ground out.

"Fuck no, we can't." I stood, shoving my palms flat against the cluttered desk. "This is the fourth restaurant in a month that's been destroyed! I thought I'd made my point clear with Polus and Manolis."

Iason exhaled, shoulders sagging. "Honestly, boss, I thought you did too. They looked like they'd been chewed up and spit out. I was sure they'd keep their distance—"

"Do I need to fucking kill them?" I slammed a fist against the desk. A pencil rolled off, clattering to the floor. "Why do they keep pushing me?"

He lifted a brow and leaned forward. "Have you considered it might not be them?"

"Who else is stupid enough to fuck with me like this?" I whirled around, pacing in circles.

"Maybe it only takes arrogance," he said with a shrug.

I stopped pacing. "What are you thinking?"

He didn't answer at first. He just folded his arms and watched me, the afternoon sun gilding the edge of his jaw.

Then, he suggested, "Lucianos, maybe?"

A cold twist gripped my gut.

"Fuck."

Dominic Lucianos was arrogant. He also leaned toward stupidity. Everyone knew this. That was why his brother was the one truly in charge of his family's empire. It was widely known that if Dominic was calling the shots, they would have lost their fortune years ago.

"I don't know." I ran a hand through my hair and stared out the window. Below, a jagged cargo ship lumbered across the harbor, its rusted hull cutting slow arcs through the water. "What does he have to gain by ransacking my restaurants?"

"Think about it." Iason stood and crossed to the window beside me. "You humiliated Dominic at that charity gala.

Humiliation's his kryptonite. Then Calista snubbed him in front of half the city. Pride like that? It doesn't heal on its own."

I hadn't considered that getting engaged to Calista would upset more than just our personal lives. Like that ship, our announcement had carved a new wake—one that rocked the underworld balance in ways I hadn't foreseen.

I had been thinking of protecting Calista. I'd been contemplating revenge on the man who'd harmed her. But I hadn't for a second thought about the problems our marriage would cause for my business.

What Iason was suggesting made sense. I'd pissed off a lot of people in my day, but most of that was in the past or had been resolved. There had been a bit of a truce between me and my enemies of late.

"We might have a fresh enemy," I murmured, my chest tightening, adrenaline pumping hot and violent. "All this time, I thought Polus and Manolis were the only ones left with a grudge."

"I heard some rumors." Iason leaned against the worn leather couch and scanned the room as if ensuring no one else could hear. "After the charity event, Dominic was in a local bar, swaggering like a peacock and mouthing off loudly about Calista. He was insulting your name too, for getting involved with her. I won't repeat the vile words he used to describe her, but I'm sure you can imagine."

"That prick," I muttered, my hands curling into fists at my sides, the knuckles turning white. "He's trying to strike back at me. I sure wish he hadn't targeted my most profitable restaurants. They'll be shut down for weeks, and we were getting the first mess cleaned up. The timing couldn't be worse."

"Yeah, it's gonna hurt," he replied with a resigned sigh.

"It's so fucking stupid," I spat, pacing the room. "There are plenty of other families with daughters ready for marriage. Cali might be smarter than most, but some less discerning women would jump at a chance to marry into the Lucianos family. It's not like she's his only option."

"He's simply a sore loser." Iason crossed his arms as he leaned back. "He's not used to getting rejected. I wouldn't worry too much about his words, though. Most people see right through his narcissistic bullshit."

"Maybe." I shrugged, though my mind was racing with the possibilities. "I can imagine what he was saying about Calista, though. There are a lot of pricks out there who would agree with him and his archaic beliefs about women."

"A few were agreeing with him," he admitted. "Said Calista was probably asking for the rapes. He said she was worthless now, and they all chimed in like a pack of hyenas. I wasn't there, but I would have torn them all new assholes if I had been."

"She's worthless now," I said through clenched teeth, fury pulsing through my veins. "But his pride is bruised because she rejected him, so he wants her? Make it make sense, Iason."

"I don't think that's possible," he replied, shaking his head in disbelief. "I can't wrap my head around that kind of thinking. I'm glad Calista saw through his facade."

"Me too," I said, the tension easing. "But what do we do about him? I'm not opposed to eliminating him, to be honest."

"That's going to cause a lot of ripples throughout our community," Iason warned as he met my gaze with a knowing look, understanding the weight of the decision.

I refused to be disrespected or seen as weak. I turned away from the window, the weight of the decision heavy on my shoulders.

"I can't ignore this," I finally said.

"Understood. Want me to handle it?"

"No," I said. "I need to find a way to make this happen without drawing too much attention to ourselves. The last thing we need is to cause other issues to deal with. Give me some time to think about it."

He placed a reassuring hand on my shoulder, his expression filled with unwavering loyalty. "I'm here when you need me. You know that."

I managed a tired but grateful smile, appreciating his steadfast support. "I appreciate your loyalty, brother."

"Always," he promised.

Switching gears, I asked, "Did you find Xenos?"

I had tasked him with tracking down Ozias Xenos, the elusive man whose presence was crucial for securing my bride's wedding present.

"Not exactly," Iason admitted, "but my men have narrowed down his location to a small village in Crete. We believe he's hiding there, protected by a tight-knit group of soldiers."

"I see," I said, acknowledging the progress with a nod. "Good work. That's enough for us to move forward with our plan."

"Just say the word," Iason responded, ready to act at a moment's notice.

"Let's give it a little more time." I leaned against my desk and glanced at the clock. "I need to consult with Elias and Avra first. The last thing I want to do is alienate my new family right off the bat. They have an interest in Xenos's death, just as I do."

"That's probably a good idea." Iason glanced at his watch, its face gleaming under the fluorescent lights. "Anything else we need to talk about? I have a meeting with the contractors in a bit."

"No, thank you, Iason." I offered him a grateful smile. "I couldn't do this without you."

"Sure, you could." He hummed. "You just wouldn't be so wildly successful."

"Yeah, yeah." I chuckled along with him as he waved and strolled out of my office, the door clicking shut behind him. I sank back into the plush leather chair with a huge sigh, rubbing my temples.

The preparations for my upcoming nuptials were causing a whirlwind of issues, but I wouldn't have traded it for the world. The mere thought of Cali made my heart race and my cock twitch. I couldn't wait to get her alone again, to kiss her, to taste her, to sink into her...

But all of that would have to wait. There was too much important business to attend to right now.

I reached for my phone, the chill of its metallic casing pressing against my palm, and dialed Elias's number. He picked up on the first ring, his voice a calm anchor amidst the surrounding chaos.

"Hello, soon-to-be brother-in-law," he greeted.

"Elias, hello," I replied, a sense of relief washing over me. "Thanks for taking my call."

"We're practically family now, Leon," he said with a chuckle.

"I hope you still feel that way after this conversation," I said as the nervous tension grew in the pit of my stomach. "Do you have a few minutes to talk? Are you alone?"

"Yes, I'm in my office by myself. What's going on?" he asked.

"I want to talk to you about your father, actually," I said, hesitating.

"Is that so?" he replied.

"I've been searching for him, and I believe I've pinpointed his location," I added, a blend of anxiety and anticipation coursing through me.

"I've been trying to locate him myself," Elias admitted. "So far, I've been unsuccessful. I'm surprised you made more progress than me."

"Don't be," I said. "I have a network scattered throughout Europe, each member adept at tracking down those who prefer to remain hidden. Their loyalty is unwavering, and they share a deep commitment to ensuring our family thrives."

"Your family, huh?" Eli asked, probing. "Is this about protection, or is it about getting vengeance for Calista?"

I ran a hand through my hair and stared at the polished surface of my desk. "For me, those goals are intertwined. Calista is all that matters. I'm prepared to do whatever it takes to keep her safe."

There was a pause, a moment heavy with unspoken thoughts, before Elias exhaled deeply. "I'm glad she chose you, Leon," he said. "But there's another issue, and it isn't my father."

My heart thudded heavily against my ribs, a drumbeat of anxiety. "What now?"

"Your rival for Calista's affection is stirring up trouble."

I frowned, my eyes shifting toward the window where the city skyline stretched out under a dimming sky.

"Oh, absolutely," I replied, as the realization set in. "Yes, I know he's been talking a lot. I believe he's behind the recent break-ins at my restaurants."

"He's been bothering both Nikolas and me, as though we can influence Calista's decision. Honestly, it's frustrating."

The rage that had simmered beneath the surface flared up once more, hot and urgent. Perhaps it would be wise to instruct Iason to address this problem without delay.

"That fucker," I said. "I don't understand why he can't just let it go. He's your friend, though, right? Eli, I need you to know that if you don't handle him soon, I will."

"I'm not sure I'd call him my friend, to be honest. Maybe

at one time. But friendships shift over time as people get older. In truth, I'm closer to Dominic's older brother. Perhaps I can have a conversation with him and ask him to step in."

"I'm not sure that will do any good," I replied. "Dominic doesn't seem like the type to do what anyone else says. I'm not opposed to eliminating him, Elias."

"Let's not go that far just yet," he said. "I don't understand why he's doing this either. Do you two have a history I don't know about? Could this be more than just the man's ego getting bruised by Calista's rejection?"

"Maybe," I said. "I don't know him well at all. I'd never met him until the charity event the other night. I only knew who he was because..."

My words faded away as a memory flashed vividly in my mind.

"Wait a minute. When I was younger, my second-oldest brother, Haris, and his wife, my sister-in-law Sophia, had quite the scandal surrounding their wedding." I paused, my brow furrowing as I tried to recall the details. "Yes, I remember now. My mother was heartbroken because they'd eloped. They claimed the only reason for their abrupt decision was that Sophie was trying to escape a marriage her family had arranged with one of the Lucianos brothers. Do you think it could have been Dominic?"

"I think it may have been," Eli said. "And if so, then Dominic must be losing his mind after being rejected twice, and both times losing to a Boscos."

"Fuck," I groaned, running a hand through my hair in

frustration. "That's it. That's what's happening. It has to be."

"I think you're right," Eli agreed. "And knowing Dominic, he'll stop at nothing until he feels avenged."

"What a fucking prick," I said, clenching my fists. "He has no idea he's playing with fire."

"Look, Leon, do what you need to do," Eli said. "I won't stand in your way. But might I make a gentle suggestion? I think it's important to increase security around Cali now. She won't like it. She'll hate it. But I think it's necessary."

"Shit," I muttered, feeling the weight of the situation pressing down on me. "You're right."

I knew my actions would make Cali feel even more trapped, like a wild animal in a cage. She had confided in me about her frustrations about the relentless protection imposed by her family, by Vik in Prague, and the ever-present security detail shadowing her every move.

All I could do was hope she'd understand my intentions and not hold it against me for trying to keep her safe. Because there was no way I was going to ignore this threat.

Dominic Lucianos needed to be dealt with, but in the meantime, I was going to do everything in my power to protect what was mine.

Fifteen

C ALISTA

Squinting through the boutique's large window, I scanned the street outside, taking in the bulky figures clad in tailored suits and earpieces. I counted the familiar faces, reaching a total of twelve bodyguards, their presence as obvious as ever, not even including the ones flanking my sisters.

The whole scene was absolutely ridiculous.

With a deep sigh, I reminded myself of the capable security already at my disposal.

Yet, here we were, with even more men stationed outside. It was clear Leon had orchestrated this without a word to me, and although I attempted to swallow my irritation, the effort was in vain.

Most of the guards were under Leon's command, with only a handful dispatched by the Vitalis family. I mentally noted to address this extravagant display with him. The potential cost gave me a chill, even though I knew Leon wouldn't be bothered by the expense.

His intentions were rooted in protection, but the spectacle made discretion a lost cause. The men tried to blend in, pretending to linger, yet their vigilant stances screamed otherwise, drawing attention to the fact that they were guarding a mafia princess.

I considered bringing this up with my sisters, hoping for some solidarity or even just shared exasperation. But as I turned back toward them, ready to voice my thoughts, Avra interrupted with a grin, pressing another sparkling champagne flute into my hand, the bubbles dancing up the glass in a silent cheer.

"Drink!"

"If you insist." I downed the sparkling golden spirit. "But if I keep this up, I won't be able to walk, let alone stand up long enough to try on another gown."

The boutique's lighting reflected off the rows of pristine white dresses hanging like dreams waiting to be tried on. I was here to find my perfect wedding dress, but the bubbles from the flutes of champagne they kept refilling had gone to my head, making my steps a little unsteady on the plush carpet.

"You're drinking for both of us," Avra teased, her hand resting on her prominently rounded belly, which seemed ready to burst with life. Her skin radiated a soft glow, and she exuded an air of serene beauty that made her look like a fucking goddess descended from Olympus, glowing with health and happiness.

"And for both of us as well." Laya indicated Constantine, who nestled against her while nursing happily. She ran her fingers through the baby's dark curls.

"Exactly," Avra continued with a playful grin. "You have to finish this bottle for us since we can't join in."

I giggled as I wobbled back to the dressing room, the champagne flute cool in my hand. "I don't think that's a wise move." I pulled aside the heavy velvet curtain. "Besides, Avra, you're on the brink of bringing a new life into the world, and I'd hate to be slumped over in a champagne-induced stupor when your little one decides to make an entrance."

"Don't jinx it," she replied with a mock-serious tone. "I want this baby to hold off until after the wedding."

"I think that decision might be up to the baby," Laya stated.

As I stood behind the curtain, I smiled while thinking of my sisters. Laya was a fantastic mother, and I had every confidence that Avra would be just as amazing. After all, she had practically raised both Laya and me when we were in hiding in Prague.

Sometimes, it felt more like she and Vik were my parents than our mother and father had been. I'd been so young when they'd died, and I had so many more important memories that I shared with Avra.

It made me sad to think of all the things our parents had

missed. And now, my wedding would be just another stark reminder of their absence.

I slipped on the third dress of the day and stared at myself in the mirror.

In the end, I decided it was way too poofy, but I walked out to my sisters anyway. They'd only make me put it back on if they didn't get a chance to see it.

"It's...so..." Laya let her gaze roam from the tiny off-the-shoulder sleeves down to the widening froth around my hips.

Avra shuffled ahead with a slight wobble due to her swollen belly. She placed her hand on her rounded belly while squinting at me.

"No. You look like a marshmallow drifting off the cake stand," she declared, warm but firm. "Why does the dress flare out like a bell? It's supposed to be a dress, not a blimp."

"Glad we're unanimous." I pursed my lips.

"Even though you look like you're about to float away like a cloud in the sky, you're still beautiful, Cali," she said. "Mama and Papa would be proud of you."

"Thanks," I said, my smile fading.

Avra seemed to notice my sadness. She grabbed the bottle of champagne and poured me another glass.

"Keep drinking," she said.

"If I keep drinking, I'm going to wind up deciding on some atrocity like this!" I protested, but I took the glass anyway, taking a sip of the delicious bubbly.

"Okay, now go and take that monstrosity off and keep going!"

I did as she said, trying to push away the sadness. This

was supposed to be a happy occasion, not a depressing trip down memory lane.

I tried on another dress, this one a heavy couture strapless beaded number that had an excessively tight bodice.

"It looks like your boobs are pushed up under your chin!" Laya cried.

I looked in the mirror and couldn't argue.

"This is excruciating," I complained, grabbing the nearby flute and downing the rest of the champagne. "I'm never going to find anything."

"Yes, you will. It just takes time," Avra said. "You can't expect to find perfection on your first try."

Her words made me think of Leon, and I felt a flush of heat rise to my cheeks.

"Oh my God, she's blushing," Laya teased, reaching out to pinch my cheek.

I swatted her hand away. "I'm not! I'm just...thinking about how lucky I was that I got to meet my fiancé on the first try."

"That was luck indeed. But finding the perfect dress? That's another quest entirely. Now, on to the next one," Avra stated.

She pushed me playfully, and I retreated again behind the curtain. I shimmied out of the beaded gown and slipped into the next dress, expecting to reject this one too.

But as I caught my reflection in the mirror, an unexpected wave of warmth surged through me, and for once, it wasn't because of thoughts of Leon.

The gown, crafted from exquisitely delicate silk, fit like a dream, hugging each of my curves in precisely the right way. The sweetheart neckline offered just a glimpse of cleavage, enough to be alluring without being revealing. The skirt flowed in an elegant A-line, cascading over my thighs in a luxurious drape that swayed with every tiny movement.

I beamed at my reflection, a certainty settling over me that this was the dress. With a grin stretching across my face, I stepped out to show my sisters.

"I think this is—"

"Fuck yes!" they exclaimed in unison, cutting me off with their excitement.

"—the one?" I finished.

"Spin!" Laya demanded, circling her fingers in the air.

With a joyful flourish, I obliged, twirling around and watching the silk whirl around me as if it had been crafted for me alone.

"Oh, Cali." Avra's eyes shimmered with tears of happiness. "You're going to be the prettiest bride who ever lived!"

"Can we go to lunch now?" Laya asked, a hint of impatience in her voice. "I swear this kid sucks every calorie out of my body!"

"Let me get out of this and talk to the clerk, and we can go," I reassured her, retreating to the dressing room once more. I lingered in front of the mirror, taking in the sight of myself in the dress.

I was going to be a wife.

Somehow, wearing this dress made it all feel so real, so immediate. Leon's face flashed in my mind, and I couldn't help but smile as I finished getting ready.

Twenty minutes later, the four of us were tucked away on plush loveseats at our favorite restaurant, the familiar chatter of patrons and the clinking of cutlery surrounding us. We indulged in olives and hummus, my sisters stealing glances at me as I sipped more champagne. I was on cloud nine, and they quickly picked up on the blissful aura that enveloped me.

"I'm assuming the fact that you can't stop smiling today means that you're happy with your choice of Leon as your husband?" Avra asked.

"I am," I admitted. "Although that dress is dreamy, isn't it?"

"You know, Cali, you can purchase the dress without a wedding being required," Laya said. "It's not too late to back out if you're having second thoughts."

I shook my head. "No, I'm sure. Leon's a great man. He's been nothing but good to me."

Too good, I thought to myself. He'd been polite, almost hesitant, in bed, and my heart thudded at the memory of every single moment. I craved the roar behind those gentle eyes, the kind of passionate intensity I needed more than he knew.

All the rumors I'd heard about him being violent and wild had left me wondering when that man would appear. So far, Leon had kept him hidden, if he existed at all.

I wanted to talk to my sisters about this, but they didn't even know we'd slept together at all, let alone what it was like.

"Well, he does seem like a good man, but don't they all?"

Avra said. "The important thing is that he's gentle and respectful to you the first time."

Heat once again crept up my cheeks.

I wondered what my sisters would think if they knew I'd already had lots of sex with Leon. I wondered what they would think if they knew what I wanted was anything but gentle or respectful.

"I don't think that's anything anyone needs to be worried about," I said with a chuckle.

I should have known they'd see right through me. They always did. There were times I was sure they were mind readers.

Avra squinted over at me.

Laya cocked her head.

And then they glanced at each other before staring back at me, full of accusations.

"Calista!" Avra exclaimed. "You've already slept with him!"

Just before they launched a full-scale attack, our server came over, leaving me uncertain whether to feel embarrassed that he'd overheard Avra's announcement or relieved to escape further questioning.

Thinking it was wise to let them wait, I grinned and told the server, "I'm starving. What's the house special today?"

After ordering, Avra frowned at me from behind her menu and whispered, "Don't think you can escape answering our questions."

"As if I would ever believe there was even a chance."

Just under two seconds after our server departed, Laya

moved, focusing entirely on me. "Spill it. I want every detail. And how long have you been keeping this from us?"

I groaned, running a hand through the tangle of my hair.

Avra leaned close, concern creasing her forehead. "He didn't take advantage of you, did he?"

I threw up my hands. "No, my God, stop—please!" My pulse flipped under my ribs.

"Then what happened?" Laya demanded, folding her arms. "Are you going to leave us in suspense?"

I sighed. "It was me. I'm the one who came on to him."

Avra's mouth fell open. "You did?"

I shrugged, my cheeks burning. "I took the lead. Pushed him, made the first move. He hesitated, tried to slow me down, but I wouldn't let him. I might've even...scared him a little."

The look of utter disbelief on Laya's face was almost comical.

"What?" Avra asked.

"I'm sorry, it's just the image of Leon, the big, bad mafia boss with the terrifying reputation, looking terrified of our little Cali!"

"Yeah, you're right, that's pretty funny," Avra agreed, smirking.

"I did hear another rumor that Leon was a very considerate lover, despite his reputation for needing to be in control at all times. Apparently, he has a dominant side, but maybe he doesn't carry that into the bedroom with him," Laya said.

I pressed my palms to my temples, willing the teasing

away. "Okay, that's enough. I don't need a play-by-play of his other...interludes. Thank you very much."

The last thing I wanted was to imagine him leaning close to someone else, tracing her jawline with his easy confidence. A hot twinge of jealousy flared in my veins, and the thought of murdering every one of them filled my mind.

I took a deep, centering breath and pushed those thoughts away.

Wow. I never realized I was so possessive.

I shifted, the fabric of my jeans bunching at my hips, and wondered if this constant fear of being handled too gently would ever fade.

Would he always treat me like I'd crack if he breathed too hard?

My pulse thundered. How could I show him I wasn't fragile and could take the weight of his dominance?

And what if he refused to hear the real me, the parts of me burning with wild cravings I barely understood myself?

What if these restless urges never went away?

A soft rustle beside me pulled me out of my spiral. Avra's dark brows drew together as she adjusted on her seat, her black curls brushing her shoulders.

"Did you tell him, Cali?" Avra asked in almost a whisper. "Does he know the details?"

"Yes, he does," I affirmed. "He was very kind, listened, and never made me feel judged. Since then, he hasn't changed. He's genuinely delightful to be around. In all honesty, I can easily imagine falling in love with him."

"Wow," Avra said. "When did you realize all this?"

"The first day I met him, if I'm being quite honest." I smiled at the thought of that first day. "I'd been so nervous. Cynical. Defensive. But as soon as he arrived, everything just seemed to fall into place between us. It was like meeting a long-lost friend."

"That's so sweet," Laya said.

Avra leaned forward. "I wish you'd said something to us sooner. You could've avoided the Dominic disaster."

"I don't think I realized it myself until later," I said. "It didn't take long, though."

"I'm so happy for you." Avra smiled first at me, then at Laya. "I'm happy for all of us."

"Look how far we've come," Laya said as she lifted Constantine from the carrier beside her and hugged him close to her chest. "I'm proud of us and everything we've achieved."

"Me too," Avra agreed.

Their confidence was like a steady flame, and I yearned to be just as unshakeable. I watched them side by side, one cradling new life, the other leaning in to share my joy, and felt my heart swell. I could be this strong too.

They were both going to be amazing mothers, and I was happy to get to watch them raise happy little humans.

"Are you aware that Leon called Eli, Cali?" Avra asked.

"Did he?"

"Yes." She rubbed her swollen belly. "He was asking about Elias's father."

"Why?" I whispered. My pulse thumped in my ears.

Avra's gaze never wavered. "Leon told Elias he's located Ozias."

When Leon had asked me if I'd rather receive Ozias's heart as a gift or cut it out myself, I wasn't sure if he was being serious or not. But if he'd gone so far as to consult with Elias about it, then perhaps he was. A bolt of surprise echoed through me. Did he truly mean to cut out the man's heart?

Laya raised an eyebrow. "What does he need Ozias for?"

I exhaled, tension rolling out of my shoulders. "He says it's a wedding gift."

They looked over at me.

"What kind of gift?" Avra asked.

"I can't say." I shrugged.

Maybe it was noble of him to dare to take such an extravagant step, but I wasn't going to be the one to tell anyone, not even my sisters. The fact that they were very perceptive, though, still existed.

"Don't you want to be the one to exact revenge on that prick?" Avra asked. She peered directly into my eyes, and it was apparent she knew what Leon was planning.

"I, for one," Laya said, "would love to watch you slit that bastard's throat."

The image of Laya tenderly holding her infant child and making such violent statements was stark and amusing to me. "Don't worry, darling sisters. You can be assured that my fiancé asked about my preferences and is committed to appropriately handling the situation. I would be lying if I said it wouldn't be a pleasure to watch him work."

They laughed, and I joined in, even if it was about a very

dark subject. We all exchanged knowing glances, the unbreakable bond between us pulsing.

"Looks like the old Cali is coming back," Laya finally said.

"No, I don't think so," I admitted. "It's a new and improved Cali you're seeing. But it sure is nice to be surrounded by people who understand every version of myself."

"We love all the versions of you, always, Cali." Avra reached over and squeezed my hand.

"I love you both too." A surge of love washed over me.

"I'm so fucking happy you found someone who cares about you and understands you," Laya said. "Leon is going to be a wonderful husband for you. He's already showing it."

"Yes, he is," I said, my heart skipping a beat at the thought of him ripping out Ozias's heart and bringing it to me.

It was so medieval and primal and savage.

And so damned sexy, it made me wet.

Sixteen

L EON

The treetops danced in the breeze as I enjoyed my morning coffee out on the terrace. The sparkling azure sea shimmered in the distance, the white puffy clouds floating overhead reflecting off its surface. The water was littered with sailboats taking advantage of this breezy morning, drifting lazily around and matching my energy today.

I was so happy, I felt intoxicated and blissful. Everything was going so well with Cali, and soon she'd be with me every single day. I never imagined things would turn out so well, and yet here we were, in almost constant communication and growing closer by the day.

Today, she was out shopping with her sisters, and I'd get to see her again later.

Footsteps approaching pulled me from my revelry, and I lifted my head to see Iason walking toward me. By the look on his face, his energy did not match my blissful outlook.

"What's wrong?" I asked, noting the tension in his clenched jaw.

He thrust a crumpled envelope toward me, frustration etched on his features.

"I'm fucking done. If you don't take care of this, I will," he snapped.

I lifted a brow, taking the envelope and eyeing him carefully. Iason wasn't in the habit of giving me orders, so I knew whatever was going on had upset him.

"He's basically putting a target on us."

He crossed his arms, his hands fisted, as he waited for me to open it.

I exhaled, a sense of dread creeping in. "What now?"

I pulled the piece of paper from the envelope with my name scrawled on it and read it, my heart racing faster with every word.

Leon Boscos,

End your engagement immediately. If you fail to untangle yourself from Calista Vitalis, the Boscos empire will suffer the consequences. The Boscos family continues to be the source of deep insults to powerful families that cannot be ignored.

Don't sacrifice your family's legacy by making this grave mistake.

"It's not signed?" I asked Iason. "Who sent this?"

"Seems obvious, right? A carrier just delivered it without any clue about the sender, but given the phrasing..."

"You suspect it's Lucianos?"

"I think so," he replied. "Who else would feel insulted by you? And with a reference to ongoing insults?"

"True," I said, anger surging through me now. "I agree, Iason. We can't let this go. Not any longer. This guy is crazy if he thinks he can fuck with me. I don't know why he's doing this, though. Calista made it clear she was never truly interested in him. It doesn't add up."

"A man whose ego is bruised rarely makes rational decisions."

His words rang true.

Whatever Lucianos's reasoning, this couldn't stand. Sending me threatening letters like this? Who the fuck did he think he was?

I'd never let him near Calista again. She'd made her decision on her own, but I would die defending it.

Lucianos must be destroyed.

"Increase security for Calista," I instructed Iason. "And then get a team together to do surveillance on Lucianos and his family."

"Maybe the cousins can help us out?" Iason suggested.

My extended family lived all over the region, ready and available at a moment's notice to help in any way necessary.

"Good idea," I said. "He won't recognize anyone."

"I'll take care of it right away," Iason said. "Anything else?"

"Not at this time," I said. "Let me know what the team finds out about Lucianos. I want to be informed of every move he makes, especially if he's coming toward us."

"You got it," he said before walking away, his footsteps determined and angry.

I sighed, reading the note again with exasperation.

Finally, I picked up my phone. Elias, Nikolas, and the sisters needed to be informed about this threat. I texted all of them in a group chat and put my phone down, my head spinning.

It was important to make sure Dominic Lucianos didn't come near any of us. With luck, my team would have enough lead time to stop him if he decided to do anything.

I was in my office later when Cali arrived.

Her sisters had dropped her off and were on their way back to Laya's estate. I was glad to have some time alone with her, but when I noticed the way she wobbled in her high heels and the faint pink flush in her cheeks, I couldn't help but smile.

"Looks like you had fun," I said as she stumbled into my office, steadying herself on my desk.

"My sisters forced me to drink all the champagne," she slurred, each vowel lingering on her tongue.

"Made you?" I echoed, feigning shock. "I didn't know anyone could make you do anything, Calista."

She straightened, lifting her fists like a boxer.

"You're right," she said. "So don't try, or I'll punch you in the face."

I pulled her forward, letting her weight settle against me.

"I understand you assigned additional security to my team," she charged, her voice sugary.

"Guilty." I shrugged, enjoying the way she pouted, her bottom lip pink and tremulous. "Does that upset you?"

She cocked her head, trying to look stern, but her lips curved. "Not at all. If it makes you feel better, go ahead."

"That's good," I said. "I would have asked you first, but then I realized I'd do it anyway—even if you said no."

Reaching up, she cupped my face in her hands, shaking her head.

"You are so very pretty and so very fuckable, do you know that, Leon?"

Her words caught me off guard. Pretty and fuckable?

She saw me that way?

"And you and I need to have a serious conversation. Eventually."

Before I could ask what she meant, she crushed her lips to mine, pressing hard enough to take my breath away.

My cock grew thick and ready for action in my jeans, my body instantly aroused and hungry for hers.

Fuck, she was intoxicated, and this was not the ideal time to want to fuck her.

I couldn't tell how much she had drunk, but this

newfound confidence was out of character for her, suggesting she was feeling tipsy. I turned my attention to the open office door when I noticed the staff moving about the house, cleaning up.

Cali's fingers dove under my shirt, but I caught her wrists and held her at arm's length. "Babe, as much as I want to flip you onto this desk and lose myself in you, I don't think the staff needs a front-row show."

She pouted at first, but she perked right up once she saw me heading to the bedroom. Looked as if she was in a mood.

And that mood seemed to match what I'd been feeling most of the day. The urge to get her naked skin rubbing against mine was overwhelming me. I wanted to be gentle with her, but the lust ricocheting through my veins felt anything but gentle.

Clearly, she trusted me.

Otherwise, she'd never have come to me being so open and nakedly assertive. I loved it, I did. But the line between being gentle and unleashing the full impact of the desire I felt for Cali was quickly blurring.

As soon as the door shut behind us, she attacked me again, as lust and unquenched need rolled off her in waves.

Her fingers fumbled with the buttons of my shirt.

"I want you to fuck me, Leon," she hissed.

Well, fuck. I wasn't expecting that to come out of her mouth. But I sure liked it. And so did my cock. It swelled painfully.

"Aren't you drunk, darling?" I asked, my voice thick with lust.

"Yes," she admitted. "And that's exactly why I want to do this."

She crashed her lips onto mine, but I gripped her shoulders and pulled back until I could see her face. "Please explain."

She pressed both palms into my chest, her nails cool through the fabric. "I want to have drunken sex with my husband. Is that so bad?"

"We're not married yet," I reminded her.

"Oh, who cares?" she exclaimed before pushing my shirt from my shoulders, allowing it to drop to the floor.

I stood still. "Wait—what did you want to talk about?" I asked. "Let's talk first."

She pouted and let out an exasperated sigh before turning away from me, walking over to the bed, and plopping down on the edge of it.

"Fine, I'll talk. But you have to promise to listen to everything I say before you say no."

"I'm not in the habit of saying no to you, but I promise to listen."

She pursed her lips, looking as if to feel me out before going on.

"Okay. I have a favor to ask you," she said, running a hand through her long hair. "Wait. Two favors, actually."

I shrugged. "I'm listening."

"First," she said, lifting her chin, "I want to be there when you confront Ozias."

I blinked, the duvet cool under my fingertips. "Why?"

"I want to watch." Her voice was steady, but a faint tremor trailed her words like a ghost.

My stomach knotted. "Calista, I'm not sure I want you to see that part of me."

I was being entirely honest with her. The last thing I wanted was to ever frighten her in any way. What if she didn't look at me the same afterward? What if she didn't trust me anymore?

The thought of that was too much to bear.

She leaned closer, as if ready to throw down a challenge. "Are you afraid I'll think differently of you?"

Had she read my mind?

"You're very perceptive. Yes, I am," I admitted.

She smirked. "And yet you are the one who presented the idea of gifting me Ozias's heart. Were you not afraid of the same thing then?"

That was a good question. What was the difference?

"I don't understand why you'd want to be there. Can you explain better?"

"I'm done with the past, Leon." She stood, staring intently at me, searching for understanding. "I want to walk into this new life with you, free and clear of all the baggage I've been carrying. Seeing the life drain from Ozias's eyes will finally help me put that chapter behind me. I'll be able to move on, fully, completely, and without the demons of the past holding us back in any way."

My heart broke for her.

For all the shit she'd been through. All the shit she never asked for, plopped on her shoulders like a death sentence.

Cali was beautiful and kind, and her heart was pure.

She was special.

She never deserved any of this, and she deserved to be able to find a way to put it all behind her.

Her request to watch Ozias die, brutal as it sounded, felt almost tender in comparison to the cruelty she'd endured. If I'd been trapped in her shoes, I might have wanted the same.

I couldn't blame her. I certainly did not judge her.

"I understand, darling," I said. "But I need you to agree to something before I agree to your request. I need you to promise me that if I think you're in danger, for any reason, you will let my people remove you."

Her brows drew together, lips parting in silent protest.

"It's the only way, Cali. Take it or leave it."

I hated to be so firm, but without that vow, I'd never be able to concentrate on the task at hand. I realized I would constantly worry about her safety throughout. Ozias held great power. He would be highly protected.

Every precaution would need to be taken.

"All right," she finally agreed.

I lowered my head and kissed her, my heart overflowing with emotions for her. I drew her toward me, holding her close. With all my being, I wished I could erase her pain, the dreadful memories and the haunting nightmares.

I knew I'd never be able to change that. Cali had been forever altered. She'd never be the same girl she once was. But I planned to do everything in my power to ensure that nobody ever hurt her again and to create plenty of wonderful memories to overshadow the bad ones she was burdened with.

I sat on the bed and pulled her onto my lap, kissing her again as she wrapped her arms around me. She straddled me until her pussy was directly against my still throbbing cock.

She moaned, pressing against me harder.

I pulled away, breaking our kiss, and stared up at her. She was beyond breathtaking, so beautiful. She made it impossible to think as she looked down at me through lust-glazed green eyes and her silky blond waves cascading around her flushed face.

"What's the other favor?" I asked, leaning in closer to catch her whispered words. Her cheeks turned a delicate shade of pink as shyness crept over her face, and she shook her head.

"Never mind," she mumbled, her gaze darting to the floor.

I studied her, attempting to understand what was significant enough to make her stop and reconsider.

"If you don't tell me, we're not having drunken sex," I teased, trying to coax a smile out of her.

She shook her head in protest. "That's not fair."

"Maybe not, but I mean it," I replied with a wink. "Tell me, babe."

"All right, fine," she said, staring down at me, still hesitating.

"You can tell me anything, Calista. We're friends first, remember?"

My words seemed to open something up in her.

She lifted her head. The soft curve of her lips trembled as she mustered her courage.

"I want to feel like the woman I used to be. And I can only do that if you stop holding back."

"Holding back?" I asked.

"Yes!" she insisted, her voice rising passionately. "I promise, Leon, I won't break! I'm not a fragile doll!"

"Is that how I make you feel?"

"Sometimes."

"Tell me what you need from me, Calista. I'll do anything, darling."

My words hung in the air between us. She seemed to be weighing them to see if I really meant them.

"You always keep me on top. You never restrain me. You go out of your way to make me feel so safe."

"And?" I asked, lifting a brow. Were these bad things?

She leaned in, her mouth brushing against mine as she whispered her next words. "I know you have a darker side, Leon. Everyone talks about it."

Her lips traveled to my ear, capturing my earlobe between her teeth and biting down with a deliberate intensity.

"I want to see it," she breathed, her desire more than evident. "I want you to fuck me like you mean it, Leon."

SEVENTEEN

CALISTA

Had I really just said that out loud?

My heart thumped in my chest like a wild drum, its rapid beats echoing violently in my ears.

I swallowed hard, trying to steady myself, while the look on Leon's face left me breathless. My head spun, and I couldn't tell if the dizzying sensation was from the alcohol still buzzing through my veins or from the sheer audacity of my statement.

Either way, I meant every single word I had spoken.

Every ounce of courage I could muster surged through me as I held Leon's gaze, determined to own my request.

I had shared my desires with him. They lingered in the

air, bold and unyielding like a blazing neon sign lighting up our surroundings.

It felt as if years passed in that silence, my anticipation stretching the moment as I waited for his response.

Yes, I was tipsy, but that didn't mean I couldn't give full consent to sex like a grown-ass adult. I had put a tremendous amount of thought into this. After talking with my sisters, it had consumed all my focus.

Their advice played on repeat in my mind, even when I sat alone in my car, piecing together my thoughts.

I knew Leon desired me. It was unmistakable in the way his eyes burned with a smoldering intensity every time we made love. I sensed he'd been holding back from the very first time. It was obvious he was worried he might trigger me. His hesitation was endearing. It was the very thing that made me trust him enough to ask for what I wanted in the first place.

And, Oh my God, did I know what I wanted...

I wanted the man I saw lingering in the shadows in the bedroom, the man with the dark, primal need that he tried to keep hidden.

The savage Leon...

The alpha Leon...

The sexy, primitive beast that I knew was pacing around inside him, itching to be let out of his cage...

I thought of Laya and Niko and what it had been like living with them. They didn't worry about what the staff heard or saw. They took their pleasure wherever they wanted, whenever they wanted. And they didn't try to hide their savage trysts or the damage caused by them. More than once, I'd walked into a room where the staff was cleaning up broken furniture that had been sacrificed for their passion. There were nights when the sounds of their escapades echoed through the entire house, and they showed their faces the next day with pride and a complete lack of shame.

That was what I wanted.

That was what I needed.

The gleam in his eyes when he smiled hinted at a level of joy he rarely showed, suggesting the longing I believed Leon kept hidden within.

"I can't," he finally said, shaking his head firmly, dashing all my hopes.

I know he saw it on my face.

He reached up and cupped my cheek with one trembling hand. "Calista, darling, I'm so sorry. I care too much about you to ever hurt you." His thumb brushed a tear I fought to swallow.

"No!" I cried. "I don't understand, and neither do you! I feel safe with you—I am safe with you, aren't I?"

He closed his eyes. "Of course! That's an absurd question!"

"Then let me decide when I don't feel safe." I pressed my forehead against his sternum, feeling his heart thump like a drum under my cheek. "Please, Leon."

He shook his head, gaze lowered to meet mine. "Calista, I just can't—"

"Are you always going to hold that night over me?" I snapped, hands clawing at his shoulders. "You use it as an excuse to keep me at arm's length. I'm sick of feeling punished!"

I flung my words at him like daggers. I knew I was hurting him, but I didn't know how else to get through to him.

"Punished?" His tone conveyed utter disbelief, which was so frustrating.

"Yes!" I shouted. I was still straddling him, his hands resting on my hips.

I felt his fingers fisting against me and the tension rolling off his body. Still, despite the anger I was unleashing on him, his cock was twitching against my pussy.

"I survived! It's over. Now, I want to thrive, not just endure."

I was practically begging him to understand me.

"I decided long ago to avoid fixating on the assault. If I hadn't, the darkness would have consumed me. Don't you understand? I need you to stop dwelling on it as well! You weren't even there! You must let go so we can create a fulfilling life together, a true life filled with passion. The kind of passion I long for!"

"No, Calista!" His voice thundered as he cupped my face, his grip firm and earnest. His eyes, wide and fierce, locked onto mine, pleading for understanding. "I've never seen you as damaged or broken! I only want to keep you safe, no matter what! That's what a good husband does!"

I couldn't take it any longer.

I couldn't be close to him any longer.

Frustration mounted in my veins, leaving me pulsing

with anger and rage. Tears welled in my eyes, and I blinked them away. No fucking way was I going to cry now.

It would only prove his point.

I pushed off him, my feet crashing against the floor, echoing the weight of my frustration. I fixed my gaze on him, the tempest of anger and desperation boiling inside me as I fought for my voice amidst the chaos of my emotions.

"Fuck off with your protection! I have a right to choose what I want."

I abruptly pivoted toward the door. I craved space. I wanted to escape his pity and narrow mindset.

"Cali!" he shouted from behind me. I ignored him and kept walking to the door.

But he sprang to his feet and jumped in front of me, grabbing my arms and capturing my gaze.

"I will never be a part of hurting you, Calista, I just can't. You have to understand. Please."

"No!" I protested. "You know what I understand, Leon? I understand that a woman has sexual needs, just like a man does. I can feel the distance between us, that invisible wall you've built, and it's suffocating. You're holding back, thinking you're protecting me, but that gnawing hunger inside you just keeps growing, festering like an untreated wound. Until it pushes you to seek what you want from someone else. I'm willing to give it to you, and you deny me."

I glared, each word slicing the charged air.

"I would never," he whispered.

"Why should I believe you?" I demanded, struggling

against his grip. He held on tightly, his chocolate eyes searching mine.

He opened his mouth, then closed it.

And then a slow smile spread across his face, as if he'd just figured out something important.

"Because I love you, Calista, that's why." His words stung. They dug deep and hit hard.

And they made absolutely no sense to me.

The anger bubbling inside me rushed to the surface, overwhelming me now.

"How dare you?" I hissed.

Surprise flashed across his face, his confusion evident, and it pissed me off even more.

"How dare you say such a thing when you only give me pieces of yourself?"

"What?" he asked. "That's not true. I am completely present with you!"

"Present?" I questioned. "Maybe partially. I want you, all of you! Not just nice Leon. Not just gentle Leon. I want passionate, primal Leon!"

"Calista..." He shook his head.

"You want me to trust you? Then maybe you should trust me too, to know my body, my desires, to know my own fucking needs!"

I couldn't help but shout now, the tears flowing down my cheeks uncontrollably.

I'd been holding so much inside—so much unhappiness and dissatisfaction, so many unmet desires—and it all burst to the surface.

I snapped, letting my anger take the wheel.

I slammed my palm into his chest, and he took a step backward.

"Blowjobs!" I roared, breath catching in my throat.

I hit him again.

"Spankings!" I cried.

My palm slapped his chest again, and he fumed, his whole body coiled tight, upset, annoyed, on the verge of fury. Undeterred, I hit him again.

"Choking!"

His mouth fell open in surprise.

"Restraints!" I seethed as I struck him once more.

"Calista," he whispered, his voice a low warning that I ignored.

"Before I met you, I had lovers—lots of them! Did you know that?"

His frown deepened, the lines between his brows growing more prominent.

"I did," I insisted, voice trembling with fierce pride. "And they did things to me—things I screamed for, begged for, cried for."

"Stop it, Calista!" he demanded. Once again, I ignored him, landing another blow to his chest.

"I won't stop. I want you to hear every word! I want you to know it all so you'll understand!" I shook my head. "I've always known what I wanted. That never changed. I like sex —no, I love it! I've never been shy about asking for it, and I don't ever want to be."

His lips were twisted into an angry grimace, and I felt my pussy quiver at the sight of him angry.

Finally!

His dark irises burned with unguarded intensity, not fury but something more predatory. I knew I was pushing things too far, perhaps beyond that, but it was too late now.

I couldn't tell if I had made any progress in getting him to understand me, but if he was going to change his mind, it would undoubtedly take a monumental effort.

I went in for the kill, fully aware of the risk I was taking.

"If you won't give me the passion I crave, Leon, what solution do you propose? Would you like me to find someone else to scratch that itch?"

Time slowed down, my questions hanging in the air between us for a fraction of a second like a bullet in slow motion.

And then, before I could think, before I could blink, and before I could utter another inflammatory word, Leon snapped.

His fingers wrapped around my neck, and he pushed me backward, all at once. I gasped as he brought his face close to mine. His fingers tightened around the column of my neck.

He kicked my feet apart until he was standing between them, his words dripping from his mouth with rage.

"Is this what you want?'

Goosebumps tingled on my skin as a shiver raced down my spine. I had been pleading for this, yet I never imagined in a million years that he would fulfill it for me.

All of a sudden, I couldn't breathe.

I couldn't think.

His eyes burned with intensity and wildness, as if I had finally unleashed the beast from its confinement.

My core clenched, and my nipples beaded. The heat deep inside me grew with an aching, throbbing rush.

He was here. He was mine.

I lifted my chin.

"Yes, this is exactly what I want." The words scraped across my tongue like razor blades, my heart racing frantically in my chest.

He tightened his grip, and I swallowed hard, watching him.

I wasn't sure if he was going to fuck me or kill me, but either way, my pussy was quivering and spasming. I was afraid to say another word. I was terrified to move. I feared that somehow I would break the curse and Leon would cool down, remove his fingers, and walk away.

The thought of him doing that was excruciating. We would never recover if that were to happen.

More than ever, I needed him inside me, pounding me, taking me.

We stared each other down like animals facing off, and then, in the snap of a second, he captured my lips in the most passionate kiss of my life. His tongue darted inside my mouth, devouring me, capturing me, claiming me.

I whimpered, taken aback by the force of his need, even though I'd taunted him into giving it to me. It was all-consuming, and I craved more. I matched him with my demands, wanting more.

"Submit," he ordered, scraping his teeth over my lower lip.

My heart pounded into my ears, and for a brief moment, I wanted to fight him, to punish him, but I knew I'd pushed him too far.

I'd gotten what I wanted.

I moaned into his mouth, letting my body fall limp as he held me against the wall.

"That's right. You're mine."

With his free hand, he reached down and grabbed the hem of my dress, pulling it up over my hips, exposing my bare pussy.

A low rumble erupted from deep in his throat. "You little slut, you aren't wearing any panties?"

I shook my head, not sure if I should speak or not.

His fingers slid between the folds of my sex and sank deep, thrusting in and out, giving me no chance to do anything but take what he gave me.

I cried out, bucking against him, riding his hand, my body responding to his touch.

"You like this? You're so wet..." His breath grew uneven as he continued to work my pussy. "Such a fucking dirty girl."

He pulled out of me, making me cry out, and then leaned in, his fingers flexing around my throat as he brought his face to mine. "You get what I give you."

He unbuttoned his pants and freed his cock, letting his jeans fall to the floor.

He lifted one of my thighs, setting it around his hip, and, with no other preamble, shoved his thick, throbbing rod, going balls-deep.

"Leon!" I cried out, electric shocks of pleasure-filled pain ricocheting through my veins.

He fucked into me, hard and fast and ruthless. His hands gripped my thighs in a brutal hold as he used me to meet the demands of his lust.

"God, yes, yes, yes!" I shouted as he slammed his cock into me over and over, harder and faster with every stroke.

It was rough.

It was deep.

It was so incredibly fucking delicious...

The pressure on my neck added to the exquisite ecstasy building inside me.

I lifted my legs and wrapped my thighs around his hips, pulling him closer. His eyes peered into mine, hungry and dark and filled with the intense shadows of the passion flowing between us.

I put my hand on his fingers that were wrapped around my neck, lifting my chin and pressing on his fingers, silently begging him to squeeze harder.

"Goddammit, Cali!" he groaned.

His cock swelled inside me, and he fucked into me with an ever more vicious intensity. The feel of his body slamming into mine sent beautiful aching shockwaves through my clit, making my core spasm and clench.

"This is what you want? To be taken like a slut?" he demanded.

I couldn't speak, but I nodded, begging him to accept my desires and needs and understand what I craved from him.

My orgasm exploded out of me, my pussy clamping down on his pistoning cock, flexing and squeezing. It was exhilarating and everything I wanted.

"Leon, yes. Like this. Just like this." I threw my head back, loving every second of this.

"Why can't you just let me cherish you?"

How could he not understand that was exactly what he was doing? I was in heaven right now.

A slow smile spread across my face as I realized that I'd achieved my goal. He was as turned on as I was. His cock was made for fucking me like this. I just needed him to get his head in the right space.

"Leon, you are cherishing me." I squeezed my pussy tighter around his hardness. "You're giving me exactly what I want. You are all I crave and need. All of you."

I kissed him then, hard, full of passion, with the purest intention of my heart, my body, my love for him.

"You have all of me," he murmured against my lips.

"Good. Now fuck me harder."

"You asked for it."

With what I could only describe as a growl, his rhythm changed, and he pounded into me even harder. The sounds of him fucking me seemed to shake the very walls of the house. Waves of thundering pleasure rolled through me once again, and I cried out his name as I shot over the edge of bliss, his cock thrusting wildly into me.

"Cali! Cali!" he shouted. His lips devoured mine, his mouth claiming mine as he exploded deep inside me.

This was passion.

This was life.

This was love...

EIGHTEEN

LEON

The time had finally come.

As the boat docked under the cloak of night, I felt the cool breeze on my skin and caught a glimpse of the island of Crete glistening beneath the glowing moon. My heart raced as I stepped onto solid ground and grasped the hands of my cousins, their grips firm and familiar. They had been waiting at the shipping port, and my men and the Boscos soldiers positioned in the area formed a dozen strong, focused men, ready to embark on our daunting mission: to abduct Ozias Xenos.

The success of our operation hinged on the element of

surprise. Only the men directly involved had been filled in on the plan. Each of us had vowed silence to protect our cause.

Elias remained unaware, a conscious decision I made for the sake of our mission. I couldn't risk him inadvertently revealing our intentions to one of his men, someone who might still hold allegiance to his father.

Not even Cali had been informed--at least, not yet.

If everything played out as I envisioned, soon Ozias Xenos would rest at my bride's feet. It was my deepest desire to offer her the closure she deserved.

Her sister's vengeance had taken care of some of her tormentors, but Ozias was the architect behind it all, the one who had orchestrated their cruel actions. The others were mere pawns, following his orders. Without his influence, the burden of trauma and stress that Cali bore would never have existed.

It was time for him to face the consequences of his actions.

I had always thought of Elias as a smart man, yet I couldn't help but think that his father was not as astute. Who in their right mind would believe they could harm one of Juno Vitalis's daughters so gravely and escape unscathed?

If I were him, I would have left the country.

But men like him were trapped in their arrogance, convinced they were always in the right, always untouchable. They believed no one would dare challenge them.

Tonight, however, Ozias Xenos would find out differently. I envisioned peeling away his power as if removing his very skin. When I was through with him, all that remained would be a trembling shell of a man, stripped of strength and dignity.

And then, I would finish him under the vengeful eye of my soon-to-be bride.

As our team transferred to a fleet of waiting SUVs, my thoughts turned to Cali for a quick moment. The wedding was coming up, and soon, we'd spend every night together. We were to be wed at Avra and Elias's estate, looking out over the sea, just as her parents had been married.

My heart raced at the thought of it. The idea of holding my bride in my arms, Cali's beautiful eyes turned up toward me as we were declared man and wife, was overwhelming.

Something had changed between us in the last few days.

She'd managed to pull me out of my head and into my body. She'd tapped into the raw sexuality that she'd been begging me to unleash on her.

It had been rough.

It had been tempestuous.

It had been fucking delicious.

Since we'd connected in such a primal way, it was impossible to keep my hands off her body. We'd made love every single night, well into the morning hours, our bodies tangled together, breathless and panting and insatiable.

I'd sunk my cock into her sweet pussy over and over, fucking her harder than I'd ever fucked anyone.

And she begged for more.

She wanted it harder. Longer. Fiercer.

No matter what I did, she wanted more.

It was a dangerous line we'd crossed, but the feeling of

wanton, sensual freedom was addictive. It wasn't just Cali who wanted more.

It was me too. The beast that I had tamed for so long had suddenly become feral, wild, and unstoppable. I needed her. The hunger I felt for her surprised me daily, growing and expanding until I was convinced it would never cease to increase.

I was starving for her body now, as if I'd locked my sexuality away and now that I'd finally let it blossom, my thirst for Cali was unquenchable.

I knew, of course, that I'd never purposefully hurt her. As we continued to increase the ferocity of our delicious fucking, I'd insisted she come up with a safe word and made her promise that she'd use it at the slightest discomfort.

It was the only way I could give her what she wanted, what we wanted, what we needed, and not worry.

After we'd set those boundaries in place, I'd found myself opening up in ways I never expected with her. We'd experimented with spanking and restraints and role-playing, and with each passing day, we grew closer and closer.

The bond of intimacy forming between us was profound.

Every day, I found myself caught between deep gratitude and awe-filled disbelief. I'd never expected to fall in love with Cali. I'd never expected to open my heart, body, and soul. Not to anyone, ever again.

The loss of my family had wrecked me, and I'd locked up my very soul to go on without them. Somehow, Cali held the key, and she hadn't hesitated to use it. And I was so grateful that she had.

I tried to refocus my energy on the matter at hand, reluctantly pushing Calista to the back of my mind as best I could. However, it proved to be impossible. Each thought that ran through my head was laced with her. Her beauty consumed me, the sweet smell of her perfume, and the deep delight her moans elicited in me.

The mission loomed ahead of us, heavy with complications, each detail crucial for success. My focus, however, slipped through my fingers like sand. I turned to Iason, nodding, hoping for a tether to reality.

"You good?" I asked, trying to pull us both out of our thoughts.

"Fuck yeah," he replied, his expression serious, lips compressed into a line. "We're getting close."

"Yeah, my contact promised it'd be easy to spot."

Iason shrugged. "Not surprised. A fucking egomaniac like Xenos? He's bound to make a spectacle of himself."

I pointed down the block, barely containing my excitement. "Look, I bet that's it."

"I'm sure it is," he said, a smirk breaking through. "It's as ugly and gaudy as he is, isn't it?"

"Fuck this guy," I muttered, my annoyance bubbling up. "I can't wait to get my hands on him."

A surge of anticipation coursed through me, tightening my chest, though the danger lurking beneath the surface was undeniable. I clenched my fists, the thought of revenge igniting a fire in my gut.

As I approached Xenos's mansion, it loomed ahead like an ominous giant, overshadowing the cramped street and daring us to move closer. Its gaudy, golden gate shimmered in the moonlight, starkly contrasting with the modest homes surrounding it, each painted in traditional white limestone. Xenos's house, however, stood bare.

Its raw stone exterior was a rebellious statement that made me wonder if he felt unique or, perhaps, superior to the townspeople he looked down upon.

Pathetic.

Whatever his motives, they only highlighted his presence. Even with his despicable acts, he paraded through life either oblivious or impossibly naive. But tonight, we were going to expose his naivety.

The mansion sprawled before us, a snake coiled tightly around its ground, full of hidden dangers. A significant distance lay between us and the inner sanctum where Ozias likely slept, oblivious to the layers of security that guarded him.

We parked our cars around the block and piled out, adrenaline coursing as we prepared ourselves. The sounds of our footsteps echoed, punctuated by the clicks of guns being locked and the rustle of armor slipping into place. Once settled, we gathered in a small circle, my heart pounding as I went over the plan.

I searched each man's gaze, ensuring they were focused and ready, before signaling our move.

We paired off into teams of three, each crew ready to tackle a different entrance and exit of the house. The air was thick with tension as I felt the weight of the moment settle over us. Iason, Alex, and I stood at the front door, the chill of the night creeping in as I fumbled for the two-way radio in my pocket, my pulse racing with anticipation.

"Team one in place," I whispered, the words almost lost in the silence that enveloped us.

"Team two, ready."

"Team three, all set."

"Team four—let's fucking do this," came the fierce reply, igniting a spark of determination in the pit of my stomach.

Iason shot me a hard look, but a cold smile broke on his face, a promise of what was to come. I returned it with a nod, swallowing my nerves.

"Count it down," I murmured, my voice steady despite the storm brewing inside.

"One..."

My throat tightened as adrenaline coursed through my veins.

"Two..."

Every fiber of my being buzzed in readiness.

Iason planted his boot against the doorframe, his body coiled tight like a spring.

"Three!"

In that heartbeat, four teams exploded into action.

Quiet as shadows, we moved to execute our plan. Iason knelt before the first door, his hands steady as he picked the lock.

When it clicked open, we were met with two men who weren't expecting us, judging by the surprised expressions on their faces. But before they could react, Iason and Alex were already in motion.

They moved like whispers, the silencers on their pistols ensuring no sound escaped to alert others. Xenos's men were dealt with in a heartbeat, their bodies crumpling silently to the ground. We had claimed our first victory, inching closer to our ultimate goal.

We advanced through the mansion, the stillness disrupted only by the footsteps muffled against the opulent marble. The once pristine floor was now marred, soaking up the crimson stains of Xenos's fallen soldiers. Each step was a reminder of the chaos we left in our wake, fueling the fire within me as we neared the main living room.

As we reached the grand stairs nearby, I raised my finger, pointing toward the looming upper levels, preparing for whatever lay ahead.

"His bedroom is upstairs, far in the west wing, last room on the right," I reminded them.

My research had provided me with a detailed blueprint of the mansion, along with the headcount of Xenos's security team.

"There should be one more guy up there," I said as we headed up the stairs.

"Let me get him." Iason lifted his chin and led the way, eager for more blood. I smiled as I climbed the stairs after him, grateful for his friendship, loyalty, and fierceness.

The last guard between us and Xenos didn't even hear us coming. Iason slit his throat, taking him out from behind before he could even whimper with pain.

I was surprised. I'd always imagined that Xenos would have the best security team money could buy, but every one of his men had failed him, and he was about to discover that painful fact personally.

"That was efficient," I murmured, as we positioned ourselves in front of the door he had been guarding. He lay bleeding out at our feet, and we stepped over him.

"Too easy, honestly," Iason joked. "I was hoping for a little more fun."

"You're evil, Iason. You think he's sleeping?" I asked, jutting my chin toward the door.

"A fat, old fuck like that? Hell yeah, he is," Iason replied, shaking his head.

"Cover me," I said as I retrieved the pre-loaded syringe from my pocket. Removing the cap, I gripped it firmly in my hand while Iason quietly opened the door.

We were met with darkness. A dim night light in the corner offered minimal illumination. The sound of Xenos's snoring resonated loudly in the silence.

I shrugged and quietly walked in, heading straight for the bastard's bed.

His round belly protruded toward the ceiling as he lay on his back, his mouth wide open as he languished in sleep.

I stared down at him for a quick second. It would be so easy to slit his throat, put a bullet through his brain, or any other number of ways to eliminate his black soul from this earth.

I was so very fucking tempted. It would make things a lot easier and be much simpler just to kill him here and leave and let someone else figure out how these assholes had expired.

But I'd made a promise.

And I wasn't about to break a promise to Calista.

I pushed the needle into Xenos's neck, watching as his breath quickened and then slowed drastically. I waited a few seconds, then grabbed his hand and lifted it, letting it drop to his side.

He didn't wake up.

He didn't budge.

"It seems the midazolam did its job," I observed, unable to hide my amusement.

"It's never failed me before. All right, let's bag him up now," Iason said. I stepped back, letting Iason and the other men work. They lifted Xenos from the bed, slipping his limp body into a body bag before quickly zipping and locking it.

I stood back, watching with pleasure and satisfaction and itching with anticipation. Cali's face flashed in my head, and I couldn't wait to see the smile on her face when I delivered this asshole to her.

"Okay, we're ready, Leon," Iason said.

"Let's all go through the back door," I said. "I'll go first and check to make sure the coast is clear."

Just three minutes later, we returned to our cars and drove to the airport, where a jet was ready to take us to Zakynthos, an island near Patras. There, one of my ships waited to complete the final transport of our package. I couldn't wait to deliver Xenos's body, all wrapped up, to my beautiful bride.

All that was missing was a big red bow.

I smirked at the thought. If I'd thought of it sooner, I'd have arranged to have one made when I presented this bastard to Cali.

With all the transportation changes, the journey back to Elias's estate in Patras lasted just over five hours. Ozias was beginning to stir, slowly emerging from his drug-induced slumber. Given the high dosage we had administered, there was a risk he could suffocate before our return, yet I took no action to avert this possibility. If the old bastard was lucky, suffocation would be a blessing, considering what I had planned for him.

The sun peered over the horizon, casting golden beams that danced on the water's surface. Our boat sliced through the gentle waves, approaching the sandy shore. I pulled my cell phone from my pocket and quickly typed a message to Elias. A moment later, I saw him jogging down the dock, his brow furrowed and a glimmer of uncertainty in his eyes.

"Thanks for meeting me," I said, greeting him halfway down the dock. I gestured behind me to the boat.

"What happened?" Elias asked.

"I have your father secured on the boat," I responded, glancing at the dock where the vessel swayed in the morning light. "I was hoping you could assist us in getting him into your house."

His gaze sharpened for a brief moment, revealing his surprise, before he stepped back, the wooden planks of the pier creaking beneath his weight.

"I apologize for not informing you earlier," I said,

running a hand through my hair. "I couldn't risk him finding out somehow."

"You think I'd be the one to tell the bastard?" Elias snapped, his brows furrowing.

"No, not at all," I reassured him quickly, raising my hands in a placating gesture. "But one small slip through the cracks would have been all it took to derail my plan."

"Why are you doing this?" he asked, searching my face for answers.

"I know he's your father, Elias," I said, my tone firm yet sympathetic. "I hope you don't mean to get in the way. I'm doing this for Calista. The man who caused all her pain needs to pay for what he's done. There's no way around it."

Elias looked out toward the horizon, the morning sun casting a gentle warmth over his troubled expression. He gradually shook his head, letting out a deep sigh.

"I won't interfere," he finally said, his voice barely above a whisper. "My father made his choices. Every man must suffer the consequences of their actions. It doesn't matter who he is."

"Thank you, Elias," I said, feeling a weight lift from my shoulders. "I appreciate your understanding."

"He's a fucking prick," he said, shrugging. "As far as I'm concerned, he deserves whatever you plan to do."

"Let's do this." I turned back toward the boat, raising my hand in a signal to my men. Alex and the others quickly lifted Xenos, who thrashed and squirmed inside the bag, his muffled shouts and curses echoing in the crisp morning air, but we remained silent.

"We'll go through the tunnels. No one will see us, just my early morning vineyard workers, and they are beyond loyal," Elias said, leading the way to a small door near the dock.

We descended a dark staircase, the air thickening as we stepped into a long maze of tunnels beneath the property. The corridors stretched out, enveloped in darkness, interrupted only by our footsteps and Xenos's muted cries, a reminder of our tense situation.

After a few moments of careful walking, we reached another door. Elias rummaged through his keys, the jangling sound loud in the stillness, and unlocked the heavy door. It swung open to reveal a well-lit series of hallways that stretched east, their sterile atmosphere stark against the earthy musk from the previous tunnels.

Rounding a corner, Elias abruptly opened another door, revealing a stairway. We climbed and emerged into a vast, open barn. I scanned the expansive space, my gaze trailing over the rafters above and the crevices allowing beams of sunlight to filter through.

"This way," Elias instructed, his voice hushed as we navigated past empty wooden stalls. We turned a corner, and he pressed his shoulder against another door, shoving it open.

"Put him in here," he ordered, leaving me standing frozen at the threshold.

The stale scent of rusted metal and antiseptic tickled my nostrils.

In the center sat a solitary steel chair, its leather straps hanging open like waiting arms. Thick iron cuffs protruded from the concrete floor, their chains clinking softly. Along one wall, instruments glinted: electric cattle prods, a tangle of braided whips, and coils of hemp rope. A rack held rows of curved knives and serrated machetes. My pulse sped.

By the far corner stood a stainless-steel surgical table, its surface polished to a cruel gleam. A slow, grim smile spread across my lips. I pointed.

"There," I said. "Tie him to the table."

Two of my men dragged Xenos into the chamber. The canvas bag slipped from his head, revealing bloodshot eyes and a desperate tremor in his chin.

Spotting Elias and me side by side, he bellowed, "You bastards!"

His words slurred, head lolling. Before he could struggle, Iason yanked a leather ball gag from a nearby tray and forced it between his teeth.

I walked up to him, watching as they tied him to the table despite his weak attempt at struggling. He was still under the influence of drugs and was practically as weak as a newborn.

I approached as they buckled Xenos's wrists to the table clamps. His fingers thrashed weakly. His breath came in ragged gasps, the residue of sedatives slackening his limbs.

Elias's voice cut through the quiet drip of water from a loose pipe. "What's the plan?"

I met his gaze. "I'll kill him. But first, I'm telling Cali. She can watch me finish this."

Elias nodded, his eyes darting to his father's bound form. His grief and hatred for the man before us filled the room with a thick electric tension, ready to spark. I waited a few moments, watching Elias, until he lifted his gaze to mine.

"So be it. His suffering doesn't belong to me. It belongs to Calista. We give her what she wants."

Then, without another word, he nodded once, turned, and left the room, letting the door swing shut behind him and leaving me to set up for the event ahead.

My team and I spread old tarps under the table, their plasticky rustle filling the silence. We arranged scalpels, saws, needles, and vials of clear liquid. Each tool landed on the surface with a familiar click.

After an hour of meticulous preparation—scrubbing every surface and lining up the implements in neat rows—I watched Iason as he methodically injected another sedative into Ozias's IV. The moment the fluid coursed through the line, Ozias's eyelids fluttered shut, and drool seeped from the corner of his mouth, a stark reminder of his helplessness.

We cleaned the sweat and dirt from our hands, shoulders, and faces before following Elias's path back through the stalls and up the twisting stairs to his home. At the top, a warm, buttery scent drifted down the hallway.

I pushed open the kitchen door and found Cali in front of the marble island, her flour-dusted hair cascading in soft waves. Her sisters moved around her, rolling dough and stamping out shapes, the clatter of baking sheets filling the air. Golden croissants, sugar-dusted Danishes, and plump blueberry muffins were arranged in neat rows, creating a feast for the eyes.

"Leon!" Cali dropped her wooden rolling pin, a flurry of flour rising around her.

She raced to me, wrapping her arms around my neck. The second she pressed against me, the warmth of her body seeped into me, easing the tension of the night.

Her lips brushed against mine, sweet and tender, and I felt a rush as I settled my hands on her hips.

A lightness blossomed in my chest, banishing the lingering shadows of the afternoon.

"Good morning, darling." I pulled back to survey the countertop: rolling pins dusted with white, a spilled bag of sugar, a mound of dough patiently awaiting its turn.

"What's all this?"

"Just some kitchen adventures," she said, her beaming smile illuminating the room. I chuckled, noticing the smudge of flour on her nose, and I reached up to wipe it away.

"You look like you're having fun," I remarked, my smile mirroring hers.

"Has Calista not told you about her baking obsession?" Avra interrupted, raising an eyebrow.

"Not yet," I replied, my anticipation growing. "But I can't wait to sample your creations. I'm famished."

"Here, try this." Before I could shift my weight, Calista had whisked a chocolate-streaked croissant from the tray and pressed it into my hand.

Warmth radiated from it, melting fudge oozing through the flaky layers. I lifted it to my lips, biting in, a burst of rich, buttery sweetness dancing across my tongue.

"You made this?" I gasped between bites. "It's the best thing I've ever tasted."

"It's my special fudge croissant," she replied, pleased at my reaction. "I'm so glad you like it."

"I'm a lucky man."

In that moment, she looked like an angel, her joyful smile outshining the morning sun. My heart swelled with pleasure at the sight of her beauty, and an overwhelming urge to steal her away to a place just for us washed over me.

But this wasn't the time for that.

I hesitated before delivering my news. All I wanted was to give my bride a life full of joy and happiness.

She was clearly having a wonderful morning. I felt a knot in my stomach as I contemplated how my news would affect her. I longed to bring her closure, a way to shut that dark chapter of her life and strip it of its power over her.

Would the gift I carried only open those old wounds?

The thought of bringing pain into her heart twisted my insides. It was the last thing I wanted to do.

Yet, I reminded myself of the promise I'd made her...

"Are you okay?" She squinted up at me, her brow furrowed. "You look so serious."

"He's probably contemplating how to make money off your precious croissants," Laya mused, her voice teasing.

I smirked. "Not a bad idea, actually."

"Stop!" She chuckled, shaking her head. "Those are just for fun. I don't want to be stuck in a kitchen every day for the rest of my life, no matter how much I love to bake occasionally."

"You can do whatever you wish, my darling," I murmured, pulling her close and hugging her tight. She felt solid against me, strong, and having her near was so grounding that I didn't want to let her go.

"Okay, so why are you here?" She pulled away after a few seconds, her gaze suddenly serious, and I knew I couldn't delay any longer.

"I brought you a wedding present."

Her face brightened with pure joy, and her delight surprised me.

"You did?" she asked, astonishment evident in her voice.

My heart raced as I brought my hand to her cheek, feeling the warmth of her skin.

"I made you a promise, didn't I?"

The smile that blossomed on her face filled me with hope. Maybe she would handle this better than I'd anticipated. I should have known better than to doubt her strength. She wouldn't have asked for this favor if she wasn't ready for it. I made a mental note to trust her more. She knew herself better than anyone else.

"You're the best, Leon!" she exclaimed, throwing her arms around me in a tight embrace. I could feel the sisters' curious stares boring into us.

Cali's hands came free, and her palms rubbed together, her eyes gleaming like a hawk on the hunt. Her gaze flicked to the chef's knife resting on the marble kitchen island, and for a moment, I feared what might cross her mind.

"No," I murmured, slipping in front of her and covering her hand with my own. My thumb stroked her knuckles, trying to ground her. "We have much better tools for the job already waiting for you."

"What job?" Avra demanded, stepping closer. She and Laya exchanged glances laden with tension. Their expectant stares were almost palpable. Cali hesitated, her chest rising with anticipation before she lifted her chin in proud defiance.

"The job of destroying Ozias Xenos, once and for all."

Avra's mouth fell open, shock written all over her face. "What?" Laya echoed, her voice a mixture of disbelief and excitement.

"Where?"

"Now?!" Their questions exploded from them in rapid succession, eyes darting between Cali and me.

"That fucker," Cali growled, a wicked grin breaking across her face. "I can't wait to see him fall."

I couldn't help but chuckle at their eager enthusiasm, the excitement sending a rush of adrenaline through me.

"I can't wait to tear that prick limb from limb," Avra said.

"Ladies, I admire your enthusiasm, but I made a promise to Calista that I would deliver something to her, and until that is carried out, I won't be able to let you near Xenos."

"What?" Laya said.

"It's his heart, isn't it?" Avra crossed her arms over her chest and shook her head. "She asked you to cut it out, right? I know she did! She's been talking about ripping that motherfucker's beating heart out of his chest for years."

I raised my hands in mock surrender, unable to deny a

thing. It was apparent that these three knew each other very well. The mood lightened, and I grabbed Cali's hand and brought it to my lips, kissing the back of it.

"Shall we get this over with?" I asked.

"Fuck yes, I've been waiting for this moment for a long time."

"We're going too," Avra insisted.

I wasn't about to argue with the three of them, so I shrugged and led them out to the barn. We avoided the tunnels, the estate filled with the morning bustle of workers going about their duties, weaving through the grounds. It felt normal to anyone seeing us walk across the property.

Just outside the room where Xenos was confined, Elias and Iason waited. Nikolas had joined them.

"Niko!" Laya gasped in disbelief the moment she spotted him, her voice a mix of surprise and joy. "What are you doing here?"

Avra narrowed her gaze at us, her arms crossing. "So, everyone knew except us?"

"No," I replied, shaking my head. "Elias got the plan first thing this morning."

Elias stepped forward, rubbing the back of his neck as if searching for the right words. "I only called Nikolas after that."

Avra studied us, some hidden truth swirling in her mind. Finally, she relaxed ever so slightly. "I promise," I offered, giving her a crooked smile to ease the tension.

"So he's in there?" Cali squared her shoulders, ready to meet him.

"Yes."

"Okay." She formed a small huddle with her sisters.

I stepped back to give them space, joining Elias and Nikolas as we waited. I knew they'd be upset that I hadn't shared my plan earlier, but this risk had to be taken. Capturing Xenos, instead of ending him in his own home, was meant to prove my loyalty.

After a quick, secretive conversation, the sisters returned to us, their resolve evident. I wanted to ask what they had decided but held my tongue.

"We're all going in together to confront him," Cali declared, her tone leaving no room for discussion.

I wasn't surprised by her pronouncement, though I hoped they didn't assume they were going in without backup.

"Ozias Xenos ruined our lives," Avra spoke with quiet fury. "We want him to see our faces, united and strong, so he knows the Vitalis sisters finally destroyed him."

I took a deep breath and looked at Elias and Nikolas. We all recognized the tremendous strength of these women, yet we cherished them. We were determined to shield them at any cost. Although Ozias was physically held on that table, what about their emotional well-being?

Worry gnawed at me, though I knew Avra and Laya were tough, fierce warriors with a strength that could intimidate the strongest opponent. I had witnessed their prowess firsthand.

But Cali? She was different. She had endured so much suffering, and fresh apprehension crept in as I considered what this might do to her. She had come so far in her healing journey. Would facing him set her back? Would it trigger old traumas and pull her back into darkness?

Would facing this asshole do more damage to her than good?

She sensed my hesitation, looking over at me with impatience.

"I'm fine, Leon, I promise," she said, her words laced with exasperation. "I can handle this. You don't have to worry about me."

She faced off with me, her steely gaze daring me to stop her.

I reminded myself of my vow to trust her more and stepped aside, providing the three of them access to the door I was standing in front of.

"He's drugged, but the effects are wearing off quickly. He's restrained. He should pose no threat to any of you, but my men and the three of us will be close by, just in case."

"As long as nobody gets in our way," Cali said, her hand already on the doorknob.

The sisters walked into the room, and we followed, closely trailed by our men, who quickly surrounded Ozias. The women stood staring for a moment, taking in the sight of him. He lay on the surgical table, his arms and legs completely restrained by thick leather straps, his head entirely covered with a black hood.

"It's really him," Cali whispered, as if she couldn't believe the day for her vengeance had arrived.

She deserved every second of this moment.

"It is," I confirmed.

He inhaled heavy breaths, still drugged and docile.

We all drew closer, surrounding the table as we stared down at him. I watched Cali, looking for any signs of distress. I was ready to have her ushered from the room in an instant if I saw any indication that this was harming her.

She momentarily looked at my gun holstered at my hip, and I feared she might reach for it, intent on shooting the bastard.

But she didn't. She took a deep breath, gazing back at him.

Avra reached forward and lifted the hood from Xenos's head. He woke slowly, and once his lids opened, he registered the group of us surrounding him.

Instantly, he began struggling against his restraints, quickly learning that it was no use. He slumped back on the table, his eyes wild. Avra pulled the gag from his mouth, and a string of slurs fell from his mouth.

"You fucking bitches! I demand you let me go this instant!"

The women peered down at him, and he began to fight his restraints again.

"Who do you think you are? This is a fucking crime! I'm Ozias Xenos!"

"And we're the Vitalis sisters, if you need reminding," Laya said, her words steely and strong.

"This is against protocol! I'm a syndicate head! Do you know what will happen to you? What will the other families do to you once they learn of this?"

Laya brought her face closer to his, shaking her head.

"Do you think we give a fuck, you disgusting bastard?" she seethed.

"You'll be destroyed." He glared up at them. I'd never seen an angrier man in my life. Xenos's swollen face was red, and a huge vein on his temple throbbed with blood as sweat poured down his face. His mouth twisted into an ugly sneer, making him look like some monster from a movie.

He shifted his focus to Avra and the man behind her, then as recognition clicked, fury reddened his face.

"Traitor! I'm ashamed you carry my blood, Elias!" He threw his words like daggers through the air, the only weapon he had at his disposal. Unfortunately, none of us were fazed as each word landed with the weight of a feather, rendering him completely useless.

"Nobody is more ashamed of the blood in my veins than I am, I assure you," Elias replied.

"You have disgraced the Xenos family! You are no Xenos," Ozias cried.

"You're right." Elias smirked. "I'm a Vitalis now. I've even changed my name. I'm still tainted with your dirty blood, yes, but I want absolutely nothing to do with you or your fucked-up legacy, Ozias."

"Let me go! Now!" he shouted, thrashing his body around the table in a frantic attempt to escape.

It was pointless, but it was entertaining to watch him struggle. It excited me to know he was suffering, realizing the first touches of fear were finally reaching his heart. Soon, the terrifying awareness of his impending death would completely envelop that black heart, and I felt a deep satisfaction at the thought of watching life slip away from this evil man.

"We're never letting you go," Calista whispered from beside me. He fell silent, his gaze landing on her.

I stiffened, ready to strike him silent at any moment.

"You!" he spat. "You fucking dirty whore! For weeks, you were used by my men. Did you enjoy it? I heard you did. I heard you spread your legs like a fucking wanton slut, begging for more. Did you not get enough? Are you back for more, slut?"

I observed her face intently for any hint of pain, yet all I detected was triumph and resilience. She looked down at him, combining pity with rage, seeming entirely unaffected by his words.

He didn't notice, eager to spout the most disgusting shit before he died.

"Your pussy is used up and damaged now, isn't it?" he growled. "You know I did that, right? I made that happen. And when my men came to me and told me that they'd completed their job, I sent them back in to start on you all over again. You might as well become a whore now, because nobody will ever want to touch you again!"

The fury that rose in my veins pulsed with urgency. It took every ounce of strength I had in that moment to stay put, to not eliminate his disgusting soul once and for all. As far as I was concerned, a man like that had no reason to remain alive. The thought of killing this man pleased me like no other person I'd killed. The satisfaction that it was going to give me would be unsurpassed.

At my sides, my fists clenched with anticipation.

"You can say whatever you want, Xenos. Get it all out," Cali hissed. "The man behind me is Leon Boscos, my fiancé. I've asked him to give me your beating heart as a wedding present."

She bent her head, staring straight down at him, and whispered, "He's about to deliver."

His eyes widened, and he began thrashing again.

"Fuck you! Fuck all of you! You're nothing but trash, and I will have each and every one of you violently destroyed!"

"You don't look like you're in any position to do that now, do you, Father?" Elias remarked, his voice calm and strong.

I was immensely impressed with everyone in the room. No matter what vile shit this asshole pumped out, we were all cool, calm, and collected.

"You won't get away with this!" Ozias claimed.

"No, Ozias," Cali said. "Don't you understand? All the shit you did. All the violence you orchestrated. All the betrayals, the pain, the suffering. You were heartless, and now, everything is catching up with you. You can't escape responsibility anymore. It's time to face the consequences of your evil actions."

"Fuck you, you ugly whore!" Xenos spat.

"Enough!" I shouted, stepping forward with clenched fists, my heart pounding with a primal urge to protect.

But before I could close the distance, Cali's hand shot

out, her fingers firm against my chest, holding me back. My muscles tensed with the overwhelming desire to silence him.

The thought of shooting him, slicing through his skin, squeezing the air from his lungs, pummeling him until not a drop of blood remained, anything to stop his vile words from reaching my soon-to-be wife, boiled inside me.

Yet, the sisters still stood unfazed, their expressions calm and unaffected by his insults. I shook my head.

"You're pathetic," I said, my voice dripping with disdain.

"Your fate is in our hands now," Cali declared with a fierce intensity. "Your words have no effect on us. Look at us! Do we look frightened? We are elated!" She paused as if taking in her triumph and savoring the anticipation. "Finally, I'll get to witness you suffering the consequences of turning me into everything you accuse me of being."

She took a step closer, her gaze never wavering.

"You may think you damaged me, Xenos, but that couldn't be further from the truth. In fact, all that damage you think you caused only served to make me stronger. It fueled my rage."

The glare of the single overhead lamp turned Cali's pupils into glowing emerald fire. Her jaw was set, knuckles whitening as she leaned over Xenos's strapped form.

"I've dreamed of this moment since the day they took me," she said, voice low and controlled, each word clipped like a blade. "I summoned it, knew without a fucking doubt it would come. And Xenos, it's far more beautiful than I ever dared imagine. My heart is soaring at the thought that you're about to draw your last breath."

No tears wetted her cheeks. No tremor shook her limbs. Her tone was precise, her fingers unmoving, her delight shining hotter than any flame.

Across the table, Xenos shook beneath the leather straps, sweat slicking his temples as fresh terror twisted through his body.

"You lose, Xenos. The Vitalis sisters are here to stay." With deliberate care, Cali forced the blood-rough gag back into his mouth.

Behind her, Avra and Laya stood in a silent semicircle. Their faces showed faint smiles of satisfaction, and all the doubts I had about vengeance melted away in that moment. This felt right.

I stepped forward and cleared my throat. "Let's get on with this."

My nod was decisive. Avra turned and offered me a grateful glance.

"Thank you, Leon," Elias said.

I lifted my gaze to Avra's. "Do you want to stay for this part?"

"No." Avra shook her head.

Laya wrapped her arm around Nikolas's. "We're leaving too."

I glanced at Calista, who had her arms crossed and one eyebrow raised.

"I'm staying," she replied.

I expected nothing less from her.

At the doorway, Avra paused. "Leon?"

I replied, "Yes?"

"Make it hurt."

With that, the sisters and their husbands filed out, boots echoing down the corridor, leaving only Cali and me amid the faint smell of antiseptic and something darker—fear, or perhaps the promise of blood. Cali drifted to a steel chair in the corner and sat, her attention fixated on the bound man's chest rising and falling in spasms.

Xenos moaned, his voice thick with panic. I wondered what cyclone of dread tore through his mind, knowing the scalpel would soon carve into his flesh. I hoped he felt every second of it.

The scalpel lay among clamps and probes on the instrument tray beside the table, its blade gleaming. I picked it up, turned it toward the lamp, and watched the tip catch the light like a shard of ice.

I leaned in, letting the cold steel press against Xenos's sternum. His chest quivered at the touch.

As I readied to make the first slice with the blade, I stopped and asked, "Darling, would you like to make the first cut?"

Joy erupted in her gaze, bright and feral. She bolted forward, her breath as quick as a child racing for ice cream, and snatched the scalpel from my hand. With a wild cry, she sliced deep into Xenos's heaving chest.

NINETEEN

ALISTA

ONE WEEK LATER

"Look up, please," Sarah, the makeup artist I'd hired for our wedding, instructed me. I blinked against the soft light, revealing my sisters just behind her, their curious gazes scrutinizing her work with eager anticipation.

"Oh my God, give her some breathing room, please?" I urged with playful exasperation in my tone.

They exchanged glances, shoulders shrugging in unison as they settled onto the bed beside me. Avra offered a flute of champagne, a smirk on her lips.

Even now, moments before my wedding, they were bent on getting me tipsy. The thought of swaying down the aisle, tripping over my gown, sent a shiver of panic through me.

I took a tentative, small sip, the bubbly fizz tickling my nose, before setting it back on the table beside the makeup clutter.

"I can't drink too much right now," I admitted as nerves bubbled up. "Why am I so on edge? Is this normal?"

"Of course, it's normal," Laya assured me, a teasing grin spreading across her face. "You're taking a big step."

"I know that," I replied, my heart thudding against my chest. "I also know Leon is the right man for me. So why the nerves? I wonder if Mama was this anxious."

The mention of her name silenced us instantly, an invisible weight settling over the room.

"I wish she were here," I said, watching Sarah glide her brush over my eyelid in a practiced motion.

"She'd be crying with happiness, no doubt," Laya offered, her voice tender yet tinged with longing.

"I'm so sorry she isn't here, Cali," Avra added. I knew she'd felt the same way at her wedding.

She squeezed my hand, our unspoken bond blooming in the shared silence.

"You two are practically both my mother, so there's no need to apologize," I said. "I couldn't do this without you. You both basically raised me when you were kids yourselves."

"We're sisters," Avra replied. "We would have done nothing less than take excellent care of you."

"Oh, I love you both so much!"

Tears sprang up, and I quickly blinked them away.

"Hey, stop making the bride cry!" Sarah said, jokingly scolding them. "At least let me finish first?"

They were both blinking away their tears. My mind wandered to our childhood and everything we had endured. There had been very difficult times, but before we were thrust into hiding by the traumatic murders of our parents, we had also shared plenty of joyful moments.

I cherished the memories of dancing with Mama in the kitchen and climbing on Papa while he drank wine and sat in meetings with his men. They always made time for all of us girls. The holidays were my favorite, with all the decorating and delicious treats and wonderful smells. It was just wonderful. Even after everything changed, my sisters tried to keep as many traditions alive as possible. They truly taught me most of what I knew. They were my mothers, teaching me about clothes, makeup, and boys. Most of what they taught about boys, they got wrong since they were learning it themselves. But they were everything a little girl needed and more in a chaotic world. As we all entered adulthood, their actions influenced my choices. Their graceful and strong navigation of their own marriages served as a remarkable example that I was eager to follow with Leon.

Just the thought of him brought a thrill to my heart.

Within just a few hours, we'd be married. We'd start our life together, hand in hand, side by side. Leon never hesitated to include me in his decision-making. The fact that he'd followed up on his promise about Xenos only endeared me to him even more. He'd shown me nothing but respect, and I expected nothing less as we moved through our life together.

He'd even been graceful when I pivoted at the last moment with Xenos.

I'd been thrilled when he offered to allow me to make the first cut into Xenos's body, and I'd done so with gusto. The satisfaction I'd felt at seeing that man in pain, at my hands no less, had surpassed every thrill I'd ever felt before then.

But it turned out that was enough. I didn't truly need his bloody heart in my hands, after all. All I needed was to hear him begging, to see the tears rolling down his fat cheeks as the knife sank into his skin. I smiled now at how it seemed Leon had predicted my change of heart.

I'd glanced up at him, hesitating. He responded by handing me a pistol and taking the scalpel from my hands. He stepped back, and I unleashed the gun, sending bullet after bullet straight into Xenos's brain.

My heart swelled with joy, a warmth radiating through me that lingered even a week later. I'd finally discovered my soul mate. Leon's deep understanding of me wrapped around us like a comforting blanket, creating a sense of familiarity and acceptance that grew richer with each passing day. Every look and shared moment echoed with a profound and effortless bond.

He had given me what I wanted and what I needed, both in and out of bed.

For the last week, we'd spent hours languishing in his bed, closed off from the rest of the world and indulging in the most wicked acts imaginable. Leon had learned how to make my toes curl, how to make me scream his name out in ecstasy, unabashedly and unashamed.

He'd accepted my kinks and proclivities toward enjoying rougher sex, and once he'd been assured that I was thoroughly enjoying myself and the delicious pain, he'd jumped into pleasing me with both feet.

Or, rather, both hands.

Leon seemed to have learned every inch of my body, knowing exactly where to touch, when, and how, leaving me gasping for breath amidst wave after wave of decadent pleasure.

"Where did you go?" Avra interrupted my wandering thoughts with a curious tilt of her head.

I crossed my legs, noting the wetness between my legs as I did. My nipples were pebbled under my robe, and I felt a blush rise to my cheeks at her question.

"She's thinking about how hard Leon's going to fuck her later," Laya chimed in.

I turned to her, glaring as if outraged.

"Oh, please." Laya waved a dismissive hand, her eyes dancing with amusement. "I know that dreamy look all too well. Tell me I'm wrong."

I let out a long sigh, the kind that releases a reluctant truth. "Okay, you aren't wrong."

"I can't blame you," Avra said, rubbing her swollen belly.

"Me too," Laya admitted.

"Honestly, I'm still like that," Avra said. "I don't know why, but pregnancy has left me constantly wanting to devour Elias."

Laya agreed, "I was the same!"

"Oh God," I replied, shaking my head. "Enough of all this sex talk!"

Avra chuckled, a playful gleam in her eye. "We're sorry, Sarah! We'll let you work your magic on her makeup. We'll be outside with our dashing husbands, Cali."

They blew a few quick air kisses my way before retreating, leaving the air humming with their joy.

The room fell quiet once Sarah applied the final touches, and I found myself alone.

As I slipped into my dress, I caught my reflection in the mirror, sparkling, elegant. It hit me like a wave.

Today, I was the bride. My heart raced as I imagined Leon's reaction when he finally saw me, and my mind flickered to the moment I would catch his gaze.

But then, like a shadow, the thought of my parents crept in, deepening my longing to share this special moment with them.

A gentle whimper at my feet broke my reverie.

I bent down to see Leo gazing up at me, her small head decorated with a delicate wedding veil that beautifully complemented Cosmo's tuxedo. Today, they would be our ring bearers, proudly carrying our wedding rings, a role they embraced with pure delight. These two shared an unbreakable bond, a duo that was nearly inseparable, moving through the day as if they grasped the importance of the occasion.

"Are you ready, Leo?" I murmured. She stared up at me,

her big green eyes wide and adorable, as she enthusiastically wagged her tail.

"All right, Cali," I whispered to myself, facing the mirror again. I lifted my chin, trying desperately to shake off the nerves. My fingers trembled as I pulled the veil over my face.

This was happening...

This was real...

I took a deep breath.

I was doing the right thing. Leon would always respect and be kind to me. I knew this without a doubt. And it was beyond time to move on with my life, to leave behind the horrors of the past and embrace the future.

My future with Leon.

I held my bridal bouquet close to my face, allowing the captivating scent of the pale pink roses to wrap around me.

"Let's go, Leo," I whispered, the words barely escaping my lips as I turned toward the door.

As I navigated toward the back exit, the murmur of conversation rose and fell in waves. Glancing through the windows, I spotted guests settling into their seats, their chatter mingling with the rustle of fabric. At the altar, the priest stood tall, and beside him, Leon awaited me, his stunning features almost ethereal, reflecting the jittery excitement coursing through me. Just looking at him took my breath away.

"My God," I whispered, shaking my head.

His tuxedo hugged him perfectly. He'd neatly slicked back his dark hair, accentuating those lovely brown eyes I adored getting lost in every day. A flash of an image of him two nights ago burst into my head. He had taken me with a violent almost possessed need, his gaze storming with heated desire as he sank his cock into me. The idea of it made me shudder with desire for him.

My heart raced as I imagined the heated moments we'd share in a private room, a sly smirk creeping onto my lips.

Leo followed closely at my heels as I stepped outside, her presence comforting amidst the swirling crowd.

A hush fell, and the bold notes of the wedding march filled the air and drew every eye in my direction.

Choosing to walk to the altar alone had been a decision steeped in reflection after my conversation with Vik.

His words echoed in my mind, urging me to embrace my solitude, celebrating the strength, resilience, and independence that had been forged in the fires of my past.

With every step I took, I sensed the strength of those qualities motivating me, and I was embracing my journey to the altar. Emanating warmth, Leon's eyes locked onto mine and held me close like an unseen hug. I cherished that sensation as we approached one another, relishing the authenticity of his love as if it were a precious gem. This man had reshaped his world for me, wagering everything—his life, his future, and even his legacy—all to bestow upon me the priceless gift of freedom.

Taking Xenos's life had unleashed a sense of liberation that nothing else could match.

Sure, I would have most likely done it myself eventually, but Leon's willingness to shoulder the burden deepened the affection I held for him.

I could hardly contain my excitement about becoming Mrs. Leon Vitalis-Boscos.

As I reached him, my heart raced, and a warm glow spread through my chest. His eyes gleamed with a mixture of love and pride, sparkling like sunlight dancing on water. A wave of emotions washed over me, both intense and thrilling, as I cherished the moment we experienced together.

He stood strong and loyal, his unwavering devotion like a beacon in the storm of life.

Against all odds, I had found my equal in Leon. His energy matched mine, and an unbreakable chord of deep respect ran between us, binding us tightly.

It felt as if the universe itself had conspired to bring us together.

As I slipped my hand into his, I felt a sense of belonging —it felt undeniably right to be with Leon Boscos.

Perhaps my parents had a hand in this, or maybe the gods were involved.

Maybe it was simply destiny.

Regardless, as Leon grasped my hand with a steady yet comforting hold, I realized I was now and always would be his.

I took a step toward the altar, and Leon stood resolutely by my side. He leaned closer, his breath warm against my ear, whispering.

"You belong to me now, darling."

His words sent a shiver down my spine. Had he read my mind? Either way, he was right. Our dogs circled each other before sitting at our feet.

We faced each other, holding hands tightly as the priest began speaking.

Overwhelmed with emotion, my brain barely registered a word the priest said until he asked me to say my vows.

I reached down and plucked the ring from Leo's collar, then stood to face Leon. I slid the ring halfway down his finger. The smile on his face was pure joy. My heart raced as I began reciting the words I'd memorized.

"Leon, you have healed me with love," I began, my voice trembling with emotion. I took a deep breath, blinking away tears. "My spirit is lighter because of you. My heart is whole because of you. My future is bright because of you. I vow to spend the rest of my days respecting you, being your friend and partner, and supporting and loving you completely."

By the time I finished, tears were streaming down my cheeks. I slid the ring the rest of the way onto his finger, etching the smile on his face into my mind to remember forever. I knew I'd never forget the way he looked at that moment.

"Leon, your vows, please," the priest said.

Leon reached down for my ring and faced me, his hands sure and steady as he slid the ring onto my finger.

"Calista, you are the light in my life. You are pure joy and sunshine, and I am a better man just by being in your presence. I vow to protect you, to deeply love you, to always cherish you, until my dying day."

He slid the ring onto my finger, and my heart skipped a beat.

I looked down at the beautiful diamond shimmering on

my hand, a vibrant display of our love and devotion to one another, and a jolt of joy hit me like a lightning bolt.

The priest inclined his head, his expression joyful and approving.

"By the honor vested in me, I now pronounce you—"

"—I object!"

The sound of gunshots rang out at the edge of the crowd, and I jumped with fear. The crowd gasped and took cover, chaotically running for the trees surrounding us, leaving only a group of three men standing and staring at us.

Dominic Lucianos, a gun in his hand, flanked by two guards.

Leon pushed me behind him immediately, barking orders to his security team.

"What the fuck?" he demanded, throwing an accusatory glance over at Iason. "How did they get in?"

Iason shrugged, drawing his weapon. From behind Leon, I struggled to see what was going on. I peered over his shoulder, cursing.

"Stay back, Cali!" Leon growled, pointing the gun he'd pulled from his boot toward Dominic.

It all happened so quickly and suddenly that we all seemed stunned.

"I can help!" I insisted.

"Stop it!" he hissed. "This fucker is here to harm you, and I'm not about to let that happen. Nobody is ever going to hurt you again."

His words were sweet but irritating. I wanted to destroy Dominic for ruining my perfect wedding. The fucking bastard was going to pay for this. Fury raced through my veins.

"Dominic Lucianos, how dare you show up here!" Leon roared, cocking his gun. "Do you have a death wish?"

"I'm not about to let you steal from me again, Boscos!" he shouted.

I frowned, wanting to punch him in the face. As if I were ever his to begin with!

"Nobody is stealing from you," Leon replied. "As for what happened in the past, if I recall correctly, my sister-in-law ran away from you. She certainly wasn't stolen."

"Think whatever you want, but I know the truth!" Dominic spat out his words, pointing his gun toward Leon. "This marriage isn't going to happen. I'm never letting it happen again."

"We're already married, you fucking idiot!" I shouted from behind Leon's back. I held up my hand, my wedding ring heavy and sparkling on my finger. "We've already exchanged vows and rings!"

"I don't give a fuck about that," Dominic replied. "It's not official until the priest blesses it."

"Are you really that fucking stupid?" I shouted, spotting Avra and Laya standing together, both of them ready to pounce.

"Cali! Stop!" Leon hissed over his shoulder.

"If anyone had ever agreed to marry your sorry ass, then you'd know that we've already signed the marriage certificate this morning! The ceremony is just a formality. My God, what an ass."

I was taunting him on purpose. I knew I wasn't helping the situation at all. But my God, was he really that daft?

"Cali," Leon growled again.

It seemed as if I'd pushed Dominic over the edge of insanity with my words, because he began walking forward, heading straight for my husband's gun that was pointed directly at his forehead.

"If that's the case, then I guess it's time to make you a widow," he stated.

His words struck a match, igniting a wildfire of fury within me. Who the hell did this arrogant prick think he was? Did he truly believe he had the right to dictate my existence? As if he alone possessed the authority to shape my destiny.

In an instant, the pent-up rage I had contained erupted like a dam bursting.

Flashes of all the faces of men who had tried to impose their will over me surged in my mind.

Then Vik, his intentions noble yet suffocating, as he tried to shield us from a harsh world.

I saw Ozias Xenos and all the faces of the men who'd raped me while I'd been held captive. I saw the faces of the men who'd beaten me after the rapes.

It dawned on me that they all thought they had control over me, over my sisters, and, in fact, over all women.

And each and every fucking one of them had been sorely mistaken.

We held the power of our own lives.

We would never back down to them.

We would never let them rule over us.

Together, my sisters and I would die before we allowed that to happen to any of us ever again. And Dominic Lucianos, of all fucking people?

What a goddamned joke this man was. Fury and rage bubbled up inside me, leaving me shaking and trembling with indignation. I was done. I was over it all. This was my fucking wedding, for fuck's sake, and he dared to interrupt it as if he had a right to do so?

The ego it must have taken to jump to such an entitled conclusion astonished me. It infuriated me that he was that stupid.

And now, it was time for him to learn a valuable lesson that was long overdue.

Fuck Dominic Lucianos. It was time to end this shit. Now.

I glanced at Leon's back, noticing the bulge in his jacket—the distinct outline of his extra gun concealed in his waistband. It was just like Leon to be so prepared.

But, as far as I was concerned, he was taking too long to deal with this asshole. Why wait any longer?

A slow smile spread across my face as I reached for his weapon. Time seemed to slow to a crawl, but I relished the fact that this time, I didn't freeze up.

Not at all.

I would never do that again, and in that moment, I was absolutely sure of it. Despite all the emotions swirling within me—anger, irritation, a sense of justice—none of them came remotely close to feeling like fear.

I'd banished fear from my heart a long fucking time ago.

Not knowing this fact was Dominic's first mistake. Coming here and fucking up my wedding while threatening to make me a widow would be his very last.

I slid my hand beneath Leon's tuxedo jacket and swiftly pulled out the gun. Leon looked back at me in alarm.

"Cali!" he warned.

I ignored him, ducking under his arm, and fired off three quick shots.

The first one took out the guard on Dominic's left, the bullet piercing his forehead. His body collapsed in a limp heap on the ground.

The second shot sank into the chest of the second guard, causing him to fall on his back, staring up at the sky, lifeless.

The third shot—my favorite—landed deliciously right between Dominic's eyes.

I watched with glee as he fell to the ground with a deeply satisfying thump.

And then, just for good measure, I ran over to him, sending another bullet straight into his groin. Standing over him, I watched the blood pool around his head, his ugly, lifeless face staring up at me.

I sighed, letting my arm fall to my side. Now that the three of them were eliminated, time started back up, chaos ensued again, and I blinked hard as the guests emerged from their hiding spots and crowded around us. As soon as they realized I was the one who shot the three men, they started shouting my name.

"Cali! Cali! Cali!"

I scanned the crowd, finally landing on my sisters. Laya and Avra stood close, watching me with a mix of concern and amusement.

I smiled at Laya, and she winked, nodding approvingly.

Avra pulled me into her arms, whispering in my ear, "Good fucking shot, sis."

My head spun.

Without a second thought, I'd managed to kill three men in mere seconds. Their bodies bled out at my feet. I stood there, amazed by the strength and power it required for me to do that.

A touch on my arm pulled me from the fog, and I lifted my head to meet my husband's gaze, desperate to ensure he wasn't angry with me for defying him.

I'd ignored every command he'd given me. A lesser man might have felt humiliated to be publicly disregarded that way. But I hadn't stopped to think. I'd just seen a problem, found the solution, and acted. I'd done it for him. I'd done it for us. For our future...

If he were angry or humiliated, we would deal with it, but I wasn't about to apologize for killing these bastards.

"Leon, I—" I stopped looking for any sign of rage.

Instead, I found love.

I found tenderness.

He wrapped his arms around me, squeezing me close to his chest as he took a deep breath and let out a long, slow exhale.

"You nearly gave me a fucking heart attack, Calista," he murmured into my hair.

I leaned back to look at him.

"Why?" I replied, winking at him. "It seems I just saved your life, actually."

A silence engulfed the crowd after my remark, and I scanned their faces, realizing they were waiting for me to say or do something to help them shake off the shock of what they had just seen.

They had been invited to a wedding and attended a bloody, violent slaughter. Not that it was something any of them hadn't seen before. Our guest list comprised the syndicate heads of our allies and our family members. They were all powerful and well-versed in the ways of mafia families.

Of course, I knew the storm I had unleashed with Dominic and his men. The whispers would begin immediately, spreading like wildfire through the streets and taverns —how Calista Vitalis, a bride adorned in white, had taken the life of Dominic Lucianos in front of a stunned audience, a scene that would etch itself into the annals of our families' stories.

That was our legacy, and moments like these were passed down as cherished family heirlooms.

And I was determined to craft a tale worth telling.

I raised my chin high, my gaze sweeping over the crowd, radiating the confidence that commanded attention. I felt the weight of their stares, each one a testament to my power, as I prepared to utter words that would echo for generations to come.

"Make no mistake," I declared, my voice rising above the

murmur, each word accentuated and distinct. "The Vitalis sisters are here to stay."

Avra and Laya came to stand beside me, the three of us claiming our place, once and for all.

The message we sent was clear.

Do not fuck with us.

Just in case, I spelled it out even more.

"We will not hesitate to protect ourselves or those we love. We have no fear of consequences. We will always seek vengeance on those who harm us. If anyone else is considering the foolish move of crossing us, consider yourselves warned that you will face the consequences of your actions."

The guests murmured to themselves, shaking their heads as they watched the three of us fearlessly face everyone down.

We were strong.

We were unstoppable.

We were the Vitalis.

And we would never, ever, let anyone fuck with us again.

TWENTY

L EON

I rubbed the heavy gold ring on my finger, a tangible and comforting reminder of my new status as Cali's husband. I couldn't help but enjoy the feeling, which blended triumph and relief. I tilted my head back in my patio chair and took a deep, calming breath.

Cali and I had just returned from our delayed honeymoon and stopped by to visit Avra. When we arrived, we saw Laya and Nikolas, which meant I might have lost my wife to her sisters for the next week or so.

I couldn't believe how much unfolded on our wedding day. It was definitely a day to remember. Aside from the shooting, we experienced a second burst of chaos at the very end, but it was worth it.

Just as Cali completed her last dance with her sisters before we headed to the airfield to board our private jet, Avra's water broke right in the middle of the dance floor while all three sisters performed a synchronized dance move.

Our nephew decided he couldn't miss the party and postponed Cali's and my honeymoon for a few days. In the early morning hours, Juno Viktor Vitalis officially made his debut, joining his cousin, Constantine Juno Vitalis, as the newest member of the Vitalis family.

Now, I was with Eli and Nikolas, enjoying the late afternoon sun setting over Eli's estate. Next to Eli, Juno slept peacefully in his baby carrier, forming fists and shoving them into his mouth while dreaming. Eli couldn't take his eyes off his son. His love for the boy was clear.

Constantine followed his baby cousin's example and napped, too. He lay on Nikolas's chest, making tiny baby snores and drooling onto his shirt.

Nikolas looked down at him and shook his head. "This is as quiet as it will get. We'd better enjoy this."

"Are you talking about the boys or our wives?" Eli asked, while continuing to watch Juno.

"Don't let Avra hear you say that if you want to live," I said. "She just had a baby and is likely to gut you."

"That is something she would do before, during, and after pregnancy," Eli retorted. "If she heard me say it, she would laugh since I only speak the truth."

"Is it always going to be like this? Chaos and power grabs?" I asked, thinking about the future and all it would hold for us.

"Probably." Niko shrugged. "It's just part of the life we live, whether the Vitalis sisters are in it or not. Though with them in our lives, the chances increase tenfold."

He turned to Elias, who was lost in thought, his gaze drifting over the sprawling trees that danced in the breeze.

"Yes and no?" he answered. "Life with our wives won't ever be simple, that is a fact. And sometimes, it feels chaotic, especially when we have to support their immense power. But at other moments?" He paused, a wistful smile forming. "To tell you the truth, when it's just the two of us at home, that's when I feel the most peace."

"Yeah, just wait until this little guy starts teething." Niko gestured toward Juno with a playful grin. "Then you can talk to me about peace."

Elias chuckled, reaching out to place a protective hand on his son's head, fingers brushing through the downy hair.

"This guy can do no wrong," he said, his voice laced with pride. But a shadow crossed his features. "However, there's always something new coming around the corner to disturb our peace." He paused, looking at me. "I think it's just something you have to get used to, Leon. It'll never be simple. It's just something you are going to have to accept."

His words settled into my mind like heavy stones. They curled around my heart, a mix of acceptance and foreboding. I had purposefully kept my world small before I met Cali. It was easier that way, never getting too close to anyone or caring about anyone. Now, everything was different.

There was so much to care about and think about now.

My life with Cali held peace too, just as Elias had described. The nights we were wrapped up in bed were profoundly peaceful and serene. Even in that space, consumed by passion, desire, and hunger, we managed to find peace between us.

"I have no doubt the girls will be stirring up shit again soon," Elias said. "Avra's just given birth, and she's already dropping hints to me about the next territories she wants to collect."

"Already?" I asked, lifting a brow. She'd only given birth two weeks prior.

"I know." He ran a hand through his dark hair. "I'm hoping like hell she'll wait until she's fully recovered from childbirth, but nothing seems to stop those women. I'm considering finding a way to use the fact that she's breast-feeding as leverage to get her to give it a little more time. I'm not sure I'll be able to do it successfully, though. Trying to change the mind of a Vitalis woman is damn near impossible."

"You're right. She's not going to wait," Niko said.

Eli groaned and looked over at me.

"I agree with Niko. Sorry, brother."

He sighed, staring down at his son again.

"It's okay—I knew it in my heart," he admitted. "In fact, if I'm being honest, Avra scares me a little. I never thought I'd have a wife that I was frightened of, but she gets riled up when I challenge her at all."

"Best not to do that," Niko mused. "I learned that lesson the hard way. Once, Laya wanted to go out for Italian food, but I'd just had it for lunch that day. Apparently, she'd had her heart set on it all week, but unfortunately, she had failed to inform me. I drove us to a Thai place instead, without consulting her."

"Oh, no," Eli replied, his eyes growing wide.

"She made me drive her home, and then she went to her favorite Italian place without me. She glared at me the entire next day! I still haven't heard the end of it."

I wondered what kind of stories Cali and I would have together. I contemplated what adventures our future held. Neither of us had expected Dominic Lucianos to crash our wedding, which had been a failure on my men's part. I'd had to fire three men after that, knowing I would never be able to trust Cali's safety with them again.

"That does sound scary," I replied.

"You haven't even seen them join forces yet," Elias said. "The three of them together are a dangerous storm that no man should face alone."

"Great," I said, my voice laced with sarcasm. "I can't wait. As if Cali obliterating Lucianos and his men right before my very eyes wasn't enough."

"Cali is a badass," Niko said. "That show of force in front of all the families? In that one act alone, she solidified the strength of the Vitalis family. She was fearless and swift.

Everyone will think twice now before planning some shit against our family."

"She's amazing," I agreed, lifting my chin with pride. My beautiful bride had saved my life in more ways than one. Sure, she'd killed Dominic, but it was my heart she'd saved along the way. I shuddered to think of how empty my life had been before Cali entered it. I'd been lonely as hell, although I never would have admitted it. I missed my family, and I'd shut everyone else out, convinced I was saving myself somehow.

Instead, I'd resigned myself to a very slow death.

Cali had breathed life back into me. She'd shown me that loving someone didn't have to hurt. That I didn't have to live in the constant fear of losing her, that I could live and love and thrive.

Yes, Cali had saved my life.

And I planned to spend every moment of my life keeping her safe, just as she would for me. I looked forward to long, luxurious nights in her arms.

"Eli, how do you feel now? You changed your name to Vitalis. Your father is dead and buried. The Xenos legacy no longer exists. You've even given Juno the Vitalis name. Do you have any regrets about that?"

Niko's question lingered in the air. I had been wondering the same things, but I was hesitant to ask such a personal, probing question. After all, I hadn't been part of this family for very long. I was still searching for my place within it.

Eli shook his head.

"I have no regrets, brother. My children will continue the

Vitalis name, of which I am proud. The Vitalis legacy embodies valor and strength. In contrast, the Xenos name is stained by evil, greed, and violence. I have never regretted rejecting it, and I doubt I ever will."

"That's awesome, Eli," I said, looking over at him.

"You know, I never imagined things would end up this way. When I received the initial marriage proposal from Avra and Vik, I thought it would just be a business arrangement, that it would strengthen the Xenos territories. I never thought I'd fall in love with her. I never expected that I would renounce my family name and take on the Vitalis name. But fuck, I am so happy that it all happened. I wouldn't have changed a thing."

"I feel you, brother. To the Vitalis women." Niko raised his whiskey glass. "Life will never be simple. But life will always be good."

I smiled, Cali's beautiful face of sunshine flashing in my head.

My heart ached at her beauty, inside and out. Soon, we'd have our own little babies to adore, and I had no doubt she would be an amazing mother, because she was an amazing human.

My wife was endlessly courageous. She'd faced her demons head-on and emerged stronger and smarter. She'd pass that courage on to our children, and I would be the lucky bastard who got to stand by her side, through thick and thin and good and bad.

She was my equal.

My partner.

My best friend.

I would protect her with my very soul.

"Fuck simple," I replied to Niko, clinking my glass against his. "Simple isn't for our family. And I wouldn't have it any other way."

"Hear, hear, brother!"

EPILOGUE

C ALISTA

SIX MONTHS LATER

My sisters and I sat soaking in the warm rays of sunshine out on Laya and Niko's terrace after a long day of training in our personal gym.

Dryad, the oak tree that Niko's parents had planted, was putting on quite a show as it danced in the gentle breeze that rippled through the air, its branches lifting and falling gracefully. The leaves threw shadows on the roses below, the light flirting with the beautiful, fragrant blossoms.

Juno and CJ were getting bigger each day, and I was

having a delightful time watching them run my sisters ragged. Juno was in Avra's lap, snuggling against her chest, while CJ crawled faster than ever, ready to walk any day. Laya was perpetually chasing after him.

As I'd expected, Laya and Avra were spectacular mothers. They were perhaps a tad overprotective, but I supposed that was to be expected, as well.

The three of us had endured so much violence and trauma as young children. The world we lived in was more dangerous than most, with the violence of the syndicates drawing closer as we became more powerful.

After just a few years since we'd returned to Greece, we had managed to reclaim power over all the territories that had once belonged to our family, along with a few additional ones. As of now, we were the most powerful family in all of Greece. In this process, we acquired an impressive list of allies, both within the region and beyond.

If anyone dared to harm the Vitalis family now, our expansive network of loyalists would deliver a swift, efficient, and potent response.

Because of this, it was rare for any of the family heads to order an attack against us. Most of them respected our power, even if it had come at an expense. We ensured that those who challenged us realized we would not hold back when it came to retaliation.

I glanced over at my two sisters, the devoted mothers who looked lovingly upon their children, amazed at the dichotomy they presented. On the surface, they were two typical maternal figures, appearing soft and peaceful. Still, they were two expertly trained, fearless assassins with a deep desire to rule over as many cities in Greece as they possibly could.

"What are you chuckling about?" Avra asked, raising a brow.

"I was just wondering what our enemies would think if they saw the two of you being so soft and gentle with your children," I replied with a smile.

"They would think they had leverage over us," Laya said.

"If anyone dared to use one of our children to gain power over us, I'd have them destroyed without a second thought," Avra said, her tone reflecting the strength in her words.

"I'd do it myself." Laya lifted her chin.

The two of them looked like they were ready to strike this imaginary enemy at any second.

"Relax, you two," I said, my voice calm despite the tension that wove itself into the air around us. "It was just a thought. Nobody is foolish enough to come after us. At least, not anymore."

My words lingered, their weight reminding us of a darkness we all wished to forget.

Memories flooded my mind: the walls of our childhood shattered, and the laughter of our parents faded away too soon. I could almost feel the chilling grip of fear returning as I recalled the night of my abduction and the days when my cries for help went unnoticed. We'd faced horrors that no one should ever have to endure.

Yet, through the ashes of our past, something fierce had ignited within us.

The three girls who once hid in the shadows of Prague were still alive in our hearts, but they wore the armor of their scars now. We had transformed that relentless agony into an unbreakable bond, a shield of resilience wrapped around our souls. We were not merely survivors but warriors, forged from the fires of our own horror, ready to face whatever came next.

"You're right, Cali." Laya picked up CJ and plopped him on her lap. "I think we've finally reached a level of power where we can expect our enemies to show us respect, for the most part."

"That doesn't mean we can let our guard down," Avra said.

As the oldest of us three, she was always the one who worried, believing it was her duty to stay alert for any trouble heading our way.

"Avra, I love you for it, but you don't have to always be so on edge," I said. "It's not up to you to protect us at all times anymore. We're adults now. Hell, we're all married now to strong, powerful, and protective men."

She looked at me as if I suddenly had two heads.

"And you think that warrants me not doing my job?" she asked, lifting a brow. "I've been looking after the two of you since you were infants. I don't see that stopping anytime soon."

"Don't you want to relax?"

"We're the Vitalis sisters," she insisted, as if it required reiteration. "Don't underestimate our enemies, Calista. We come from generations of families who have fought for this.

The moment we look away, they will strike. Remember my warning."

I wasn't going to argue with her when it was pointless. I had hoped that becoming a mother would ease the tremendous weight of responsibility on Avra's shoulders. Since our parents' murder, she had been endlessly burdened by it.

Yet, after giving birth, it seemed she was carrying even heavier loads. I realized she would never be free of this duty with another child to protect.

I sighed as I gazed at the fluffy clouds gliding through the bright blue sky, feeling my worries float away with them. I had dedicated far too much time to fretting about the past and the future.

These days, I caught myself savoring each moment. The vibrancy of now enveloped me, urging me to stay present.

Leon was by my side.

Our days unfurled like a gentle stream, flowing effortlessly as we navigated life together. Each shared glance deepened our connection, weaving intimacy into a beautiful tapestry of love, each thread spun from raw passion and the softest whispers that lingered between us.

Somehow, we managed to find a balance that left both of us physically and emotionally satisfied.

Leon was an amazing person, a fantastic lover, and most importantly, he had become a great friend to me. He was precisely what I needed in my life. Selecting him as my husband was the perfect decision.

I shuddered at the thought that I had even considered Dominic Lucianos as a possibility. After Dominic had rudely interrupted our wedding, his brother reached out. He tried to make amends for his brother's rogue behavior, insisting they were already trying to oust him from the family before I'd killed him.

I accepted their apology, but I did not extend my hand any further. I wanted nothing to do with any of them. His brother was much more intelligent because he didn't press the matter any further, keeping his distance from me and my family.

I reached down and petted Leo's head as she lay at my side. My sisters had their babies, and I had my loyal dog. She was just what I needed right now, and Leon too. But soon, there would be one more addition, which was why I was staring so adoringly at my sisters this morning.

My hand fell on my lower abdomen, a soft, dreamy smile spreading across my face as I considered just how perfect my life had turned out to be.

CJ dashed across the terrace once more, with Laya in pursuit. The moment she retrieved him and set him down, he beamed at her, releasing an adorable giggle.

"CJ!" Laya exclaimed with joy.

Avra clapped her hands and shouted, "Oh my God."

"Yes, CJ!" I cheered. "Go! Walk!"

He let go of Laya's hands and did just that, taking three more steps before he fell on his butt. He looked back at us, surprised by what he'd accomplished.

The three of us jumped to our feet, clapping and cheering. Laya rushed over to him, picked him up, and spun him around. Tears rolled down her face.

"Oh, you look so happy!" I said, going over and gathering them both in a big hug.

"I'm crying because my job has just gotten much harder!" CJ wiggled and squirmed in Laya's arms, but she held onto him. "How am I ever going to be able to keep up with him now?"

"Uhh. I just realized I'm next." Avra put Juno into the baby carriage next to her.

"Yes, you are," Laya replied, giving her a pointed look. "And I'm going to laugh at you, just as you've done to me this whole time!"

"Hey, it was good-natured," Avra protested.

I pulled away from Laya and CJ, figuring this was the best time to share the news I'd been keeping to myself for far too long.

Keeping secrets from them was nearly impossible, but this one had been excruciating.

I took a deep breath and glanced at their expectant faces. My heart raced in my chest, and I fiddled with the hem of my shirt, feeling the weight of unspoken words.

"You guys," I finally said, my voice barely above a whisper, as if the very act of speaking it would make it more real. I hadn't shared this yet, not even with Leon, and the air thickened with my uncertainty.

"It looks like I'm going to be next."

They stopped, cocked their heads, and stared at me.

"Next for what?" Avra shook her head. "I'm confused."

I laid my palm on my stomach, raising a brow, waiting for them to catch on.

"Oh my God! Calista!" Laya shouted. "Are you pregnant?"

Tears formed as I spoke those words for the first time. "I'm going to be a mother, just like the two of you."

They rushed over to me, hugging me with pure joy.

"We're going to be aunts!" Avra said. "Again!"

"You're going to be the best aunts ever!" I assured them.

"Cali, I'm so happy for you and Leon. He must be over the moon."

"Actually," I admitted, "I haven't told him yet."

Laya asked, "Why not?"

"I wanted to share this with you two first." I smiled at the two most important people in my life. "You're my sisters, and revealing this to you before anyone else felt right. I love Leon with all my heart and am excited to have his child. I've always told my sisters significant news first. Why should that be different now? I'm sure Leon will understand."

"Oh, Cali!" Avra exclaimed, tears flowing down her face in sync with mine. "You're going to be an amazing mother."

"If sharing blood with the two of you is any indicator, then yes, I will be."

We laughed and cried, hugging each other until CJ wiggled to be let go again, scrambling down Laya's legs until his little feet hit the ground.

And in the next second, he was gone again, fleeing from his mother and venturing out into the world, another formidable Vitalis eager to demonstrate the strength of the blood coursing through his veins, now and forever.

If you haven't read the full journey of the Vitalis
sisters, start at the beginning with *Legacy* and witness
the enemies-to-lovers storm between Avra and Elias
that started it all.

Or dive into an entirely new, indulgent world of power,
sin, and seduction.
Begin the *Gods of Vegas* series with *Master of Sin*.

Prefer something darker and grittier?
Enter the dangerous underworld of New York in
Dangerous King.

https://geni.us/LegacybySiennaSnow

A Marriage of Convenience. A War of Obsession.
Avra Vitalis never expected to walk into her family's stolen empire dressed as a bride—but this isn't a union of love. It's a declaration of war.

Her husband, Elias Xenos, is ruthless, powerful, and dangerously possessive—the heir to the family who destroyed hers. He views Avra not merely as a pawn, but as a prize he's determined to claim.

Yet behind their bitter rivalry burns a forbidden attraction too intense to deny. As lethal secrets surface and hidden betrayals emerge, Avra realizes revenge isn't the only thing at stake. In this world of blood oaths, passion, and deceit, trusting Elias could lead to salvation—or complete destruction.

LEGACY is the explosive first book in the *Sisters of Wrath* series, a dark mafia romance filled with powerful alpha males, fierce heroines, high-stakes passion, and dangerous family loyalties. Perfect for fans of Sophie Lark, Danielle Lori, and Natasha Knight.

NOTES

Books By Sienna

Rules of Engagement

Rule Breaker

Rule Master

Rule Changer

Politics of Love

Celebrity

Senator

Commander

Gods of Vegas

Master of Sin

Master of Games

Master of Revenge

Master of Secrets

Master of Control

Master of Fortune

Sweetest Sin

Intrigued By Love

Street Kings

Dangerous King

Vicious Prince

Deceptive Knight

Ruthless Heir

<u>Violent Delights</u>

Claim

Defy

Own

<u>Sin and Lies</u>

Sin and Betrayal

Sin and Deception

<u>Sister of Wrath</u>

Legacy

Influence

<u>Sinful Gods</u>

Forbidden Empire (Oct 8, 2025)

Dark Alliance (2026)

Broken Crown (2026)

<u>Collections</u>

Reckless Romeo

About the Author

USA Today bestselling author Sienna Snow loves to craft dark and extremely sexy stories centered on anti-heroes and the strong, unapologetic women who bring them to their knees. Her books immerse you in a world of indulgence, suspense, and undeniable steam.

Her heroines are vibrant and self-assured, often discovering love and romance under unconventional circumstances. Sienna offers her readers enticing glimpses of steamy romance filled with empowerment and indulgent satisfaction.

Sienna loves a life filled with travel and adventure. She plans to explore even the farthest corners of the world and revel in experiencing the diverse cultures along the way. When she isn't writing or traveling, Sienna is focused on her "happily ever after" with her husband and children.

Sign up for her newsletter for notifications of releases, book sales, events, and so much more.

http://www.siennasnow.com/newsletter

contact@siennasnow.com